ALL THAT
WILL REMAIN

Richard Snodgrass

A Novel

Calling Crow Press

Pittsburgh

Also by Richard Snodgrass

Fiction

There's Something in the Back Yard

The Books of Furnass

All That Will Remain

Across the River

Holding On

Book of Days

The Pattern Maker

Furrow and Slice

The Building

Some Rise

All Fall Down

Redding Up

Books of Photographs and Text

An Uncommon Field: The Flight 93
Temporary Memorial

Kitchen Things: An Album of Vintage Utensils
and Farm-Kitchen Recipes

Memoir

The House with Round Windows

Published by Calling Crow Press
Pittsburgh, Pennsylvania

Book design by Book Design Templates, LLC
Cover design by Jack Ritchie

Printed in the United States of America
ISBN 978-1-7373824-1-6
Library of Congress catalog control number: 2021911547

For Kim Harrison
and, of course, as with all things,
for Marty

They are all gone away,
There is nothing more to say.
from "The House on the Hill"
Edwin Arlington Robinson

All That Will Remain

. . . it starts in an empty wing of the old wood house, a wing intended for use by one of the grown children and his or her family though that never came to pass, the flames spreading quickly across the floor of the empty sitting room following the splashes of gasoline and up the walls, the heat growing now, the glass shattering in the window frames, the fire building of its own intensity, out the open door and down the hallway and into the empty rooms along the corridor, into the main body of the house, into the kitchen, the gas range exploding setting off like explosions from the smaller gas heaters in the upstairs bedrooms and the gas light fixtures throughout the house that were shut off when electricity came but never removed or fully deactivated, the entire house now, those rooms that aren't engulfed in flames, filling with thick black choking smoke, the furniture in the dining room, the grand twelve-place dining table and matching chairs and china cupboard and linen bureau and buffet outlined as glowing embers before flaring into sparks, the fire at last traveling into the room at the front of the house known as the study, the room used as office and retreat and sanctum sanctorum by his grandfather who built the house and then his father, the room lined with barrister bookcases full of ledgers and engineering works and the books of fiction and nonfiction that are considered to be the most important of Western Civilization, a purposeful gesture and intellectual sophistication even if the books were never read, the remaining sections of the walls crowded Victorian-style with photographs of farm and road-building and well-drilling machinery along with pictures of his father receiving various awards and meeting with various dignitaries, none of the pictures portraying this man however, Augustus Malcolm Lyle, commonly known as Gus, not an old man at all, only in his late-forties or so, who is or should be in the prime of life, who after setting the fire comes back to this room and takes the 1 inch = 1 foot model of the latest *and final version of his beloved Lylemobile and collapses into his grandfather's tall leather wingback chair, the model of the Lylemobile on his lap because he wants no question when his charred body is found who it is and what drove him to set the fire, barely making it back to this room before the roiling smoke catches up to him, dead within a few minutes from smoke inhalation before the flames consume him and the scale model and the chair and the room, the house midway up the slope of the hill overlooking the town, as he intended, free of everything once and for all. . . .*

PART ONE

Sunday, July 2, 1916

The shafts of sunlight angled down from the row of clerestory windows through the gloom of the old foundry, slanting columns of light spacing off the darkness at mid-afternoon; along the walls the hammered glass of the tall shop windows, pitted and singed from decades of sparks and flames and smoke, glowed dully with half-light, providing little illumination. The two women, one white, the other dark-skinned—the white woman in her late eighties, ramrod straight though walking with the aid of a cane, dressed all in black, the dress with black pearl buttons extending from throat to the floor, with just the hint of a bustle, a style decades old, hopelessly out of fashion, a bustle-era hat with small brim and lots of ruffles tied on her white hair like a bonnet; the dark-skinned woman thirty-five years younger at least than the other, equally dressed out of fashion though of a different sort: likewise buttoned up from collar to toe but her dress light with a Caribbean flair, narrow red and white and tan and blue and yellow longitudinal stripes though the colors were muted and blended together, faded from sunlight and years of wear, the dress high-waisted and tucked up under her breasts, a matching brimless hat that was more of a turban—made their way down the central aisle of the long narrow shop, the older woman a step and a half in front of the other, the *tick, tick, tick* of her cane marking the beat of their progress, the hems of their floor-length skirts dipping back and forth with their footfalls leaving a trail of interlacing circles in the soot that covered the dirt-packed floor. The two women passed in and out of the shafts of murky sunlight, light to dark, dark to light, past workbenches of ancient machinery, castings of monstrous wheels and gears and discarded machine parts, scrap barrels of ruined castings and scrap metal, the walls above the workbenches lined with blackened tools, pry bars, shovels, picks, files, sampling ladles on long poles, toward the far end of the shop where a figure on horseback rose like a vision, larger than life, even without its pedestal the figure nearly twelve feet tall, the arm pointed into the farther darkness, in the direction across the river, the Union Army officer's cape shielding the left arm of the figure, the horseman surrounded now with ladders and scaffolds with several workmen scrambling over horse and rider with grindstones and brushes and buckets of wax. As the two women approached, one of the men saw them coming.

"Ah, *grazie, grazie!*" he said, delighted. He left his brush in his bucket and hurried to climb down.

"Why does the man always thank you?" the black woman, Perpetual, said to the other. "Every time he see you, Mawm— *grazie, grazie, grazie.* It makes Perpetual think the sculptureman don't know the right word for things."

"Remember, you didn't always know the right word for things either, when you first came to this country."

"Do say," Perpetual said, pretending to look askance, her wrist folded against her hip, hip cocked in Libby's direction.

"I told you, it's *Do tell*, not *Do say*."

"Perpetual knows what Perpetual means."

Libby shook her head, pursed her lips. Impossible. "Hush now."

The man hurried toward them, wiping his hands on a piece of burlap. "*Grazie*, Mrs. Lyle. *Grazie*, it is so good to see you."

"Ennio," Libby, said, ignoring his greeting, looking past him at the statue.

He was in his late fifties, short and stocky, powerfully built, what was left of his gray hair nested around the dome of his sunbaked skull, wearing a canvas sculptor's smock tied at the waist. He glanced at the woman in Caribbean dress but nothing more.

"I wasn't sure if you would visit us today or not."

"Why wouldn't I visit you?"

"It being the Sunday and all. . . ."

"I needed to make sure everything is in readiness for the move tomorrow," Libby said, walking past him, away from him, still looking at the statue. "Sunday or not."

"Of course, of course," Ennio said, continuing to wipe his hands, though more like wringing them now, long after he needed to, trailing after her. "I said I would have it ready for its unveiling on the Fourth of July, and ready it is. The protective wax is almost finished, there are only a few more areas to touch up before we prepare him for his journey."

Libby placed her hand against the sculptor's upper arm to brace herself as she got closer to the statue, looking up. "And is my son cooperating, giving you everything you'll need to move it?"

"Oh yes, yes. Very cooperative indeed. He was here this morning, going over with the foreman all that is needed for the dunning and bracing. He is calling in a crew specially on a Sunday, they should be here shortly to begin their work and get it loaded on one of the steamworks' drop-bed lowloaders."

"And what in heaven's name is a drop-bed lowloader?"

"I have no idea, Mrs. Lyle. A cart of some kind, I assume. But your son said they use it to transport steam shovels and the like, so I guess they know what they're doing."

Libby, knowing her son all too well, was tempted to question it, but decided it was too late to say anything. Her companion, Perpetual, separated herself from the other two and moved around behind the figure, studying it from different angles. Libby moved a few steps closer—the sculptor moving with her, step for step, a willing portable support for the elderly woman—gazing up at the figure on horseback, at the features of his face under the brim of his cavalry officer's hat. From this close, the figure on horseback towered over her like some guardian out of antiquity, like an idol or a god; in the shadows at this end of the shop the bronze glowed a burnished reddish-brown, the waxed surfaces catching the glow from the shafts of sunlight, the highlights splaying off in tiny rainbows. The eyes of the horseman, two blank holes sunk deep in the skull, gazed down at her, appeared to follow her wherever she moved. She met his stare, gazed right back at him.

"It's sad in a way," she said after several minutes, leaning with two hands on her cane, speaking to no one in particular, thinking out loud. "This is the last time we'll be with him when he's ours. As soon as he leaves here, he'll belong to the community. He'll be part of the town."

"But isn't that what you wanted?" Ennio said, gazing up at his creation. "You wanted a statue for the town. A tribute to the town, you might say."

"No, I wanted a tribute to him. To this . . . Union cavalryman, whoever he is. That the town will take it somehow as a tribute to themselves is only another example of their misguided folly. They don't know what is right before their eyes."

For a second Libby and Perpetual, on opposite sides of the statue, looked at each other through the legs of the horse, an understanding passing between them.

"Do not distress yourself, Mrs. Lyle," Ennio said. "The statue will stand as you intend it for centuries to come. A tribute to this heroic soldier of the Republic. How could it be otherwise?"

"How could it, indeed?" Libby said, cocked an eyebrow at him, and stepped back again. She took a handkerchief from her sleeve and blew her nose in ladylike fashion.

"It is all the soot and ash," Ennio said, turning away in equally gentleman-like fashion until she was finished.

"Yes," Libby said, tucking away the handkerchief again.

"Those special details we discussed. You said it would be necessary to detach the left arm and the drape of the cape from the mold in order to cast them. Was there any problem reattaching them again? From here I can't see any telltale lines or seams."

"No, no problems," Ennio said, obviously proud of his work. "It is standard procedure. It was necessary to detach a number of the elements in order to cast them. Though I still don't understand why we went to the trouble of making such details that no one will ever see."

"All for the sake of authenticity. Let's just say they are our little secrets."

"As you wish, madam." Ennio smiled his best patron smile. "Well then, is there anything else? I need to get back to work. . . ."

"Yes, of course, don't let me delay you. . . ." Libby turned to leave, the sculptor bowing slightly as she passed by as if caught in her wake.

"You missed a spot," came a voice behind them.

Perpetual came around the statue, adjusting her turban. "On the horse's belly. Right where his tallywags are supposed to be. Before you or somebody else made him a gelding."

Ennio sputtered. "Mrs. Lyle. . . ."

"It's all right, Perpetual," Libby said. "We decided early on that the horse would be a mare. Though frankly I can't remember now if that's what it was, if I ever knew." She turned and continued on. "You'll have to excuse my companion. We were just discussing differences in language. Come along, Perpetual."

"Yes, Mawm." As she passed Ennio, Perpetual said, "Don't forget, sculptureman. There be a spot." She raised her eyebrows at him, gave a brief tug to the ties of his smock, and smiled. "A spot."

Ennio drew himself up, straightened the front of his smock. Harrumphed.

When the two women reached the front of the shop, Libby stopped. "You go on. I'll be with you in a few minutes."

"Are you all right, Mawm?"

"I'm fine, fine. You go think about your story or whatever it is that's on your mind lately. I just want to look at something. Alone."

Perpetual cocked her head at her, the attitude of someone used to appraising someone else, then pushed open the door and went on outside. Libby leaned on her cane as she looked back through the shop, through the dust and the gloom and the shafts of sunlight, at the statue of the horseman glimmering in the distant shadows, standing like the figure in a shrine. Thinking, What would Colin say if he saw this here, in the shop he was so proud of once upon a time? How could I explain it that he would understand? As always he would believe only what he chose to. Dear man. I knew you once. You came to me but you left me too. In those years I would see your kind riding in the clouds above the hills, along the top of the valley's hills, monster figures, gods, guidons snapping in the wind, sabers at the ready, bugles blowing as they wheeled in formation and charged down the sky toward me, above the treetops, froth flying from the mouths of the horses, their eyes wild—beautiful, oh beautiful—a sword glinting in the sunlight as it slashed down at me, the pain above my eyes like a blade piercing my temple, the swirl about me of dust and screams and horses' hooves—but that was years ago, lifetimes ago, yours and mine, before everything changed. But I know you still, in my own way now, what all you gave to me. What I will never forget. We will see, we will see. . . .

She took one last long lingering look down the expanse of the shop, aware that in all probability this would be the last time she would have reason to visit the steamworks, Colin's steamworks, with or without the statue—Good-bye, old love—and followed Perpetual out the door.

2

A short time earlier, Malcolm Lyle, in his waistcoat and shirt-sleeves because of the heat, was in his office—his father Colin's office originally, directly over the passageway into the large enclosed yard of the steamworks so he could keep his eye on all the comings and goings of his company—pacing back and forth in front of the windows, keeping an eye now on the activities in the yard, idly rubbing the scars on his hands, the puckered skin, as he tried to decide what to do about the telegram he received this morning, when the surrey with his mother and Perpetual rolled into view below him. A mixed blessing.

Good Lord, Mother! Would it be too much to ask that you let me teach Perpetual how to drive a motorcar? It doesn't even have to be one of Gus' Lylemobiles. Just so the Lyles aren't seen around town as stuck in the horse-and-buggy era?

Still, her appearance at the steamworks solved his problem of the telegram. Malcolm Lyle was a thick burly man with unruly salt-and-pepper hair, old-fashioned muttonchop sideburns that met under his nose, and eyebrows like small thickets. He watched as the surrey crossed the yard and pulled up at the far side of the compound, in front of the old foundry that Malcolm had let them use to cast her statue. Waited until the two women had climbed down from the surrey and went inside. Then he checked a few items on his desk, giving his mother plenty of time for whatever it was she was about, before putting on his brown tweed suit coat and leaving his office, making his way down the back stairs and into the compound, the heat of midday hitting him like the opening of a furnace. He was just approaching the surrey when Perpetual came out the door of the shop.

"Is everything all right? Where's Mother?"

"She be inside having herself a think," Perpetual said. "She be out in a few minutes, I would expect. And how is it with you?"

"Me?" Malcolm said, surprised she would ask. "Why? What would be wrong with me?"

Perpetual shrugged, puffed out her lower lip, all innocence.

Malcolm thought she was having him on, as she liked to do, Perpetual being Perpetual. He was mad at himself for letting her get to him again, it seemed to be her favorite sport. "And the statue is to Mother's liking?"

"The sculptureman missed a spot with his wax. Right where the horse's tallywags should be. But Perpetual set him straight."

Tallywags, is it? Malcolm wasn't going to let her flummox him again. "I'm sure you did, Perpetual."

Perpetual looked a little disappointed. She walked over to the surrey and took Malcolm's hand when he offered it to help her up—grasping only his fingers; he was never sure whether the condition of his hands bothered her or if she was afraid she might hurt him, and of course Perpetual would never let him know one way or the other—not looking at him, a smile like she knew a secret playing across her face. Look at her, it's like she thinks we work for her, rather than her working for us. Though maybe she's right, she doesn't work for us, she's my mother's paid friend— come to think of it, the only friend my mother ever had, including her children. As Perpetual got settled with the reins, she said, "Here's Mawm now."

Libby came out the door of the shop, preoccupied with pulling on a pair of black cotton gloves.

"Oh, hello, Malcolm," she said absently, barely glancing at him. "Fancy meeting you here."

"Why wouldn't I be here, Mother? It is my company, you know."

"Don't be touchy, dear. Of course it's your company. Now." Finished pulling on her gloves, she looked at her son as she worked the webs of the fingers on one hand against the webs of the other. Smiled to no one in particular.

Blazes, Mother! Can't you give it a rest for one minute? Blazes to hell! But all he did was smile in return. "How is everything with your statue? Everything to your liking?"

"It's fine, fine. Ennio says you've been very helpful."

Well, that's something. "I have men scheduled later today to get it ready for transporting the first thing tomorrow."

"That's fine, dear."

So what did she mean by that? Blazes. She smiled again and offered a gloved hand for him to help her into the surrey.

"Ah . . . before you go there's something I need to discuss with you," Malcolm said, holding her hand as if they were engaged in a minuet. She stopped and looked at him expectantly, waiting for him to go on; when he didn't, she made a face as if to say, Well?

"Hmm . . . I don't know if we should discuss it in front of Perpetual."

She shook her head once impatiently and proceeded to climb up into the surrey. When she was settled beside Perpetual she looked down at him. "My son, after thirty-some years I would think you would know that there's nothing you can say to me that you can't say in front of Perpetual. Besides, it saves me the trouble of recounting events to her afterwards."

Malcolm knew it all right, he just didn't like it. "I got a telegram this morning from John Lincoln—"

"What? Here at the steamworks? Why wasn't it delivered up at the house?"

"I made an arrangement with the telegraph office. I asked that all telegrams to anyone in the family be delivered here. To me directly."

"And why is that?"

"Because I thought there might be some communication either from or about John Lincoln and I wanted to be the one to see it first."

"But why on earth. . . ?"

Malcolm sighed, as if it should be self-evident. "Because if we received word of any kind about the boy, do you really want his mother to be the first to have the news? Missy can barely handle what happens to her as it is. You've seen how she's reacted to Mary Lydia's condition. Can you imagine what she'd be like if something happened to John Lincoln too?"

"Perpetual hasn't noticed any difference in the way Mrs. Missy's reacted to Mary Lydia's condition," Perpetual said. "It always be like it isn't there at all."

Libby looked at Perpetual as if to say she should keep her opinions to herself.

Malcolm frowned before going on. "And I particularly do not want Missy to be the one to tell any news of John Lincoln to Mary Lydia. The girl is ill enough as it is."

"True, so true," Perpetual said, wagging her head. "The love of the twins is very strong for one another, maybe too strong. . . ."

"Perpetual—" was all Malcolm could say. Blazes to hell, can't someone make that woman shut her mouth?

Libby reached beside her and patted Perpetual's hand, held it for a moment. Her black-gloved hand covering the woman's dark-skinned hand. "Please go on, Malcolm. We interrupted you. What did John Lincoln's telegram say?"

"He's joined a group of young men going to England to join the British army."

"Really?" Libby said. "Well, that would be like John Lincoln. I know he was very upset that we've been so slow to join the war against the kaiser. Did it say when he leaves?"

"He's on a boat leaving New York the day after tomorrow."

"So he won't be coming back before then."

"I don't see how he could make it," Malcolm said. "Even if he wanted to."

"*C'est mauvais* for Mary Lydia," Perpetual said. "*C'est mauvais,* indeed."

"Mary Lydia has been heartsick that her brother went away without saying good-bye or telling anyone what he was up to," Libby said, looking out across the expanse of the compound. "When she hears that he's not only going to England to join the war, but won't be coming back before going overseas . . . oh, I see." She focused again on Malcolm. "You not only want me to break the news to Missy, you want me to be the one to tell Mary Lydia."

"You know her mother would only make things worse, telling her news like that. If Missy is in any shape herself after hearing that her darling baby boy is going to war."

Libby studied her hands resting on top of her cane for a moment. Now it was Perpetual's turn to fold her dark-skinned hand over the other's black-gloved hand. "You don't be worried, Mawm. We will help Mary Lydia with this news."

"And Missy can take it any way she pleases," Libby said, and nodded once, so there, to Malcolm.

"Mother—"

They were interrupted by a commotion across the yard. A large cloud of steam erupted from the passageway to the street, swirling around a peculiar box-shaped vehicle that emerged from the cloud like an apparition, a tall black oblong automobile surrounded by its own fog, puffing into the yard, issuing a new cloud of steam with the shriek of its whistle. The horse in the shafts of the surrey shifted uneasily, the traces jingling. Malcolm stepped away from the surrey and waved to the driver to stop where he was.

"Is that Augustus' latest Lylemobile?" Libby said.

"I'm afraid so," Malcolm said, coming back to stand beside where his mother was seated.

Libby looked at him with a questioning expression, then shook her head. "Well, I'll leave you to your devices."

"And you'll tell Mary Lydia and her mother John Lincoln's news?"

"Walk on, you there!" Perpetual said, snapping the reins before Libby had a chance to reply. Almost running over Malcolm's foot.

"What the!" he said, jumping back, calling after them, "Blast you, Perpetual!"

3

Malcolm absently rubbed the burn scars on his hands, first one hand then the other, his fingers tracing the familiar ridges and valleys of fibrous tissue, a nervous tick, as he watched the surrey circle the yard and head back toward the entrance, the two women, one in black, one in muted candy stripes, waving to Gus as they passed the idling Lylemobile. When the surrey was safely into the passageway under the building, the Lylemobile released a large cloud of steam and chuffed across the compound, a fresh cloud of steam engulfing Malcolm as the vehicle pulled up beside him. Gus closed the throttle and ratcheted home the handbrake as the engine gave a hiss, trickled a stream of scalding water into the dust at Malcolm's feet, and sighed.

"The two witches of Furnass," Gus said, looking after the surrey. "No, that's probably not fair to Grandmother. Birds of a feather, though."

And that's too kind to Perpetual, Malcolm thought. But decided he shouldn't help spread family discord. "Remarkable for her age, though."

"Grandmother or Perpetual?" Gus said. Looked down at his father from the window as if to say, Touché.

Augustus Malcolm Lyle—no one ever considered he was up for

the name, even as a baby; he was always Gus—was a pug-faced man in his early thirties, his pushed-together though not unpleasant features associated with someone much older, coarse-skinned, with the air about him of something of a bumbler whether he was or not. Despite the heat he wore an ill-fitting gray pin-striped suit too heavy for the season, a rounded tab collar with a red polka-dot four-in-hand tie pulled off-center; on his head was a gray fedora that had been crushed at some time so its shape was a bit crimped and lopsided. In deference to the demands of piloting the steam car he wore heavy gloves and brown leather sleeves over the sleeves of his suit coat.

"Did our guests from Washington arrive safely?" Malcolm said.

"Yes. None the worse for wear. I got them settled into a suite at the Grand."

"And did you pick them up in this?" Malcolm looked over the steam vehicle in front of him. It was a box of a vehicle, larger than most other motorized vehicles on the road, built more like a steam tractor than the current fashion for automobiles that looked like carriages or sleighs; large rubber tires raised the vehicle several feet above the ground, requiring the use of inset metal steps to enter or leave, and the interior was tall enough that the occupants could stand up and walk around, more like a small omnibus than what was beginning to be called simply a car. As if in response to Malcolm's scrutiny, the Lylemobile gave another small hiss of steam.

"I only walked them across the street to the hotel. But I pointed out the Lylemobile to them and they commented. Favorably, I might add. I told them I would give them a ride when I picked them up and brought them here tomorrow."

"We still don't know if it's the Lylemobile they're interested in or not."

"Why else would the government send a special delegation?"

"Don't be naïve," Malcolm said. When it was obvious his son did not appreciate being referred to as naïve, Malcolm added, "I can think of a number of things. A well-driller designed for specific conditions, maybe a road grader built to specifications, or a new type of crane. Regardless, if you are going to meet them tomorrow with this, I trust it's running top-notch."

"You don't have to concern yourself with that," Gus said, looking around the cab, then back down at his father. His face was drenched with sweat, his coarse skin glistening, beads of water dripping off him, but he was evidently unaware or unconcerned. "And I'll tell you, it makes all the difference, having the controls up here at the front rather than at the back. It's a lot easier to pilot through city streets."

"I seem to remember mentioning something of the sort to you before that last prototype."

Gus sighed, closed his eyes. "I know, I know, but Grandfather's original design had the controls at the rear."

"Your grandfather's designs weren't carved in stone, he was limited as to the materials and processes he had on hand at the time. I've had to rework all his designs for the new machines we put into production. The wonder is that he came up with them at all."

"I know, you've told me—"

"His idea for a motorcar was based on one of his designs for a steam tractor. The boilers back then were still gigantic, we hadn't learned yet how to compress the proportions—"

"Father—"

Malcolm caught himself; Gus was right, he was rambling on about things his son knew as well as he did. Malcolm took out his handkerchief, mopped the sweat from his forehead, around his neck. No wonder he thinks I don't respect his ideas; fact is I don't most of the time, I never give him enough credit for what he knows or is trying to do with these autocars. "So," he said, putting the handkerchief back in his pocket, "did our visitors give any indication at all what their interest is?"

"Nothing that I could tell. And I didn't want to come right out and ask."

"No. Better not to. The letter said it was regarding a secret project and we weren't to discuss their visit with anyone, so I guess we will know in good time. We did get some news, though, about your brother."

Malcolm told him about the telegram from John Lincoln, and that he had asked Libby to tell his stepmother and half-sister.

"Yes, I suppose that would be best." Gus thought a moment. "Do you actually think he will go?"

"To England? Why wouldn't he?"

Gus laughed like a puff of air. "He's already got what he wanted, doesn't he? He's got everyone in the family all worked up, especially Mary Lydia who hasn't been out of bed since he up and disappeared. He's the center of attention, plus now he's got everyone thinking he's some kind of hero, a moral leader taking a stand in support of our involvement in the European war. There's no need for him to actually get on that ship."

"I think he was quite serious about joining the war effort and doing his part."

"I'll believe it when I see it. I think everyone misjudges John Lincoln's intentions. They're not always so grand and high-minded as everyone wants to believe they are." Gus looked down at the gauges in front of him. "I'm starting to build pressure, so I either need to shut it down or be off. All things considered, it seems I'll do better if I'm off."

They agreed to talk at home later that evening and Gus chuffed away, Malcolm once again engulfed in steam. As he walked back across the compound, watching the block-like vehicle disappear in the shadows of the passageway to the street, Malcolm thought, The same old battle, the same old war. It had been going on between Gus and the twins since the day John Lincoln and Mary Lydia were born. Irreconcilable differences. So much for brotherly and sisterly love, at least as far as Gus is concerned. Was that the reason John Lincoln and Mary Lydia were so close, drawn up into themselves against the onslaughts of their older half-brother? Or were Gus' antagonisms brought on because it was apparent, even from the time John Lincoln and Mary Lydia lay side by side in their crib, that their older half-brother was excluded from the twins' closed society? Whatever the source, the conflict was still alive and kicking, no question about that. He began to trace again the scars on his hands, the patches of mismatched skin, before jamming his hands in his trouser pockets. No matter, he couldn't change it regardless. For now, all he cared about was to get out of this heat, back to his office.

4

The house sat by itself halfway up the slope of the valley's hills, alone in a level space among the trees and the sandstone and granite bluffs, above the reach of the town, a large white wood multifaced structure with an open porch extending across the front of the original house. The house was built by the first of the Lyles in the area, the first Malcolm Lyle, who along with a man named John Buchanan founded the iron furnace along the banks of the river that eventually grew into the mile-long Allehela Works of Buchanan Steel, with the town of Furnass growing up the slope of the hill from it. In time the first Malcolm turned his share of the steelworks over to his son Colin, who soon grew bored with the raw industry of making iron and steel; instead, he became interested in the developments the British were making with steam engines, and broke away to form his own company, the Keystone Steam Works. The first Malcolm meanwhile built what he named Sycamore House on the slopes above the smoke and clamor of the mills and the town, though he kept his eye on things from the window of his study at the front of the house on the first floor, and, just to make sure he didn't miss anything, had French doors opening from the master bedroom to a balcony over the front porch.

When Malcolm Lyle died in 1853, Colin and his wife, Libby, and their beginning family took over Sycamore House—though by this time it was known in Furnass more by the name of the Lyle House—until Colin toward the end of his life took up residence in his office and workshop at the steamworks. When he assumed Colin's departure would mean his own ascendency to take over the house, Colin's son, Malcolm Hayes Lyle—the Malcolm of our story—extended the house with the addition of a wing on either side: one wing to accommodate his son Gus and his own family when he had one; the other to accommodate his aged mother, Libby, into her golden years. As it turned out, however, Libby had other ideas.

This day when Libby and Perpetual arrived at the house after their visit to see the statue at the steamworks, they found an unfamiliar automobile parked in front of the house.

"That isn't one of Gus' experiments, is it?" Libby said as Perpetual stopped the surrey before the front steps.

"I don't think so, Mawm," Perpetual said, wrapping the reins around the brake and getting down to help Libby from the surrey. "That's a gasoline car, and Gus only works with the steam cars."

"Then we must have a caller," Libby said, brushing herself off, straightening her dress, before attempting the three steps up to the porch. At the top, proud of herself to have made it on her own, she looked down at Perpetual, who had climbed back in the surrey. "Maybe one of those nice handsome well-spoken gentlemen who come to visit Malcolm from time to time. What do you think?"

"If you say so, Mawm. Walk on, you," Perpetual said, snapping the reins and heading to the barn up the slope behind the house.

Libby was glad to get inside, into the shadows inside the house, out of the direct sunlight, but the heat inside the house was just as oppressive, in some ways worse than outside, the house stuffy and close the moment she stepped from the foyer into the front hall, like stepping, plunging into warm water, the same sensation of suddenly being unable to breathe; and dark, the drapes still drawn that would later be pulled back from the open windows to allow the evening breeze, if there was one, to course through the house. She stopped in front of the hall tree, watching herself in the tall mirror as she removed her gloves and hat, then turned to face whatever it was the world was going to present to her this time. The answer came in the presence of Missy, a small figure of a woman dressed in a white gossamery peignoir, floating out of the shadows at the rear of the downstairs, coming toward her down the hallway.

"I expected to see a businessman or two waiting to talk to Malcolm," Libby said, looking in the doorways of the parlor and then her son's study. "I saw the autocar parked out front."

"It belongs to the doctor. I called for him to have a look at Mary Lydia."

"Really," Libby said. Wanting, more than anything, to comment about her daughter-in-law's uncharacteristic initiative and concern, but caught herself, decided for Mary Lydia's sake it was best to keep her thoughts to herself. She checked herself once more in the mirror to make sure she was all present and accounted for. "I trust she hasn't taken a turn for the worse."

"No, she's still the same as far as I can tell. I just got tired of trying to deal with any more of the girl's hysterics and decided to have a medical person tell us what's going on."

Ah yes, of course that would be the reason to make the call, Libby smiled. She's grown weary of dealing with Mary Lydia. Certainly stopping into her daughter's room a few times a day, to make sure Perpetual or someone else had delivered the girl's meals and changed the chamber pot, would interfere with Missy's usual routine of looking at women's magazines and eating chocolates. Libby gave her son Malcolm the benefit of the doubt for marrying the woman—it undoubtedly had something to do with the tragic end of his first marriage—but for the life of her she found it hard to see Missy's redeeming qualities. But no matter now, there were more immediate concerns.

"So, has the good doctor given his conclusion?" Libby said as Perpetual came down the hall from the back of the house, sandwiching Missy between them, much to Missy's obvious discomfort.

"I can tell you what's wrong with Mary Lydia," Perpetual said, "but nobody wants to listen to Perpetual."

"I've heard it all before," Missy said, looking to see if she could squeeze by Libby in the one direction, or Perpetual in the other, so she wasn't caught between them, eventually giving up, resigned to her fate. "I know very well that she's upset because her brother up and disappeared without saying good-bye. Well, he didn't say good-bye to me either, and you don't see me mooning around the house staying in bed, do you?"

Perpetual folded her wrist against her cocked hip, closed her eyes, and nodded three times for emphasis: "Mm-mm-mm."

"You don't 'Mm-mm' me," Missy said, drawing herself up to her full four foot, eleven inches. "Now we'll know for certain what the problem is with the girl. Dr. McArtle should be down in a few minutes with the results of his examination."

"Dr. McArtle?" Libby said, feeling as though the air had just gone out of her.

"Mawm, you all right?" Perpetual said, brushing past Missy, sending the smaller woman reeling against the wall, to take Libby's arm.

"Well, I never—" Missy said, righting herself.

"Yes, I'm fine," Libby said, leaning momentarily against Perpetual, forcing a smile. "I don't know what got into me, I guess the name, McArtle, surprised me. There was a Dr. McArtle here many years ago, surely it can't be. . . ."

"That would be my father," a male voice said coming down the stairs, his shoes, ankles, legs, torso, head emerging from the shadows of the second floor. He was a tall narrow-shouldered man in his late forties or early fifties, clean-shaven as was the fashion and with a full head of hair, in a tailored gray four-button suit, carrying a doctor's bag. "And you must be Mrs. Lyle," McArtle said, offering his hand. "I've heard my father speak of you many times."

Libby felt confused, as if things were going too fast. "You're Eugene's son. Of course, but what are you doing here? Is Eugene. . . ?"

"I'm afraid my father died many years ago. And what am I doing here? Well, I helped my father with his practice for a time, but after he died I didn't want to stay in Lancaster, and I heard there was need of a doctor here . . . so. . . ."

"Lancaster," Libby said, thinking. "I never heard where he went after he left Furnass. . . ."

"Furnass always seemed to be a special place for him. . . ," Dr. McArtle said.

"This is all very touching," Missy said, sloshing her words as she tended to when upset, looking at the doctor somewhere in the area of his rib cage, "but it doesn't tell us anything about the state of my daughter and why she's taken to her bed."

"Ah," Dr. McArtle said. "I'm pleased to say there's nothing at all wrong with her. She's a very healthy, and very pregnant, young woman."

"Hah!" Perpetual said. "Perpetual, she could have told you."

"Hush now, Perpetual," Libby said. "Pregnant? Are you sure?"

"Yes ma'am," Dr. McArtle said, taking his hat from the hook on the side of the hall tree. "As sure as sure can be. Probably close to two months, I'd say—"

"Well, that's nonsense," Missy said. "How can she be pregnant when she doesn't have a husband?"

"Then perhaps we should be looking for a bright star in the sky," Dr. McArtle said, a conspirator's smile to Libby, "and three wise men on camels."

"Hah!" Perpetual said again.

"You are your father's son," Libby said, trying not to be amused. "He always said things at inappropriate times too."

McArtle seemed unfazed or perhaps unaware of anything improper. "I'll send over a tonic she needs to start taking. And I'll send some written instructions she should follow in these early weeks. I also should see her at my office in a week or so, if she's up and about by then. If not, I'll come back. Nice to meet you, Mrs. Lyle."

As McArtle backed down the hallway and out the front screen door, Perpetual trailed along to escort him out, then turned around and said again, "Hah!"

"Hah indeed," Missy said, looking at no one in particular. "Utter nonsense. The girl is no more pregnant than I am. The man doesn't know what he's talking about." She headed back down the corridor muttering to herself.

"I told you, Mawm, Perpetual just knew it," Perpetual said to Libby.

"Hush now, Perpetual. Help me upstairs, I need to lie down."

She was suddenly very tired, as if all her energy had drained from her in one great gush. Perpetual came beside her and the two women made their way slowly up the stairs. On the second floor, Perpetual followed Libby into the master bedroom at the front of the house. As Libby sat on the edge of the bed and took off her shoes, undid the top buttons of her dress, she asked Perpetual to pull back the drapes and open the French doors onto the balcony.

"Don't you want them closed, Mawm? For your sleep?"

"Thank you, Perpetual, but at my age I want to see as much sun as possible. As often as possible."

With the drapes open, mid-afternoon sunlight took over the room. For a moment Perpetual looked at the view down the slope of the hill, at the town descending in steps to the mills along the river, the steamworks where they were earlier this afternoon, the wall of trees on the opposite side of the valley, the drift of clouds as the sun angled west, before turning around to look back in the room, at Libby getting herself comfortable on the bed.

"So. Mr. Malcolm, he did a good thing. Keeping John Lincoln's telegram to himself, down at the Works."

"So it would appear," Libby said lying back, arranging the pillows under her head. "But then I've never doubted Malcolm's intelligence or managing skills, though I suspect Malcolm doesn't believe that. Where he gets these ideas . . . but that's his concern, not mine. There was never any question that Malcolm was and is a better businessman than his father, he took Colin's ideas and figured out not only how to make the machines but how to market them to the world. Left to his own inclinations his father would have given away all his designs if someone had asked for

them, the dear man. The Keystone Steam Works became world-renowned under Malcolm's guiding hand. I only wish I could say I had the same faith in the next generation coming along. Gus is a sweet young man and he's certainly eager enough, but. . . ."
Libby felt herself starting to drift off and didn't care to fight it.

"And it doesn't seem to Perpetual that Mary Lydia needs to hear any more news today. The sweet child has enough to think and worry about. I think we just forget telling Mary Lydia any news about her brother going off to fight somebody else's war. That's what Perpetual thinks."

Libby opened her eyes again. Perpetual was a silhouette before the sunlight coming through the open French doors, without definition or shading, expressionless, a shadow's shadow—what the ancients called a shade: I wonder if that's what happens after we die, if that's what we see, how we see the others, our loved ones, not as how we knew them in life but only in outline, recognizing them by something other than physical description, I guess you would call it their spirit, that would certainly solve the age-old question of how someone will look in the afterlife, whether they are as you first knew them or when they died or somewhere in between, you just know them from something deep within yourself, oh it would be wonderful to see Colin again, and Father and Mother, and Judson of course, ah yes, Judson, you to whom I owe so much, all the more present for your absence, I stopped taking Eugene's laudanum that day—and Eugene too, I met your son, the young doctor, you did well with him—I never took your dream potion again after my handsome Confederate knight in shining armor came to rescue me and I was too hazy to recognize what was happening, what could have happened, though maybe it was all to the good in the long run, if I had come to myself that morning and gone with you how would the world be different for all of us now, you, me, Colin, Malcolm, but oh the stories we could tell, the stories could tell about us. . . .

5

Perpetual watched as Libby drifted off to sleep, waiting until she was certain that the elderly woman was away from the world, before going across the room and placing a throw over Libby, making sure everything was as it should be for when Libby woke up, then went quietly through the connecting door to her room, knowing from practice over the years where to step to avoid the floorboards that creak, and closed the door behind her. Safely in her own room, she sighed, a relief that she got the old woman back safely from the day's outing. She stood for a moment looking out the front window at the myriad shades of green of the sycamores in the front yard. Then she knew, even without the confirmation from Dr. McArtle that Mary Lydia has a baby coming, that it was time. It was time to put to paper the story that had occupied her waking thoughts for the past few weeks. Ever since she and Libby had their talk. Perpetual, still careful to make as little noise as possible, sat down at her tall secretary desk, unlatched the slanting cover and lowered into place the writing surface, took the sheaf of paper she'd been collecting for this moment, uncapped her pen and, after refilling the reservoir in the barrel from her bottle of ink, started to write:

> "Ow!" said Mole Rat. "You spiked me!"
> "Ow yourself!" said Hedgehog. "You're the one who bumped into me!"
> Hedgehog ran her paws down the length of her snout as if to make sure it was still in place. The small animal had stopped on the path to admire the view of orange and yellow leaves as the trees changed in autumn.

Mole Rat rubbed her chest where Hedgehog's spines had spiked her.

"I'm sorry. I try to warn folks I'm coming by tapping this stick," Mole Rat said, holding up the tree branch she was carrying. "I'm blind, in case you didn't notice."

"Well, I'm sorry too," Hedgehog said. "I'm afraid I don't hear very well these days. Where are you headed?"

"I'm on my way to talk to The Crow."

"And why would you want to talk to some flighty bird?"

"Not just any bird. I heard people talking one day while they were having a picnic. They said The Crow was the wisest of all the creatures in the forest."

"What?" Hedgehog said.

Mole Rat sighed, and then spoke louder. "I want to know why I'm blind and was born to live underground. Other animals have eyes, and spend their lives in the light and the warmth of the sun and the cleansing rain. Why was I fated to spend my life in darkness and dirt? Why can't I live in a nice place too?"

"Funny you should say that," Hedgehog said. "I've wanted to know why I'm covered with all these spines, like an inside-out pin cushion. Folks think I'm so cute, but when they try to get close to me they stick themselves. So everyone stays away. Why can't I have friends like everybody else?"

"That's certainly a prickly question," Mole Rat said, looking off somewhere to Hedgehog's right.

"I'm over here," Hedgehog said.

"Oh. Sorry," Mole Rat said. "Maybe you'd like to come with me and ask The Crow about yourself."

"Oh good. An adventure. I'm tired of being an old stick-in-the-bush."

"We'll make quite a pair. I can't see, and you can't hear."

"What?" Hedgehog said, leaning closer.

"Easy," Mole Rat cautioned, feeling the first tingling of Hedgehog's spines. "Here, I'll throw away my stick and take your arm. Very, very carefully take your arm."

"You let me know if I start to get bristly," Hedgehog said.

"Don't worry. I'll stick close, just not close enough to get stuck." Mole Rat grinned, her buckteeth glimmering, proud of her clever wordplay.

"What?"

Mole Rat sighed. "Just go."

. . . and Perpetual stops her writing and listens for a moment, hearing Libby stirring in the next room, then the old woman settles down again, goes back to sleep again, but Perpetual decides that's enough writing for today, she's got a good start at it, and she's at a good stopping place; she gathers together the pages she's written, tapping them on end into alignment, then secures them away in a drawer of the secretary desk and closes the lid, feeling somewhat proud of herself, unsure when she started if she could do such a thing as write a story, waits a moment to make sure there are no more stirrings from next door, then gets up quietly, making sure the legs of her chair don't drag across the wood floor, crosses the room and out the other door into the hallway, closing the door carefully behind her, the room that had been the nursery when Libby and Colin were raising the children here but became Perpetual's room the day she arrived, the same day Colin, an old man then, moved out of the house to take up his final residence

at his beloved steamworks, the day Libby announced she would remain in the master bedroom on her own and that Perpetual's room would be next door so that she would be close by in case Libby needed her, establishing Perpetual's position in the household from her first day that she was Libby's helper and companion exclusively, different by definition from Margaret the cook and housekeeper and her husband, William, who tends the grounds and stable—both born to slaves on her father's South Carolina plantation who Libby brought here and made a home for in the years after the Civil War when the Reconstruction turned violent and vindicative—Perpetual untouchable as it were, unreproachable, her mistress' agent and confidant and voice too when necessary, though both women understood the limits and limitations of that too; the woman whose dark skin color is genetically determined for equatorial sunlight, endless sunny days, heads now down the hallway, moving through the dark upstairs of the house like a spirit of the house, quiet as a whisper, the floorboards creaking softly like distant voices talking to one another, the house her domain as if the house is hers alone though she knows she is here only to serve, glides around the railings of the stairwell and into a room at the rear of the house directly opposite the door of Libby's room at the front of the house, into the darkness of Mary Lydia's room, Perpetual opening the door only a few inches at first, then stepping inside as her eyes adjust to the lack of light, only a thin bar of sunlight and not even that, a thin bar of gray light extending from a crack in the drapes falling across the figure in the bed, and then the voice, "Perpetual?" and Perpetual steps into the room and approaches the bed, "Yes, my girl, it's Perpetual, she's come to see how you are," and the figure on the bed stirs a bit, stretches and tries to sit up or at least raise her head, Perpetual reaching over to help the young woman get adjusted on the pillows as the young woman says, "I'm all right. Did you hear

*the doctor was here?" and Perpetual, finished plumping the pil-
lows, stands beside the bed, the figure lying there in the white
nightdress and the white sheets and coverlet, "Yes, your grandmother and Perpetual, we met him when we came in. So it's what
we already knew," and Mary Lydia, a not particularly attractive
girl, a fact that she's well aware of, having heard all her life that
her twin brother is actually better looking than she is, her hair in
long ringlets along the sides of her face only serving to accent the
more that she is unformed, a personality in progress, younger
than her twenty-one years, "Yes, it's what we thought. How did
Mother take the news?" and Perpetual says, "That was as we
expected too, she doesn't believe it," and the two women scrunch
their shoulders at each other in appreciation of the joke before
Mary Lydia sobers again, "And is there any word from John
Lincoln?" and Perpetual makes a point to look her in the eye as
she says, "No, my darling child, Perpetual is afraid not," and
Mary Lydia says looking off somewhere in the distance, "I didn't
think there would be, he won't come back now, I told you when
we first knew what was happening to me," and Perpetual says,
"There's no reason for John Lincoln to know anything about
what's happening to you, and there's no reason for that to have
any bearing on why John Lincoln went away," and Mary Lydia
looks at her hands folded on the bedsheet a moment then looks up
at her and says, "But he does know about it, I told him a few
weeks ago when you and I were first sure what was happening to
me," and Perpetual says, "What are you saying, child?" and
Mary Lydia says, "I'm sure that's why he went away, because I'm
pregnant," and Perpetual hits at the sheet, "Don't talk nonsense,
child. You don't know no such thing," and Mary Lydia smiles
beatifically, secure in what she knows of her twin, "Yes, I know
all right," and Perpetual leans close to the figure in the bed and
takes the young woman's face in her hands and speaks with deadly*

certainty, *"Don't you say a word of this to anyone in this house. You hear me, child? Perpetual, she cannot help you unless you promise Perpetual,"* and Mary Lydia tries to move her face out of the other's grasp but hasn't the strength, can only look into the dark features and brimming eyes in front of her, aware that indeed this dark-skinned woman is probably her only hope, and says, *"Yes, I promise,"* and Perpetual continues to hold her face for several seconds more, then leans closer and kisses her full on the lips before straightening up again and without saying anything more leaves the room . . . and the house falls silent again as it settles into its late afternoon routines, the life of the house as it has for decades continuing with a life of its own, the mortise and tenon joints of the timber frame construction working in concert with one another, the elements of the construction swelling or shrinking as the temperature of the day progresses or recedes, the soft but unstoppable push and pull of wood against wood creating its own dimension of life, its own separate reality, with its own life- and-death cycle, to say nothing of the life-and-death struggles going on within the walls and floors and ceilings themselves, hundreds, thousands of insects and vermin in violent daily conflicts against each other and themselves fighting to survive, flies, ants, lice, bedbugs, cockroaches, earwigs, silverfish, centipedes, millipedes, spiders, moths, mites, mosquitoes (actually they're not in the house itself, they're hatching in a stagnant pond under the back steps), beetles, termites, spiders, mice, rats, squirrels, field mice, a lone and sexually frustrated garter snake, to say nothing of plant life, the seed pods from the sycamores in the yard blown here by spring rains pushing up through the dark loam in the fruit cellar, the acorn buried underneath the porch by a cautious squirrel sending up its tendrils looking for light, the moss covering the edges of the stones of the walkways, the grass pushing up between the foundation, the ivy starting to cover the kitchen wall, the *house a living, and dying, thing secure in its patterns, at peace with its normalcy, as if the secrets and untruths and outright deceptions that drift through the dark rooms and corridors are no more than a wayward breeze or unwanted sunlight that can be blocked off with a closed drape, a shuttered window . . . as back in her room Perpetual waters and prunes the small forest she maintains close to the windows, pots and hanging baskets of herbs and native plants she brought with her as seeds and seedlings from her home in the Caribbean, plants that the Lyle family have come to assume over the years as having something to do with Perpetual's religion but that they don't understand and don't want to understand, and Perpetual certainly isn't going to tell them differently, talking to her plants in her soft soothing voice as she tells them the latest happenings in the family and how they may be called on for help in the near future, listening for the stirrings from next door that will tell her that Libby has wakened from her nap and will need help getting ready for dinner . . . while downstairs Missy, Malcolm's wife, dressed as she has for years in a white lacy peignoir and pom-pom slippers, hovers in the kitchen keeping an eye on Margaret as she sometimes does at mealtime to make sure the woman prepares the meals correctly, never saying one thing or another about the food preparations as she stands in a corner beside the broom closet wringing her hands because the truth is Missy hasn't a clue how to cook or bake or do anything in the kitchen, even after a couple of decades of watching Margaret prepare the meals, Missy only doing so because of some nagging feeling that she is in fact supposed to keep track of things, the truth being that even after all these years she is fruitlessly trying to fulfill the role of mistress of the household, her misguided hope that her presence will in some way intimidate the cook and housekeeper, though her presence in the kitchen no more worrisome or bothersome to Margaret's work than if a floor mop had*

*taken up residence in the corner, a rather short blond floor mop
at that, having accepted years ago that she has to make allowances
for monied white people, they are basically crazy and it is up to
her to help them as much as she can . . . while in the back of the
house in the left-side addition known as the Nearer Wing—for
the simple reason that it seems closer to the main part of the
house than the one called the Farther Wing, though in truth both
wings are equidistant from the rest of the house—Augustus Malcolm Lyle, better known as Gus, home from the steamworks after
picking up the representatives from Washington and getting them
settled at the Grand Hotel and then reporting back to his father,
wanders through the suite of rooms that make up his home totally
lost now that his wife, Lily, has taken their eight-year-old son,
Augustus Malcolm Lyle II, better known as Mal, on a visit to see
her family in Kansas, her father a Covenanter preacher of the
fire-and-brimstone variety that Gus hopes the close exposure to
won't ruin Mal's sweet nature (and that Gus hopes will do something to bring back some of the sweet nature Lily had when they
were first married), never for a second imagining when Lily first
announced her intentions for the trip that he would ever miss his
wife and child, the first time she had returned home since she
graduated from Covenant College and married Gus, the truth being that it isn't that's he's missing either Lily or the boy as much
as he's missing the feeling of normalcy that their presence gives
him, the feeling that he's like everybody else in the world with a
wife and family, someone by definition in his corner at least nom-
inally, enough to make him feel stranded without them, fleeing
the house now out the wing's private entrance and into the side
yard, walking up the hill to the stable where he left his latest
prototype for the Lylemobile, the steam car sitting in the first
stall inside the door, the brass fixtures on the engine and casings
of the headlamps catching the gleams of sunlight in the shadows*

of the stable, the particles of dust hanging suspended in the air as if the old building is holding its breath, where he finds William the groundsman and stable hand hanging over the wall of the stall studying the vehicle, "So, William, would you like to go for another ride?" and William says shaking his head, "Would admire to, Mr. Gus, but Margaret said she'd beat me again with her wooden spoon if she saw me in your autovehicle again," and Gus laughs, "Well, we wouldn't want that, would we?" "It is not a pleasure, Mr. Gus," William says and then adds, "Tell me again how many horses are inside?" and Gus smiles to himself, "It's hard to judge, as I explained before, the criteria of horsepower for a steam car and an internal combustion car being rather different. But the boiler on the Lylemobile is rated at thirty horsepower, though at certain times it probably reaches closer to a hundred," and William shakes his head, "It's a marvel," he says walking back into the shadows of the stable, "A marvel," and Gus takes a rag and begins to buff again the fixtures and the metal sides of the machine in preparation for the meeting with the Washington representatives tomorrow, "A marvel" echoing in his thoughts, his marvel, his alone . . . and the afternoon wears on till it's close to six thirty and Malcolm arrives home having walked from the steamworks as he does every evening, in the heat or cold, rain or snow, his way he says to keep in physical shape as well as to keep in touch with the goings-on in the town, though he also knows he does it because his father, Colin, always walked home in all weathers, stopping at the water pump behind the house just as his father did to splash cold water on his face after the walk, drying himself with the towel Margaret leaves for him on a hook beside the kitchen door, also aware that it was Colin's wife, his mother, Libby, who always left the towel for his father, but no matter, he wouldn't expect Missy to remember such a nicety much less perform it each evening, carrying his coat over his arm into the house and putting it on again before entering the dining room, where the family is gathering for its evening meal, another tradition started by his father and continued on because of Malcolm's insistence, the family such as it is this evening reduced in size because Gus' wife, Lily, and son, Mal, are away to Kansas, John Lincoln is on his way to go to war (though Malcolm is resolved to say nothing of the telegram about his son on a troop ship heading to England unless Missy or someone else brings up the topic, unaware that Libby never told Missy or Mary Lydia that particular bit of news), and Mary Lydia is upstairs in her bed, the family such as it is, Malcolm, Missy, Gus, Libby, and Perpetual sitting down at the table that's too long for their reduced numbers, the family stretching to pass the platters of roast beef and ham, the tureens of beans and summer squash, mashed potatoes and corn, everyone eating in silence as Malcolm ponders what exactly he can say without asking for trouble and finally hits upon it, thinking as he says it that a good father probably should have said it sooner, "Well, what did the doctor have to say about our Mary Lydia?" and as soon as he says it, from the raised heads around the table all looking his direction, realizes that without meaning to he's stepped in it this time though he has no idea what it in this case is, Missy looking at him across the length of the table, her fork on a flipped wrist aimed his direction, sloshing her words worse than ever, a sign in itself that there's deep trouble ahead, "Oh, well, listen to this: We not only ended up with the son of the doctor you told me about who kept your mother drugged up with laudanum for several years and carried on a love affair under your father's nose, but the man had the nerve to say that our Mary Lydia is pregnant. Pregnant! Whoever heard of such a thing! How can a girl get pregnant if she's never been with a man, just tell me that? Tell me that!" and tosses the fork in the general direction of the roast beef, gets up from the table and heads out of the room, back through the shadows and down the hall to the living room where she spends most of her days to the point that it's now referred to not as the living room but "Missy's room," leaving Malcolm and Libby looking at each other, "Mother, I don't know where she got all that about Dr. McArtle and being drugged—" and Libby silences him with a look as she touches the corners of her mouth with her napkin and says, "It's all right, Malcolm, I'm sure she got it from you at one time or another, and I'm sure you had your reasons, but I think for now I'll go back to my room" and gets up and heads out of the room toward the staircase, Perpetual getting up as well to follow her, saying as she passes him on her way out of the room, "She be all right, Mr. Malcolm. Perpetual, she knows you never said a word about that to nobody that Miss Libby hasn't thought herself," and Malcolm says, "Is that supposed to make me feel better?" and Perpetual stops in the doorway, half in and half out of the light in the dining room, considers a moment then says, "Mr. Malcolm, I don't think there's a thing in the world that would make you feel better about anything," before leaving the room and following Libby up the stairs, Gus taking one look at his father's face and gets up and leaves the table on his own, leaving Malcolm sitting there by himself, wondering what just happened, "Blazes to hell, Mary Lydia's pregnant? Why didn't somebody tell me? What's going on around here?" as Margaret comes in from the kitchen, surveys the half-eaten meals on the plates, sighs once and says to Malcolm, "You want me to redd the table or you still hungry. . . ?"

6

"So, are we to believe Mary Lydia is pregnant or not?" Gus said, sitting down in the wing-back leather chair in front of his father's desk.

"I'm afraid we have to," Malcolm said, lighting his cigar. "Why wouldn't we?"

"Well, Mother said—"

"Your mother has many sterling qualities, despite what your grandmother might say." Malcolm waved the safety match to extinction, took the cigar from his mouth, and looked at the lighted end. Satisfied, he put it back in his mouth and took a healthy puff. "But between a doctor's word and your mother's. . . ." He let the rest of the sentence float away with the cigar smoke, gradually filling up the room with a gray haze.

It had become another of the family's traditions that after dinner Malcolm and Gus would retire to the study at the front of the house to discuss the day's events at the steamworks and plan the next day's agenda. The two men sat in silence for several minutes, Malcolm occasionally taking a puff on his cigar, Gus sitting across from him watching the smoke rise to the level of the ceiling as he tried not to cough. There was no breeze from the open windows, where the evening sky above the town flickered orange and white from the Buchanan Steel Works along the river; the light in the room came from sconces with bare bulbs high up on the walls, the green-shaded desk lamp. The walls of the study were lined with glass-fronted barrister bookcases holding Malcolm's and his father's collection of engineering books, folios of the steamworks many patents, along with leather-bound editions of the classics that every well-born gentleman of the era should have read—Thucydides, Marcus Aurelius, Shakespeare— and which, for the record, Malcolm and his father had, and Gus had not. Above the fireplace was a large painting of the Keystone Steam Works as it would be seen from the air, the cluster of reddish-orange brick buildings with their distinctive saw-toothed clerestory windows along the roofs, the painting done during the heyday of the plant when the steamworks rivaled Buchanan Steel as the largest employer in town, with a border of inset medallions depicting the manufacturing processes going on in the plant—the stamping mill, the mammoth forge, the annealing furnaces—as well as scenes of various Keystone Steamers at work in the field—a mobile well-driller, a steam shovel, a steam tractor—and scenes of the supposed genteel fin de siècle life of Furnass, ladies with parasols and men in top hats promenading under fashionably spindly trees along the sidewalks in front of the plant. After several minutes, Gus uncrossed, recrossed his legs.

"Mother does have a point, though. We are certainly unaware of Mary Lydia keeping company with anyone. Much less spending enough time to get pregnant."

"It's been my experience," Malcolm said, "that it takes an astoundingly short amount of time for a woman to get pregnant."

At that Gus allowed himself a cough. "I think you know what I mean, Father."

"Yes, I'm afraid I do." Malcolm again regarded the burning ember at the end of the cigar. "That's why I want you to go to the college tomorrow morning and find out what you can about any relationships Mary Lydia might have had. I remembered there was a picnic or some outing last spring she went to, she showed us a Brownie snapshot of a group of them afterwards."

Malcolm opened the center drawer and took out a small framed photograph and handed it across the desk to Gus. There were eight or ten young people grouped together on the slope of a hillside. Mary Lydia was lying on the grass with a young man in a pin-striped blazer and bushy hair kneeling behind her. John Lincoln was at the other end of the group, hugging his knees.

"Where did you get this?"

"Mary Lydia had it on her dresser."

"Did you talk to her? How is she feeling after the doctor—"

"She was asleep."

"You just took it?"

Malcolm ignored him. "I want you to take it up to the college and find out who she was with that day. I especially want to know the name of the young man kneeling behind Mary Lydia."

"It's summer vacation, Father. There won't be anyone at the college now."

"There are a few summer classes going on, I believe. Besides, the deans and administrators will be there, they're the ones you need to talk to regardless. Tell them who you are, that I sent you, if there's any question. The Lyle name should still carry some import there, if anywhere. Despite your own unhappy sojourn with them."

"And what do I do if I find out that she was involved with someone in her class? Organize a lynching party?"

"Don't be ridiculous," Malcolm said, taking a particularly impatient puff. "But we do need to know if such a person exists and if he's a prospective suitor and what his intentions are. So far Mary Lydia isn't forthcoming about such information."

"Well, if you don't mind my saying so, it sounds like a fool's errand to me."

Malcolm did mind Gus saying so, but decided for the moment not to comment.

"But more to the point," Gus went on, "I can't go to the college tomorrow because we have the meeting with those government reps in the morning."

"I don't want you at that meeting tomorrow."

Gus blinked once. Stared at his father.

"I'm sorry to be blunt about this, but I'm afraid I have to be. I don't want the subject of the Lylemobile to be brought up under any context, unless of course they bring it up on their own. But I don't think they will. I think the reason for their visit here is on account of something else entirely, though I have no idea what that might be. The point is that I want them to present their proposal without any distractions or influence of what we might want from them."

"And you think I'll bring up the Lylemobile regardless what they propose."

"I can't be assured that you won't." Malcolm sighed, leaned forward and folded his hands on the desk blotter, the lit cigar projecting from the barricade of fingers like a smoking gun. "I know you're passionate about the project. I know it's what you're basing your future on with this company. I admire you for that, I truly do. But I also have to be wary of it. There's too much at stake here for the good of the company."

"And you don't think I have the good of the company in mind?"

"You'll have your chance to show off the Lylemobile when you pick them up at the hotel and bring them to the office. And once you return from the college and the reps are on their way back to Washington, I will tell you everything that went on in the meeting. Lord knows, whatever it is they're proposing, I'll need your help to fulfill it."

Gus sat for a moment, then shook his head as he got up from the chair, deciding not to say what he was thinking. "Good night, Father," he said without looking at Malcolm again as he left the room.

You do what you have to to protect your children, Malcolm thought. You do what you think is best, even if it hurts them. He probably thinks that if the Lylemobile were John Lincoln's project that I'd take an entirely difference stance, but that's not it at all. At least I hope it's not. No, I would feel this way regardless, that we have to wait and see what it is the government has in mind for us, we can't be pushing ideas at them, we can't impose our agenda on theirs. And Gus doesn't know that yet, he's too one-sided, he's too . . . oh, I don't know what he is and what he isn't. The poor boy, I want to help him, and I fear there's just not enough there to help. How can I feel that way about my own son? And Missy's certainly no help with him, there's no help for her either. Oh Lydia, if only you had lived, you would know what to do, you would have raised our children to stand on their own and be their own persons, but then I snuffed out her life too when the moment of truth came about, I carry her bones and charred flesh with me every day of my life. Little wonder that I'd doubt my own ability to make the right choice, I certainly didn't when it mattered most. Well, this line of thinking will only dig me deeper into my hole. . . .

Malcolm got up from his desk and stood at the window, looking at himself repeated in the double panes of glass from the open lower sash, the double view of the room behind him imposed on the night landscape of the lights of the town stepped down the slope of the valley, the flames of the Bessemers at Buchanan Steel in their berths aimed at the night sky, matching the stuttered glow of the cigar in his hand. Then he violently stubbed the end of the cigar into the glass in front of him, grinding it to ash against the glass, smudging, singeing the glass, sparks raining down on the sill and his shoes, thinking, Blazes to hell, I don't know why I even bother with these things, I can't stand the taste of them anymore. . . .

PART TWO

MONDAY, JULY 3, 1916

7

So, with Mole Rat holding on gingerly to Hedgehog's arm, the two little animals set off through the dark wood. They hadn't gone very far when they encountered Rabbit, who wanted to know where they were going.

"We're on our way to see The Crow," Hedgehog said. "Mole Rat wants to ask why she's blind and has to live underground, and I want to know why I'm covered with spines so no one can get close to me."

"Sounds like big questions to ask a bird who basically lives on waste," Rabbit said, twitching her nose as if she smelled something unpleasant. "But maybe I'll come with you. I'd like to know why everybody chases me. Apparently all I'm good for is food for somebody else, but when there's danger all I can do is run away. Why wasn't I born with fangs, or maybe scary claws?"

"An armed bunny," Hedgehog said. "Now, that's a concept."

"But she has a good point," Mole Rat said. "The world is as unfair to Rabbit as it is to you or me."

"Then Rabbit should come with us," Hedgehog said. "The more the disgruntled, the better, I always say."

"You do?" said Mole Rat.

"What?" said Hedgehog.

"Go."

With that the trio of adventurers continued along the path through the dark wood. But Rabbit, as rabbits are wont to do, kept charging ahead and the smaller animals had trouble keeping up. After a while when they came to a quiet pond, they decided to take a rest, sitting together on a large rock. Hedgehog and Rabbit admired the view of the water and Mole Rat took a little snooze. For a moment all their troubles seemed far behind them—when suddenly beyond the edge of the rock appeared a large green head.

"Large green head! Large green head!" shouted Rabbit and Hedgehog in unison as they tumbled off the rock and ran for the bushes.

"Where? Where?" shouted Mole Rat, unable to see what the others saw and having to stay put.

"Here! Here!" shouted the large green head. "Where else would I be? You're sitting on the roof of my house!"

When they realized they had been sitting on a turtle, Rabbit and Hedgehog laughed raucously, perhaps a bit too raucously as folks do when they're embarrassed at their own foolishness. But Turtle was unamused.

"I don't know what you think is so funny. When I heard you coming I didn't know if you were friend or foe, so I did the only thing I could do, duck back into my shell. I don't know why I wasn't given some way to defend myself, I can't even run away. When danger comes, all I can do is hide."

"Hmm," said Mole Rat. "This sounds familiar. Another animal unhappy with her lot."

"Then Turtle should come with us to see The Crow too," Hedgehog said.

When Hedgehog explained the nature of their quest, Turtle was anxious to join them. But Rabbit was concerned.

"We're having trouble keeping up with each other as it is," Rabbit said. "I'm afraid Turtle will only slow us down more."

"I may be slow, but I'm steady," Turtle said. "Unlike some animals I know."

"That story of the tortoise and the hare is grossly overrated," Rabbit said, her ears collapsed like fallen flags.

"I know what we'll do," Hedgehog said. "We'll all ride on Turtle's back. That way we'll all get there at the same time."

Mole Rat, Hedgehog, and Rabbit climbed up on Turtle's shell and continued through the dark wood. The slow, peaceful, rocking back and forth made the trio sitting on top of Turtle drowsy. They were half-asleep when they rounded an ancient oak tree and came face-to-face with a fox sitting in the middle of the path.

"We're goners!" Turtle said.

Rabbit took one look at the fox and went into shock, sliding off Turtle's back onto the ground; Hedgehog rolled into a small spiny ball and tumbled off into a bush; Turtle, for her part, ducked into her shell and hung out a sign that read NOBODY HOME. All Mole Rat could do was just sit there, repeating "What? Somebody tell me what's so terrible!"

"My point exactly," said Fox.

Hedgehog chanced to poke her little black snout out of her ball of spines. "What point is that?"

"You took one look at me and think the worst," Fox said.

Hedgehog opened her cloak of bristles a little farther to expose her face. "Tell me you're not a born killer, fast enough to run anyone down, clever enough to find any hiding place."

"Yes, but aside from that," Fox said. "I'm very pretty, my fur is extremely luxurious, and I'm quite intelligent. I can actually be very nice, given half the chance, but all you see is a violent killer. Why is that?"

Turtle, who was just coming out of her shell, said, "Sounds like our common plight."

"Will somebody please tell me what's going on?" Mole Rat said. After Hedgehog explained the situation, Mole Rat said, "Well, maybe Fox's cleverness will help us find The Crow."

"Sorry," Rabbit said, her nose twitching nervously, "but I'm having trouble getting past Fox's eating habits."

"I'm not sure why you're putting so much faith in Crow," Fox said, ignoring Rabbit's reservations. "Personally, the bird never showed me all that much, and her singing sounds like claws on a blackboard. But if you're still determined to talk to her, take a look at the clearing up ahead."

The other animals looked to where Fox indicated— except for Mole Rat, who gazed off unknowingly in the opposite direction until Hedgehog turned her friend's head. Sure enough, through the autumn trees they saw a large black bird strutting back and forth, amusing herself kicking the leaves.

8

Perpetual Guadeloupe Coeur di Lion Panettiere-Gray stopped writing and put down her pen, gazed out the window beside her secretary desk, her *secrétaire* as she liked to call it. She hadn't written anything since she was in convent school, those days as a teenager when she wanted to become a writer, the Jane Austen or maybe one of the Brontë sisters of her Caribbean island, but then harsh reality set in and she had to put away such dreams in order to survive, to find work for herself in a new country. When she felt the urge to start writing again—no, it was stronger than an urge; it was more a need, almost a calling—and she realized her life had settled to a point that she could actually do so, it had taken some time and effort to arrange her writing space in her room. She wanted to keep such activity secret; she knew Libby would understand, but there was no telling how the rest of the Lyle family would react; at best they would think it presumptuous, if not outright ludicrous, that a servant, as they considered her, an uneducated person as they also considered her, a woman of color, would have pretensions to an intellectual pursuit such as writing. The Lyles considered themselves the intellectuals of the town—and if it were ever questioned they were quick to enlighten them—surpassing the acumen and acuity of even the professors at Covenant College. No, it was best to keep her storytelling to herself, at least until the baby was born.

Because it was her awareness that Mary Lydia was pregnant, weeks before the doctor made his official determination, that gave Perpetual the desire to write again. There was a story growing in her imagination, preterm in her mind much the same as Mary Lydia's baby was preterm, driven by the idea that there would soon be a baby in the house, a young child that Perpetual could look after and coddle and teach about the workings of the world; she had the inspiration for a story that she could read to the child both as a comfort and an instruction. It was then that she asked William and one of his friends from Black Town to move the secretary desk she found in the attic, one day when none of the family was about—she knew that once the desk was in her room no one would know it was there, the family over the years doing everything it could to overlook her presence, or admit that she was there at all, including the fact that she had a room of her own. Now the *secrétaire* sat snug and secure and hidden from anyone looking in the door from the hall, tucked away in a corner next to the window with its view of the side yard. To make it her own, under the latticework that fronted the glass doors, Perpetual had placed the few photos that held meaning for her: a colored picture from a newspaper supplement of a beach on a Caribbean island—it was actually Barbados, not her home of Martinique, but it was close enough to bring back memories—; a picture of Perpetual standing with her family in front of their stucco house, a hut really, Perpetual the eight-year-old girl to the left standing resolute off to the side of her seven brothers and sisters; a picture clipped from a magazine of a group of Caribbean women on the steps of the administration building at Ellis Island, a news photo to show the influx of immigrants to America's golden shores, twenty black women, Perpetual in the front row, in their finest muslin dresses and head scarves, in reality an advertisement for servants-to-be, women brought here by a kind of brokerage firm offering a way out of the poverty of their island homes in exchange for service to the well-to-do. Reminders to Perpetual of where she came from and who she was determined not to be.

The pen she used for her writing she had liberated from Malcolm's study one day while he was at the steamworks, a Parker Lucky Curve Fountain Pen with a transparent barrel so you could see its inner workings, one of half a dozen pens scattered across his desk among the clutter of papers and books; she doubted that he would ever miss it, or if he did would never dream of looking in her room to find it. She discovered the pen while she was in the study looking for paper to write on, settling for a ream of heavyweight letterhead from the steamworks that she decided would do nicely as long as she wrote on the back. She had begun to write her story when Libby became aware of what Perpetual was doing—few things in the house or in the town for that matter got by Libby's notice, a quality that not only made Perpetual smile but also made her a little proud—and asked

Perpetual to write a story for her, to read to her at the chosen time. At first Perpetual was unsure, but then realized the story she had in mind of Mole Rat and Hedgehog applied to Libby— and to Libby and herself—as well as to Mary Lydia's future child. Now she gathered together the sheets of her story so far, tapped them on end against the surface of the drop-down writing desk, and put them away in a drawer; it was enough for today, she was at a good stopping place, the introduction of The Crow, and it was time to become once again the Lyle family version of Perpetual.

It was thirty-one years earlier that Perpetual first knocked on the Lyle front door with her tied-together suitcase in hand. And it was Libby who answered the door that spring morning.

"Hello?" Libby said, not unfriendly, just surprised as she gave this stranger the once-over. "Who have we here?"

"My name is Perpetual. Mr. Colin, down at the Keystone, he told Perpetual to come here."

"He did, did he?" Libby said, then looked beyond Perpetual at the horse-drawn wagon in the front yard, the half dozen work-men in their shirtsleeves, a couple of them whom she recognized. "And who all is with you? What's going on?"

"You don't know a thing about this goings-on, do you, Mawm? I told Mr. Colin that Perpetual didn't want to be a messenger of bad tidings. I told him that Perpetual didn't think it right for Perpetual to be a messenger at all."

"Well, it seems my husband has delegated you to be a mes-senger, whether it is right or not. So, would you please tell me what this is all about?"

"Mr. Colin, he sent these men to move his things down to the Keystone. And he sent Perpetual to be with you now that he be going away."

"Going away? Where's he going away to?" Libby said.

"Perpetual don't really know, Mawm. Perpetual only arrived this morning, on the train. But from the way he was talking and telling the men what to do, Perpetual got the idea that he was planning to live right there, at the Keystone."

"That's the most ridiculous thing I ever heard in my life. . . ." A second wagon pulled up in front of the house and her son Malcolm jumped down from where he was sitting beside the wagoner. As he hurried up the front steps and across the porch, he brushed past Perpetual as if she wasn't there.

"Malcolm, will you please tell me what this is all about?" Libby said. "This woman—"

Malcolm glanced Perpetual's direction but obviously dismissed her from further consideration. "It seems Father has decided he's moving out of the house and down to the steamworks. He's fixed an apartment for himself there next to his workshop—it's actually rather Spartan but it seems to suit him, with the way he's thinking these days."

"Do you know the way he's thinking these days?" Libby said. "Because he hasn't said anything about this to me, his wife."

"He says he wants to spend the rest of his life concentrating on his work. His ideas for other developments for Keystone steam engines, new applications for the technology, things like that."

"I thought he gave the operation of the steamworks over to you. I thought you were now president of the company."

"Well, he did. But this isn't about the operation of the company, the day-to-day operations of manufacturing. He says his mind is full of ideas for the engines and machines, he says he knows he doesn't have much time left and he wants to spend every minute possible bringing them to life. He said it doesn't have anything to do with you or how he feels—"

"He did, did he? That was very nice of him," Libby said,

pushed by her son and headed down the steps.

"Mother, where are you going?"

Libby walked over to the wagon Malcolm had arrived in, hiked up her skirts, and climbed up beside the wagoner, settling herself on the seat beside him. The wagoner, an older man with a spiked mustache and goatee, his shirtsleeves puckered by armbands, looked at Libby as if a wildcat just sat down beside him. Which in certain ways she had.

"Take me down to the steamworks. Now."

"I can't do that, Mrs. Lyle. Mr. Lyle gave me orders to—"

"Either you take me down to the steamworks or you can jump off and I'll drive myself. And if you think I can't handle a team of horses you're very much mistaken."

The man looked helplessly at Malcolm—who sucked in his mustache, said, "Blazes to hell," under his breath, then nodded for the man to drive on.

"And don't you be swearing in my house, Malcolm Hayes Lyle," Libby said as the wagoner turned the team around in the yard and headed back down the slope toward the river. "I don't care if you are outside," she called back over her shoulder.

"We'll see whose house it is," Malcolm said as he watched the wagon head down the road, then looked at the men standing around in the drive. "What the hell are you looking at? Get your damn asses into the house and start loading stuff. Now!"

Perpetual watched as the men unloaded the empty crates and barrels from the wagon and carried them into the house. Inside, Malcolm, reading from a list, was directing things, instructing the men as to what to take from the study on the first floor—the specific books on technology and philosophy his father thought he might read from the barrister bookcases; the specific files his father thought he might need from the wooden files of legal papers, patents, mechanical drawings, and designs; a few personal items from the large mahogany desk and the mantle over the fireplace—a one-inch scale model of a Keystone well-driller, a framed picture of Libby at a happier time. Then Malcolm led the men upstairs. In the large bedroom at the front of the house, he directed the men to empty the closet and wardrobe of his father's suits; then they emptied the bureau drawers of the dress shirts, underwear, socks, before carrying the bureau and wardrobe and boxes of clothes down to the wagon. As the men finished up, Malcolm conferred about something with the foreman. Then Malcolm shook his head adamantly and said to the men, "When you're done with those things, I need you to take the rest of the furniture down the hall to my bedroom and bring the furniture from that room in here."

"Do say," Perpetual said, hand folded on her hip.

Malcolm looked at her as if to say, What are talking about? Then shook his head. "Whatever. This is the master bedroom where the master of the house sleeps. And now that my father is no longer living here, I will be taking it over."

"This is still Mrs. Lyle's bedroom, as far as Perpetual knows. Mrs. Libby's room."

Malcolm laughed uneasily. "You don't know what you're talking about, for one thing. And for another, you don't have any say in the matter."

"Perpetual knows what Mr. Colin told her this morning. That Perpetual's job is to take good care of Mrs. Lyle, Mrs. Libby. And that's what Perpetual is going to do. And Perpetual says that nothing of Mrs. Lyle's, Mrs. Libby's, is leaving this room until Mrs. Lyle, Mrs. Libby, says so."

"Who's this Perpetual you keep talking about," Malcolm said.

"This is this Perpetual," Perpetual said.

"Ignore her," Malcolm told the workmen, standing in the hallway. "Go ahead and start removing the furniture like I told you. . . ."

Perpetual, who had been watching the goings-on from beside the French doors to the balcony, took a parasol from a bucket of parasols and canes beside Libby's closet and waved it at the workmen as they started to enter the room. "You! You stop where you are, you!"

Malcolm pushed past them and approached Perpetual, his face burning red. "I've had enough of this foolishness. Who do you think you are—?"

And with that, as Malcolm reached for the parasol, Perpetual hit him over the head with it.

Malcolm stopped cold and stared at her. "Ow! You hit me!"

"Yes indeed, Perpetual did, and she broke Mrs. Lyle's, Mrs. Libby's, parasol doing it. But that won't stop Perpetual from hitting you again if you don't be careful."

"She hit me!" Malcolm looked at the workmen half in and half out the bedroom door. "Men, take this woman out of here!"

The workmen took one look at the look on Perpetual's face, turned around, and headed out the door and down the stairs. "Not me, mate," one of them muttered. "I'd rather face a wild dog than that woman."

When Libby arrived home an hour or so later from the steamworks, she found Malcolm standing in the hallway outside the door to the bedroom, and Perpetual sitting on the bed, holding the broken parasol on her lap.

"She hit me," Malcolm said to his mother as she looked in the doorway, staying behind her, apparently afraid to come further into the room.

"You hit him?" Libby said to Perpetual.

"Indeed Perpetual did. And I told him Perpetual would hit him again if he tried to move your things from this room without you saying it was all right."

Libby looked at Malcolm in the doorway. "You were going to

remove my things from this room? From mine and your father's bedroom? What, so you could move in here, now that your father is living down at the steamworks?"

"Well, I just thought that—" Malcolm started to say.

"Thank you, Perpetual," Libby said. "You were absolutely right to do what you did. And as for you, my son—"

"Mother, I—"

"—you can tell those workmen of yours who are standing around the front yard to come back in here and remove the nursery things from the room next door and put them in the spare bedroom, and put the spare bedroom furniture in the room next door. From now on, that room is to be Perpetual's room. There's a connecting door, she'll have easy access to this room whenever I need her. And just so we're all clear on this: with Mr. Lyle out of the house, for whatever reason, that means I am in charge of this household. For now and forever, as far as you're concerned. And Perpetual and I will reside in these respective rooms until we're carried out feet first, and after that you'll have to deal with our ghosts. Do you understand?"

"Yes Mother," Malcolm said, head bowed, and headed back down the hallway.

Perpetual swung her feet over the edge of the bed and stood. "I'm sorry, Mawm, about breaking your parasol."

"Oh piffle," Libby said. "I never cared for it anyway. And it's 'Libby' to you."

"No, Mawm. It's not. It's Mawm."

Libby studied her a moment, then another thought crossed her mind. "You hit him over the head? What did he say?"

"He said Ow," Perpetual said. "It was glorious, Mawm, glorious."

Libby smiled slightly, then headed toward the connecting door between hers and Perpetual's room as the workmen appeared to start removing the furniture from what once had been the nursery. Talking to herself: "She hit him over the head with it. That's what she did. She hit him over the head."

Perpetual stood at the window beside her desk in her bedroom, looking out into the branches of the sycamores in the side yard, lost for a moment in memories. She was brought back to reality by the sight of two squirrels chasing each other along the branches of the trees, round and round the trunk, then racing along the network of branches, though she couldn't tell if they were playing, courting, or fighting. In the distance a crow was calling, calling. For some time she had been aware of the distant sounds of Margaret in the kitchen at the back of the house, the smells of coffee and bacon. She had heard Malcolm leave his and Missy's bedroom on the other side of the hall, do his morning ablutions in the bathroom, then return to their bedroom before going downstairs for breakfast; she knew Missy wouldn't stir for another several hours. So far she hadn't heard anything from Libby's room next door to indicate the elderly woman was awake. Which was just as well. Perpetual wanted time to speak to Mary Lydia before she had to tend to Libby this morning, she wanted to find out more of what Mary Lydia meant yesterday when she said her brother John Lincoln knew she was pregnant. Find out more of what she meant when she said that was the reason that drove John Lincoln away.

On her way past she stopped by her garden of hanging plants in the other window to check on a recalcitrant prune mombin, a plant she had to keep cutting back so it wouldn't develop into a tree, this particular plant still able to produce clusters of tiny white flowers though it took harshly to its last trimming. Perpetual caressed it and spoke fondly to it, "Come now, my darlin', don't you be pouting, everything be okay, Perpetual still loves you, Perpetual just had to trim you back a ways so you wouldn't outgrow yourself, you'll be fine now, Perpetual is here to take care of you. . . ." She bent down and kissed the plant, cupped it in her hand again, gave it a playful tousle, then opened the door quietly and slipped out of the room, easing her way down the hall to Mary Lydia's room at the head of the stairway.

She opened the door and edged inside. The drapes were still drawn from the day before, the room in darkness except for a slight glow along the baseboard, a crack of light marking the bottom of the cloth. Perpetual went to the window and pulled open the drapes, flooding the room with gray morning light. She turned and found Mary Lydia in the same position on the bed that she was when Perpetual tended to her last evening, propped up on pillows against the headboard, watching her.

"What are you doing, child? Did you sit up like that all night the way Perpetual left you? Didn't you sleep, then?"

"I must have nodded off at some time," Mary Lydia said. "But I don't know, the night just seemed to unroll on its own, without me having anything to do with it."

"Days and nights will tend to do that, if you're not careful. So what was on your mind? What were you thinking about so hard that it kept you awake like that?"

Mary Lydia stretched, scrunched her shoulders to the left then to the right, adjusted the sheet about her waist. "Oh, you know. The baby and all. . . ."

"Yes, and all," Perpetual said, straightening the sheet and blanket over the young woman's feet. "Perpetual thinks it's that 'all' that's got your family so troubled. Why not tell Perpetual who the father is, so Perpetual can put everyone out of their misery?"

"I can't do that."

"Cannot, or will not?"

Mary Lydia made a regretful face. "It's the same thing."

"Oh *sacré tata*," Perpetual said, and slapped at the young woman's feet under the sheet. "'Tis nothing like the same thing at all. Well, it's no matter, your father has sent Gus up to the college to find out if someone there knows who you were involved with."

"Gus?" Mary Lydia said, sitting up straighter. "Why Gus?"

"He is your brother, child, or half-brother. If your father is going to send anyone, of course it should be Gus."

"But why would he send anyone? Why to the college?"

"I guess your father tried to think when or where you'd have the time or opportunity to be involved with someone. And the college is the only place where you spent any time away from the family. And you went on those picnics with your friends last spring, and even a good Covenanter boy isn't beyond the temptations of sweet flesh—"

"But Gus? No, not Gus," Mary Lydia said, almost a croon as she turned her head into the pillow.

Perpetual stopped fussing with the covers at the foot of the bed and looked at the girl. "Why does that bother you so, child? Is there something about Gus that makes it worse than if it was somebody else asking the questions? I never thought there was dislike between you and your older brother. . . ."

"No, no, it's nothing like that," Mary Lydia said, close to tears, obviously distressed.

Or maybe it's not something that's wrong with Gus at all, Perpetual thought. Maybe it's something else entirely. Maybe it's the opposite of dislike, maybe it's more of like, maybe it's more that she wants Gus to like her, that she doesn't want Gus to know ill of her. . . .

Mary Lydia was crying softly into the pillow. Perpetual went to her, sat on the edge of the bed beside her and took her in her arms, Mary Lydia collapsing into Perpetual's lap, sobbing hysterically.

"There, there, child. I be here, Perpetual won't let harm come to you, you're safe with Perpetual, your secret is safe with Perpetual, we'll take care of *de bébé* too, Perpetual will make it all right for you, you'll see, you'll see," Perpetual said in her sing-song. Wondering if Mary Lydia was beginning to recognize that she had for too long given her best feelings to the wrong brother.

9

After Gus delivered the two government representatives to his father at the steamworks, he felt surprisingly positive about himself, something out of the ordinary for Gus; under most circumstances, he labored under a cloud of self-doubt and general apprehension, fueled by the suspicion of his father's continual disappointment in him, a disappointment brought on by comparisons of Gus to his younger half-brother, John Lincoln. But lately he felt his stock was looking up, first with John Lincoln's surprise disappearance, and then with word that his brother had run off to join the war in Europe. True, John Lincoln's enlistment could be seen as the action of a patriot and hero, personal qualities that certainly fit how the family considered itself to be perceived in the eyes of the town. But still, his kid half-brother's running off was simply that, a running off, and it served to highlight Gus' steadfastness, his stick-to-itiveness. If nothing else, John Lincoln's defection showed Gus to be the son his father could depend on, there could be no denying that now. A bumbling son in the hand was worth more than a golden-boy son in a far-off land.

He was particularly pleased with how well his delivery of the government agents went. Following his father's cautions—they were more like warnings—Gus didn't talk up the Lylemobile during the ride from the hotel to the steamworks, rather he let the Lylemobile speak for itself in its performance. The agents had several good questions about the autocar, questions that went beyond polite conversation, such as torque ratios, the size and displacement of the engine, the time it took to warm up before it was ready to travel—all questions they should be asking if the government was interested in the development of the steam car's technology. And Gus was proud of himself too, how he handled himself around the agents, providing thorough, informative answers, with just the right amount of technical terminology to let them know they weren't talking to just anyone, he wasn't just a glorified errand boy the way it might appear, he was someone to take into account in future dealings with the company. A bumbling son in the hand indeed.

Now he piloted the Lylemobile up steep Eleventh Street from the steamworks along the river, turned right onto the main street, and continued up through town toward the college. That his father sent him on this fool's errand, rather than include him in the meeting with the government representatives, regardless of what the meeting was about or which of the Keystone machines the government was interested in, was disappointing. But Gus could see why his father wanted him to oversee finding out who was responsible for Mary Lydia's pregnancy; it was a grave responsibility, not something that could be trusted to just anyone. The implications for the family's reputation, its good name in the town, were far-reaching, to say nothing of what people would think of Mary Lydia. He supposed now they'd have to send her away someplace to have the child, isn't that what families like the Lyles did in a situation like this? He had little doubt that this trip was a waste of time, he certainly didn't think someone at the college, some classmate of his sister's, was going to step up and claim the baby as his own, offer to do the right thing by marrying her. But if this was what his father wanted him to do, check out any connections of Mary Lydia at the college, Gus was willing to do it to stay in his father's good graces; now that he had an advantage, for once in his father's favor over John Lincoln, Gus couldn't afford to jeopardize it, the future of the Lylemobile depended on it.

Covenant College sat on the edge of Orchard Hill, a hill within the hills of the valley, overlooking Furnass and the curving river. The town had developed first along the flatlands close to the river with the original iron furnace that became the Allehela Works of Buchanan Steel; later came the Keystone Steam Works, as well as a boat works, and other heavy industries. In the meantime the town grew from a few scattered houses on the hillside to blocks of steep streets rising like steps to the main street and on up the valley wall, dwindling farther up the slope with Colin Lyle's Sycamore House isolated at the edge of the woods. As the town developed transversely spreading up from the river, it also developed parallel to the river following the contours of the three lifts or plateaus of the slope on this side of the valley. There was the Lower End, the flatlands closest to the Ohio River at the end of the valley, where many of the lowest-paid workers at the mills settled; then up a two-block-long hill to the business district, a shelf stretching a half mile or so along the slope of the hillside; then up the several blocks of Orchard Avenue to Orchard Hill, its own plateau within the confines of the valley. The name Orchard Hill came from the apple orchards that originally populated the area; after the college located there in the mid-1860s and the professors and administrators built houses close by, it became known as a "better" place to live in town.

The college, even fifty years after its founding, had an unfinished air about it, a feeling of a work in progress; the lawns that were supposed to be covered with lush grass were still patchy; there were several buildings that seemed permanently under construction; the trees, those that were planted when the campus was initially landscaped, were still spindly and appeared bare even in mid-summer. Gus drove up the paved main drive and parked in the circle in front of the administration building, a three-story structure of native gray stone with a tall wooden bell tower to chime the hour. With only a few classes in session during the summer, the walks were deserted, no one was standing along the curb of the street, the only place students were allowed to smoke. Gus left the Lylemobile ticking cool and headed up the granite steps and through the heavy oak doors.

His boot heels ticked along the empty corridor. He recognized the smell of the place—one he instantly associated with pretension and high-mindedness—a mixture of floor wax, vinegar, and uncirculated air. His time here, however short, was not a happy memory; because the professors and instructors were aware of his grandfather and father—Colin Lyle donated the steeple on the building; Malcolm Lyle cast the bell in the forge at the steamworks—Gus felt under the weight of unrealistic expectations from the first day. When he left after only a few weeks into the first semester—despite his rationale that he found the courses at the college superfluous and pointless; despite his argument that he wanted to go to work at the steamworks so he could learn the business from the ground up, which was true in a way—his father made no effort to hide his displeasure and disappointment with his first-born son. It didn't help his father's opinion of him that John Lincoln, when it came his time to go to the college, was an honors student, king of the Maypole celebration for two years running—Gus took a particular satisfaction that the Covenanters never realized the pagan origins of the celebration—and president of his class. To Gus the college represented everything hypocritical about religion and those who professed belief in a wise and judicious God, which included to his way of thinking most everyone in town, whether they were Covenanters or not; he had felt that way about religion since he was six years old, from the time he witnessed the tragic accident that killed his mother, and his father's hopeless, hapless attempts to save her. It only made matters worse that both his grandfather and father were elders in the church, though for the most part in name only, their participation consisting mainly in making large donations on behalf of the steamworks. If there was any satisfaction to be had on his current errand, it was the possibility, however unlikely, that he might actually find some holier-than-thou young man who had impregnated his sister, that would certainly show the college's high moral values for what they were; though he was obviously going to have to be careful how he approached the subject with anyone he spoke to, he could end up spreading the word of Mary Lydia's condition without meaning to. That sounded like something he would do, by most people's reckoning, didn't it?

Behind the hammered glass panel in the dean of students' office door, a vague figure floated back and forth as if underwater. Should he knock or just go in? He waited for a moment until the figure stopped moving, then tried the door, then opened it farther and stepped inside, his hat in hand. The figure was a tall elegant older woman in a black high-waisted ankle-length skirt and white blouse with puffy sleeves, her gray hair piled high on her head, in the midst of sorting papers on the front counter of the office. She turned and looked at Gus as if she had discovered an unpleasant bug.

"Can I help you?" she said, before continuing to distribute the sheaf of papers in her arm onto the piles of paper on the counter.

"I guess I'm looking for the dean of students."

"You guess?"

"Heh heh," Gus said. "I mean, I actually am looking for the dean of students."

"You are aware that the college is closed today, because of the Fourth of July holiday tomorrow."

"No, I wasn't aware of that," Gus said. "Though that certainly sounds appropriate. That the college would be closed for that. Because of the holiday and all."

The woman turned her head to look at him briefly before returning to her papers. This isn't going well, Gus told himself.

"I was wondering if the dean was available."

"Available. In what context?"

No, not going well at all. "Let me start over. I was wondering if the dean is available for a few minutes of his time. I am looking for some information and I'm hoping he can . . . shed some light on a couple of questions. . . ."

The woman placed the remaining papers on their respective piles on the counter, looked over her handiwork, then turned once again to Gus. "You're speaking to the dean of students. Elizabeth Quigley." She offered her hand, then brushed past him along the counter to her office in the next room.

Gus, Gus, Gus. He sighed and followed her into the office. Elizabeth Quigley walked around her desk and sat down, straightened a few papers, then folded her hands on the blotter, waiting for Gus to proceed. Her smile was short and fleeting.

Gus sat in the chair opposite her, his rather crumpled fedora in his lap, yanked his lapels to straighten his suit coat, trying to regain his composure. He felt fifteen years old again, called to the principal's office for some infraction or other; he felt the sweat inside his shirt trickling down the sides of his chest. Good grief, man, get ahold of yourself, you're the one in control here, these people here owe you, owe the Lyles, she's the one who should be sweating.

"I'm remiss, I should have introduced myself. I'm . . . Augustus Lyle—"

"I know who you are."

"You do?"

"Yes. I do. There's no reason why you would remember me. But I worked here in the office when you attended Covenant. I was here when you made your rather infamous departure, a few weeks into your first semester. It was quite the subject of conversation, I must say."

If you must. Mention of the incident brought back mixed emotions—a slight smile crossed his lips and was quickly erased by an old hurt. His disenchantment with the college had been growing since the day he first set foot on campus, his weariness with the expectations laid upon him because of his family. Things came to a head one morning in a required Bible class, when the instructor, a lay preacher named Ian Cameron, on the subject of the physical presence of God, drew on the blackboard a large rather lumpy circle, added a number of flecks inside it, and said he thought it helpful if the class imagined God as an immense tapioca pudding floating in the void. "That's it," Gus had said, gathering up his books and leaving the room. "I'm away."

As soon as he was outside the classroom, he felt a great weight lifted from his shoulders; without knowing beforehand that he was going to, he kept on going, out of the building, off the campus, discarding his books along the way. He grabbed the first trolley car that came along and rode it downtown, walked on down the steep side streets to the steamworks and announced to his surprised and not-pleased father that he was done with college, that he was there to begin work, even as a laborer if need be. Which, as it turned out, was the case for a while until his father realized that he wasn't going to discourage his son from his intention to learn the business and relocated him as an apprentice in the machine shop.

"I heard later," Gus said to Elizabeth Quigley, "that Professor Cameron used me as an example in his class as someone of low moral character on account of my departure, someone who would never be successful in this world and was a disgrace to his family."

"And yet here you are," Elizabeth Quigley.

"Yes, here I am," Gus said. "I'm hoping you can give me a little information about my sister, Mary Lydia. She was a junior this year—"

"Yes. I know Mary Lydia. Of course. John Lincoln's sister."

"Hmm," Gus muttered. Thinking, even here, even with her. He wanted to, but he couldn't let it go. "You probably haven't heard. John Lincoln won't be attending his senior year. He's left town."

"Why would he do a thing like that?" Elizabeth Quigley said, picking up a pen beside the desk blotter and holding it as if ready to write something.

"We only heard yesterday—he never said why he was leaving, he just up and left. As it turns out he's decided to join the war effort in Europe, he's shipping out tomorrow with a group that plans to join the English army."

"That certainly sounds like something John Lincoln would do."

"Yes, the family is pretty upset, as you can imagine. Just taking off like that without an explanation or a fare-thee-well—"

"No, I mean it sounds like something John Lincoln would do: volunteering to serve for the greater good."

"Hmm, yes," Gus said. Even her, even here. But he came to the college with a job to do; from his suit coat pocket he took the framed snapshot his father had removed from Mary Lydia's bedroom and handed it to Elizabeth Quigley. "But getting back to Mary Lydia. I was hoping you can tell me about her social life on campus."

"Her social life," Elizabeth Quigley repeated. "Why am I looking at this photograph?"

"The family is interested to know how Mary Lydia has been getting on. Socially speaking. Such as, you know, who her friends are. Such as who the students in this snapshot are."

"Why would you want to know that?"

Gus shifted his weight uneasily. Coughed. Smiled like a burp. "Mary Lydia, as I'm sure you know is a . . . high-strung young woman, and we, my parents, that is—I'm making these inquiries on their request—want to make sure that she is, uh, making the right acquaintances."

"The 'right acquaintances,'" Elizabeth Quigley repeated. "Well, Mary Lydia has a circle of young women she's friends with, just like any of the other young women. Though, as you say, she can have an edge to her. There are times when she can appear standoffish. . . ."

"She seems like she's having a good time in that snapshot." Gus nodded to the framed photograph.

Elizabeth Quigley thought about something, then remembered she was holding the picture. "Yes, I'm fairly sure this was taken on the annual outing to paint the *C* on the hill across the river. Everyone seemed to have a good time that day. . . ."

"I think I recognized a few of the people—"

"Well, I would think you would recognize John Lincoln." Elizabeth Quigley pointed to a figure in the photo.

"Yes, of course." Gus tried not to let his impatience show as he leaned around to have a better view of the picture. He pointed to the dark-haired fellow kneeling behind Mary Lydia. "But this fellow, for instance, I don't recognize him."

"Ah, Dimitris. I'm not surprised you don't know him. He is, or was, one of our Greek Covenanter students."

"Greek?"

"Yes, though actually he belonged to a Greek Covenanter church in Turkey, he was from Constantinople. It's a sad story, the church there is under a lot of persecution and he decided to go back home to make sure his parents are safe. We haven't heard anything since—"

"So there's no way to talk to him? Do you know if he and Mary Lydia were, you know, seeing each other, like maybe she was his girlfriend or something. . . ?"

Elizabeth Quigley studied him a moment. "What is this about, really?"

"I told you, the family is concerned that Mary Lydia is—"

"What you're asking me is if Mary Lydia had any romantic involvements, is that correct? Well, even if I thought such a question acceptable, which I don't, how would you expect me to know something like that?"

Careful, careful. He tried his best to be off-hand, casual. "You know, word gets around. People talk, that sort of thing." Gus smiled. "Especially at a place where, as I remember, it's forbidden for students of the opposite sex to even hold hands on campus."

Elizabeth Quigley fixed Gus in her gaze for a moment. "In the time I've worked in this office, such an inquiry has only come up a few times. And those circumstances were never very complimentary to the young women involved."

Be careful, now. It's time to apply some leverage. . . . "I think you're aware of my family's position in town—is it *Mrs.* Quigley?" Elizabeth Quigley didn't answer; Gus went on. "And I think you can understand why the family would want to make sure that an impressionable young woman such as Mary Lydia did not associate with other young people, especially young men, who might not maintain the high values and moral standards that she is accustomed to."

Gus was proud of that, but he didn't like the look on Elizabeth Quigley's face as she settled back in her high-backed chair. "I'm sorry to be the one to tell you this, but it's apparent that somebody needs to. You grossly overestimate your family's position in town, both as to its prominence and its perceived, as you referred to them, moral standards. Yours may have been a leading family in Furnass at one time, but there are others, such as the Buchanans and the MacKinnons from Buchanan Steel, to name just two, who have far surpassed the Lyles in their influence. For instance, your family hasn't made a significant contribution to this college for more than twenty years, and I think those were inspired more from a guilty conscience than from any philanthropic spirit. And as for your family's perceived moral standards, I'm afraid those have been questioned in town since your grandfather is said to have collaborated with the Confederates during the Civil War and his wife had a well-known dalliance with a certain doctor. And then there was all the suspicions surrounding the terrible business of your mother's death. But be that as it may. I understand you're undoubtedly sick and tired of hearing all the praise heaped on your younger brother, or I guess it's half-brother, John Lincoln, but in the town's mind he's the first one of your clan to come along in a long time who seems to hold up to the promise of your family's name." She sat forward again, folded her hands on the blotter again, and made a face as if to say, Well, you're the one who brought it up.

Gus had no idea what Elizabeth Quigley was talking about. Driving back down Orchard Avenue toward the main part of town, he tried to understand what had just happened, going over in his mind the conversation with Elizabeth Quigley, but he was having trouble making sense of it; he went to the college to ask about his sister's friends and contacts and social life, and ended up facing a diatribe against his family extending all the way back to his grandfather Colin. Elizabeth Quigley said people in town thought his grandfather colluded with the Confederates during the Civil War—was that true? Gus had always heard a very different story, that Colin was a hero, that indeed he had worked with some disguised Confederate raiders to outfit a couple of steam road engines with armor plate and Gatling guns. But when he found out that they were Rebels and intended to take the engines to General Lee as he invaded Central Pennsylvania, Colin sabotaged the engines before they could leave town; he mined the bridge and sent the engines and crews tumbling into the river. That didn't sound like colluding with the enemy to Gus. Where did Elizabeth Quigley get such an idea?

And people thought there was something suspicious about the death of his mother, where did that come from? It was a tragedy to be sure, something Gus never got over, watching his mother burned alive in front of their house. Gus most certainly blamed his father for not doing enough to save her. But was Elizabeth Quigley implying that there was something questionable about the circumstances of her death, that his father perhaps did it on purpose, that he intended to kill her? Were there actually people in town who thought that? Or where did she get the idea that his grandmother had been involved with a doctor in town? Gus knew that his grandfather, in his later years, had moved down to the steamworks, holed up in an apartment and workshop developing new applications for their steam engines—the Lylemobile he was driving was a direct result of those last designs—but did people think his grandfather moved to the steamworks because he and his wife had separated? Could that be true? And could it have been the result of Colin's wife having an affair with a local doctor? His straightlaced grandmother Libby? He had grown up around his grandmother, lived in the same house with her all his life, ate three meals a day with her, timed his visits to the downstairs bathroom according to her schedule, was careful even now as a grown man not to stomp up or down the stairs or tread too heavily in the hallways for fear of her reprimands. He knew her as aloof, withdrawn, rail thin, and stiff as the cane she carried, buttoned up in black from her ankles to her high-necked collars, an elderly force of nature; a stern and ancient presence moving through the house with Perpetual, her attendant, churning behind her in her wake. He could no more imagine a younger Libby naked in the arms of a lover than he could see her climbing a tree. But whether such accusations were true or not, the fact that Elizabeth Quigley brought them up must mean that somebody thought such things. Gus was shaken.

So who were the Lyles in the eyes of the town? At this point he wasn't even sure who they were in his own eyes. As he entered the main part of town, the business district along Seventh Avenue, the fire department was busy installing the decorations for the Fourth of July celebrations the next day, their ladders propped against the light poles as they draped strings of American flags and patriotic bunting over the street. He detoured up the hill on steep Fourteenth Street and turned onto Eighth Avenue, past the new park where workmen were hanging more banners and bunting, erecting a temporary speaker's platform for the ceremony after the parade; a Keystone Steam Works portable crane was in the process of hoisting the statue of a Union cavalryman onto its pedestal in the center of the park, the statue his grandmother had funded and would dedicate the next day, in the park his father and the Keystone Steam Works had donated to the town. Perhaps a block-long city park and a bronze statue weren't in the same class monetarily as the college's Buchanan Library or the MacKinnon Gymnasium, but surely the town's opinion of his family couldn't be all bad. Could it?

He wished Lily hadn't chosen this time to take little Malcolm and visit her folks in Kansas, though he supposed there was never a time that he'd like it any better; he needed to talk to her, to get her perspective on things, tell her what all Elizabeth Quigley said, help him sort it out. For that matter, who knew what the town thought about her leaving as she did—that he and Lily had

had a fight? That his marriage was breaking up? Stop it! Get ahold of yourself, man! He had to stop worrying about what people thought one way or the other about his family. People would think what they will, there was no way to change it, no way to control it. Oh Lily, Lily. Sweet Lily. His Lily of the Valley as he liked to call her—he knew she hated it, hated the idea for reasons he couldn't fathom that she belonged to *this* valley, but he called her that regardless, hiding his true feelings in a tease. And he knew what she'd think about his concerns about the family's image, if he had courage enough to express such concerns around her—in his mind's eye he saw his wife standing in the kitchen in their wing at Sycamore House, in her ankle-length apron and housedress, her flaxen hair pulled up into a chignon, not for fashion or for beauty but simply to get her hair out of her face, this transplanted Kansas Covenanter preacher's daughter, as determined as a cornstalk, as irrepressible as a prairie wind, waving a wooden spoon in his direction, saying, "Stop this nonsense, Augustus, and stand up for yourself!" She would be right, too.

At the next corner he turned left on Eleventh Street and chuffed down the hill toward the river and the steamworks, stirring up a warm breeze for himself through the open windows under the canopy, the air puffing up his sleeves and slipping under the lapels of his suit coat. It occurred to him that maybe he wasn't too late, that maybe the government reps were still at the plant and he'd be in time to take them back to their hotel and he could make an additional pitch for the Lylemobile. That would help clear away the bad taste left in his mouth from his talk with Elizabeth Quigley. In addition to having his worldview challenged in regard to his family, he was also aware that he had failed at the mission his father sent him on, namely, to find out if Mary Lydia had been involved with someone at the college. What he found out was that their prime candidate for the baby's father was a Greek national or maybe a Turk who was far, far away and liable never to be heard from again. What would his father say to that? Somehow, Gus just knew it would come out looking like it was all his fault. Well, so be it, at least he had found out there might be somebody, that was more than they knew before his visit; if that didn't placate his father, his father could go to the college and talk to Elizabeth Quigley himself. He was fed up being thought of as nothing but an errand boy. Stand up for yourself, Augustus! He'd like to see how far his father got, talking to Elizabeth Quigley.

And as for Elizabeth Quigley's impressions of his family and their standing in the town, the old biddy be damned, he wasn't going to let the likes of her get him down. There was nobody more important in Furnass than the Lyles; maybe they weren't the wealthiest family these days, but they were certainly the oldest and still the most influential, the fact was there would be no Furnass if not for the Lyles. And when it came time for him to take the helm of the steamworks, he was certain he would lead the town into greater prosperity with his ideas for the Lylemobile and the company. Chugging through the intersections of the cross streets on his way down the hill, jamming his hat farther down on his head against the wind, standing on the brake pedal against the insistence of the slope, he blew the whistle long and shrill, releasing fresh clouds of steam—Watch out world, here I come! He was sure Lily would be proud.

10

"You have quite a modern manufacturing facility here, Mr. Lyle," Charles Adams said.

"You say that as if you're surprised," Malcolm said, getting seated after greeting the two government reps and directing them to the chairs in front of his desk.

"It's just that these brick buildings are rather old, aren't they?" Julian Taylor, the younger of the two reps, said. "They must have been built in . . . what? The 1850s?"

Adams silenced his companion with a look. "I think what my colleague is trying to say is that the age of your physical plant would lead an observer to think that the manufacturing facilities within would be of the same vintage. And such is obviously not the case."

"I think the Keystone Steam Works can certainly hold its own," Malcolm said, clasping his hands on his blotter, smiling to both visitors, "when it comes to modern manufacturing facilities and techniques. In fact we take pride in the number of our innovations."

"As well you should," Adams said, straightening the crease in his trousers. "If what we saw on our tour yesterday is any indication."

Taylor smiled wanly, touching the tips of his long slender fingers to the side of his mouth. Both men were clean-shaven, dressed in identical trim black suits, without shoulder pads, of the kind advertised as featuring the "military high-waisted effect," echoing a serviceman's uniform. In his bulky boxy padded brown tweed suit, Malcolm felt hopelessly old-fashioned. He decided on the spot that it was time to lose a little weight.

"You may not be aware," Malcolm said, "that Keystone was one of the leaders, if not *the* leader, in developing the use of the steam engine in vehicles in this country, such as the steam tractor and road engines."

"Indeed, we are aware of that," Adams said. "As I . . . we understand it, your father—was that Colin Lyle?—was responsible for applying some of the English developments of the steam engine on the technology here. . . ."

"He took some of those ideas and developed them further—"

"That's right," Adams said quickly. "I didn't mean to imply in any way that he simply copied ideas—"

"Your father is the one who outfitted steam tractors with iron plate and Gatling guns for the Confederacy, is that right?" Taylor blurted out.

Malcolm sat back in his chair. Thinking, People just aren't going to forget that, are they? Is that why they're here? Is the government dredging that up again, is there still some question about Father's loyalty? Or is it my loyalty they're here to question?

"My father didn't come up with the idea of outfitting the steam engines that way—"

"But from what I've read, they could never have done it without his knowledge and expertise—"

"I think we're getting ahead of ourselves here," Adams said, again throwing a withering look in the direction of the younger man.

"I don't know what you've read or where you read it," Malcolm said. "It's a footnote to history that I'm afraid is little understood. Yes, my father helped some Confederate agents mount armor plate and some Gatling guns on a couple of his road engines. But he did so believing that they were representatives of the United States government in Washington, which is who they said they were. As soon as he realized that they were actually Rebels and what their intentions were, he risked his life to sabotage the project so that the engines were destroyed before they could leave town. He had no more reason at the start of the project to doubt who they were than I have reason to doubt who you are."

"Mr. Lyle, if there is some question about our credentials. . . ," Taylor said, reaching inside his coat pocket. But Adams stopped him.

"I'm afraid we've gotten off on a tangent here, Malcolm—may I call you Malcolm? The only reason we brought up that incident from the past is because it demonstrates that Keystone Steam Works has a history of innovation and a willingness to attempt the difficult problem. For instance, on the way here this morning, your son Augustus was showing us some of the many technical innovations you've made with the Lylemobile."

Malcolm relaxed a bit. So it is the Lylemobile that they're interested in, I probably should have had Gus here after all—no, it's best for him not to be involved just yet. But what is it with this other rep, Taylor, one minute he's mute in the corner and the next bouncing up and down with excitement? Looks like Adams and I share having a younger man working under us who can't always be trusted to show the best judgment. . . .

"Yes, the Lylemobile has been pretty much Gus' . . . Augustus' project. He's been able to take some of his grandfather's original ideas for such a vehicle and develop them for a more modern age. Though I'll admit I've toyed with the idea of replacing the steam engine he's used with an internal combustion engine."

"What on earth for?" Taylor broke in. And for once Adams didn't try to correct him.

"Well, it certainly seems that progress is favoring such an engine. I think that Gus' ideas for the body are sound. The development of most motor vehicles has been to simply adapt the basic design of the buggy or sleigh—the 'horseless carriage' is an accurate description. But Augustus, following his grandfather's original designs, has developed the body into something stronger, and safer actually—"

"The subject of the body type aside," Taylor said, leaning forward in his chair, becoming animated again, "the application of the new smaller steam engine used in the Lylemobile is much more important than the vehicle's design, why, it's revolutionary, it's . . . it's. . . ." He looked to Adams for support.

"And the ability of this smaller engine to be ready to run in just a few minutes' time is equally important," Adams said, more restrained but equally forceful. "What do you call it, the forced air induction system? That's positively brilliant. Surely, that wasn't part of your father's concept, was it?"

"No," Malcolm said, wondering where this discussion was going. "Father could never solve the size and weight problem of the engines they had then. We've only developed the smaller engines in the last few years—"

"Well, there you are," Taylor said, slapping his knee and looking from Malcolm to Adams and back again. "That engine opens up entirely new opportunities for steam-powered vehicles, it's a different ballgame, as the sports writers say. . . ."

"I agree, I think it's an important development. And I'm glad you're interested in the Lylemobile, Gus—Augustus will certainly be pleased. We were speculating before you arrived as to which of our machines you were interested in—"

"No, it's not the Lylemobile we came to talk to you about," Adams said.

"Then a well-driller?" Malcolm said. "We haven't used one of the smaller engines in a well-driller so far, but I suppose we could—"

Adams nodded to Taylor. The younger man opened his valise and took out a rolled-up sheet of paper, standing up in order to spread it out on the blotter in front of Malcolm. His hands with their long slender fingers were trembling with his excitement. "Allow me to show you a drawing, Mr. Lyle. . . ."

11

The hoop within the hoop held the coarse cloth taut so the needle could find its way through the warp and weft, dragging its charge of colored thread through to the other side; then it was mostly a matter of not sticking her finger with the needle while it was on the blind side as she reversed its course, using feel and intuition to guide the needle back through the cloth again, the silver tip appearing among the leaves and flowers and buds of the design, asking to be pulled through again to start its journey again. Meanwhile, the slice of morning sunlight from the space between the drapes, pulled closed to keep the cooler night air in the room as long as possible, moved slowly but determinedly across her legs, her hands holding the needlework, the arms of her rocking chair positioned in the corner of the room across from her bed, the glass of amber liquid sitting on the end table beside her chair. Now Libby stopped her needlework to take a sip of the rye whiskey. Thinking for a moment what a beautiful morning it was. Thinking there wouldn't be many more such mornings for her, there couldn't be now, though she never expected to live this long. Each day, whether sunny or gray, too hot or too cold, a blessing. A gift.

Her thoughts were interrupted by the ringing of the front doorbell downstairs. That and the silence that followed, indicating that no one was making an effort to answer it. Sigh. She was fairly sure that Missy, Malcolm's wife, was somewhere downstairs, probably sitting in the living room reading one of her women's magazines, too self-absorbed to answer it herself, expecting someone else to do it for her. If Lily were around, she would answer it, even coming from her and Gus' apartment at the back of the house, but she wasn't around, she had taken their son, Mal, for whatever reason, to visit her folks in Kansas. What do you suppose that's about? When the doorbell rang a second time, she heard Perpetual, in her room next door to Libby's, scrape her chair as she got up from her secretary desk, muttering

to herself in the patois that Libby suspected was of her own de-
vising, knowing full well that Missy was closer to getting it,
sweeping out of her room and down the hall, down the steps to
answer the bell. In a moment she heard voices below in the hallway, Perpetual talking to someone, then Perpetual's footsteps
coming back up the stairs. She came into Libby's room without
knocking, a look on her face that said she was in no mood to be
trifled with.

"Mrs. Whitticom, Mrs. Edgeworth, and Miss March are downstairs to see you, Mawm."

"Good heavens," Libby said. "The local chapter of the
Women's Christian Temperance Union. What on earth would
they want to see me about?"

Perpetual came over to the rocker and picked up the glass of
whiskey, holding it up in the slice of sunlight intruding on the
room. "I can't imagine, Mawm."

"That'll be enough, Perpetual," Libby said, putting her needlework aside and reclaiming the glass from Perpetual, taking a
sip before putting it back on the end table. "It's possible they're
not here for the temperance union at all. Those three notables
like to stick their collective noses in every civic organization that
will have them. So, how is Mary Lydia this morning? I heard you
go into her room earlier."

"She be the same as yesterday," Perpetual said, folding her
hands against her waist. "Perpetual got her some breakfast,
helped her with the bedpan, seeing as how her own mother won't.
It seems to Perpetual that Mary Lydia be thinking about things
a little bit. But the girl didn't say anything to Perpetual."

Libby looked at the dark-skinned woman; I don't believe you
for a second, if it didn't serve your purpose, you wouldn't tell me
if the girl told you the house was on fire. Though I know it's
nothing against me, it's everything for the girl. Your special

charge. Libby started to get up from the rocker; Perpetual moved over and helped the elderly woman to her feet.

"So, what will you say to the temperance ladies?" Perpetual said. "Would you like Perpetual to get them something to drink?"

"I know very well what you'd like to get them to drink, but I'm not wasting my precious resources on women who wouldn't appreciate them. No, Perpetual, thank you very kindly, but I will see to these three worthies on my own."

Perpetual got Libby's cane for her from the bucket of canes and parasols beside the bureau and stood beside the door as Libby shuffled out of the room. "Perpetual hopes you give them the what for," she smiled. "Imagine, going around and disturbing good Christian folk with the evils of demon rum, and it's not even a Sunday, neither."

Libby took her time moving down the hallway along the banister of the staircase and going down the stairs, two feet to a tread, making sure she made a loud *Thump!* with her cane with each step. The temperance ladies were waiting for her in the parlor, the three of them managing to squeeze together onto the love seat, bumps on a log, even though there were other chairs available. They were all dressed similarly as if in a kind of uniform, white cotton blouses and long white skirts—two of them, Mrs. Whitticom and Miss March, with blue kerchiefs around their necks, a nautical look—with large straw hats, the brims upturned in front as if in surprise or astonishment. Libby gave them the once-over, welcomed them, and sat herself down across from them in a straight-backed chair, folding her hands over the knob of her cane and giving them each, one, two, three, her best hypocritical smile.

"We hope you are well, Mrs. Lyle," Mrs. Whitticom said, the tallest and most buxomly of the three, who seemed to be the appointed spokesperson.

"No reason that I shouldn't be," Libby said. "And to what do I owe the honor of your visit this fine morning?"

"I'll get right to the point," Mrs. Whitticom said, nodding in turn to her companions on her left and her right.

"Always the best course of action," Libby said under her breath.

"On behalf of the people of Furnass, we wish to thank you in advance for your generous donation of the Colin Lyle Memorial Park. It is a display of civic-mindedness that is unequaled in the memory of the town."

"Above and beyond," Mrs. Edgeworth said.

"Yes indeed," echoed Miss March.

All three women looked at Libby, nodded, and blinked.

"Well, that's very nice of you," Libby said. "But to be absolutely correct, it was my son, Malcolm, through the auspices of the Keystone Steam Works, that donated the park to the city. My personal contribution is the statue for the park."

"Well, I'm sure that you contributed your part to the development of the park," Mrs. Whitticom said. "After all, what good son does not include his mother in important decisions?"

The other two ladies tittered, nodded their agreement.

"And what would a park be without a statue?" Miss March said.

"The focal point of interest for all who visit there," Mrs. Edgeworth said, an ample-bodied woman who always gave the impression of having just risen from her bed, with red curls dawdling down under the brim of her straw hat. She leaned forward to encourage the agreement of her two companions; all three nodded their approval.

"It's the statue of a Union cavalryman, we're told," Mrs. Whitticom said.

"You're told correctly," Libby said. Thinking she must have

been wrong in suspecting that the reason for their visit had something to do with temperance. But then what was the reason for the visit? She knew these women and their ilk too well to believe they would go this far out of their way just to thank her for a civic donation that they probably didn't approve of in the first place.

"And isn't it wonderful," Mrs. Whitticom said, "how the town has been able to forgive and forget, and allow the return of your husband's name to its good graces."

"It is a testament to the town's basic Christian nature," Miss March said, "that it has allowed the family name this rehabilitation after a bad patch."

"A bad patch?" Libby said.

"Well yes," Mrs. Whitticom said. "I'm sure you are aware that there was much speculation at the time and after that your husband was actually a Confederate sympathizer back in the Civil War days, that he was fully aware of who he was building those war engines for, regardless what he claimed. There was even talk that he did it for you, you were originally from the South I believe. . . ."

"South Carolina," Libby said.

"Well, there you are. It would certainly be within the realm of possibility that a husband might fall sway to his wife's inborn sympathies. But no matter certainly, I'm sure you knew all this when you decided to erect the statue. In fact I imagine it was a determining factor for you to erect the statue, a celebration of the return of your husband's good name in town."

"I should have known you would be able to see through my intentions," Libby said without expression.

The three women smiled, nodded their agreement to each other. For several minutes the women sat in awkward silence. Libby thinking I'll be damned if I'll make it easy for them, whatever it is they think they're truly about. . . .

"There is one thing. . . ," Mrs. Whitticom said finally.

"Yes," Miss March said. "We were wondering if. . . ."

"You know, to make something even more positive out of—" Mrs. Edgeworth said.

"We are hoping," Mrs. Whitticom broke in, "that you will make your remarks, in addition to a glorification of the past, a heralding of the future. A clarion call for things to come."

"Really," Libby said. "And how exactly would I do that?"

The trio was obviously emboldened by Libby's reaction. They clucked among themselves like self-satisfied hens.

"We are hoping," Mrs. Whitticom said, "that you could add to your remarks some mention of the efforts of the good women of Furnass to create a sober and pure world through abstinence, purity, and evangelical Christianity. Particularly the abstinence of alcohol."

"Ah," Libby said. "So you are here on behalf of the Women's Christian Temperance Union. I wondered—"

"Not necessarily," Miss March put in. "We like to think we represent all the women's organizations of Furnass, the women's *Christian* organizations. . . ."

"I'm sure you do," Libby said.

"We took the liberty of drawing up a number of talking points that you could include," Mrs. Edgeworth said, taking a piece of paper from her purse and handing it across to Libby as she continued. "As you may be aware, our members are inspired by the Greek writer Xenophon, who defined temperance as moderation in all things healthful, and total abstinence from all things that are harmful. Obviously, that includes total abstinence from alcohol, which we all know is a major cause of crime and unrest among the lower classes, particularly the large number of immigrants who are finding their way to our hallowed shores."

"We all know," Libby said, perusing the list.

"The inclusion of such noble thoughts would not only lift your remarks into a higher sphere," Mrs. Whitticom said. "It would also—how shall I say this?—help to resurrect your own good name, along with your husband's, in the good graces of the town."

"Which, of course, your dedication of the statue, and your family's dedication of the park, has already done much to achieve," Miss March added quickly. The trio of straw hats nodded to one another.

Libby placed the piece of paper with the list of talking points on her lap. "Well, I have no idea of my son's motives for his donation of the park itself, we never discussed it one way or the other. But as for funding the statue in order to resurrect my own name in the good graces of the people of Furnass, I can assure you that was the farthest thing from my mind. In fact, I must say I wasn't aware that my name needed resurrecting."

"Oh it doesn't, it doesn't," Mrs. Edgeworth cried. For emphasis she fluffed up one of her red curls with the back of her hand.

"Most certainly not," Miss March agreed.

"You understand we certainly don't feel that way," Mrs. Whitticom said. "Certainly not. But I would be remiss if I didn't note that a number of people have commented to me over a period of time on your reticence to take part in the civic life of the town. In fact, some people might even think that you considered yourself above such participation."

"Well, we certainly wouldn't want the people of Furnass to think that, now, would we?" Libby said, placing the list on the end table beside the chair and getting to her feet. Signifying that the conversation had come to an end.

"Our point exactly," Miss March said, and the trio stood up as well.

"Then we can count on you to include our message in your

dedication remarks?" Mrs. Edgeworth said.

"I will be happy to include a message about your efforts to promote tolerance among our fellow citizens," Libby said. "You can count on it. And I thank you for calling my attention to the issue."

"Oh splendid!" Mrs. Whitticom said, as the three women fell in line behind Libby, following her out of the room and down the hallway to the front door.

As Libby shook hands with each of the women in turn, Miss March said, "Thank you, thank you, thank you, Mrs. Lyle. How can we ever thank you enough?"

"Yes, how?" Mrs. Edgeworth said. None of them waiting for an answer.

Libby stood in the doorway and watched as the three women in white made their way down the front steps to a waiting surrey. Perpetual came up behind her, standing in the shadows of the vestibule, as Mrs. Whitticom turned the team around and directed the surrey back down the hill toward the town, the rooftops stepped down the hillside visible through the leaves of the trees, and over all the smoke and steam rising from the mills along the river, clouding the morning sky.

"I heard what it was they asked you," Perpetual said.

"I assumed that you would," Libby said. "You always manage to hear most of what goes on in this house. One way or the other."

"And will you honor what it was they said?"

"Honor," Libby said, turning away from the door to face Perpetual, studying her before walking past her. "Such a formal way to put it. Honor."

"As you say, Mawm." Following Libby back into the darkness of the house.

12

"First of all," Adams said, leaning closer to Malcolm across the desk, "I must impress upon you the highly sensitive nature of this drawing. No one is to know that you've seen it. No one. It's a matter of national security. If you decide to take the assignment, we'll need to work out certain clearances. . . ."

Malcolm looked at the drawing, looked at the two men standing across the desk from him. He knew the answer to his question, but decided it was best to play uninformed. "What is it?"

"The British refer to them as *caterpillar machine-gun destroyers*, but for secrecy's sake call them *tanks*, to foil any German attempts to find out what they're working on—"

"This is a French model FT-17, made by Renault," Taylor broke in, unable to contain his excitement any longer. "None are in production yet, but they're hoping to start soon. We haven't been able to get any drawings so far as to what the British are developing."

"How did you get this one?" Malcolm said.

"It's unimportant how," Adams said, straightening up. His face was nondescript, he could have fit in anywhere, not bland, just ordinary, an Everyman, or maybe an Anyman; he could have been a shoe salesman, a drummer with a line of ladies' gloves. "And unfortunately we don't have any more detailed drawings or blueprints of the FT-17 to go on. This one was actually done from memory."

"I assume the entire vehicle is covered with iron plate."

"Steel."

"And the turret turns, with the machine gun?"

"There's lateral movement ninety degrees from its central axis in both directions," Taylor said, remaining bent over the drawing, eager to talk more about it. "Both the French and the British are making larger vehicles with larger crews, some of the tanks we're told even have cannons. But this size is what we're interested in for now, the French call it *Mosquito* because of its ability to flit around." Taylor smiled; in his long esthetic face, the expression looked almost obscene.

Malcolm studied the drawing but his mind was wandering. Thinking, Why are they showing this to me? What do they have in mind? Surely they're not asking me . . . for Keystone to develop such a machine of this nature, we've never done anything of the kind, though we have done caterpillar treads on the well-driller, and we did an earthmover a while ago, there has to be another reason. . . . But all he said after several moments was, "It's very interesting, of course."

"It's the future of warfare," Adams said, sitting down again, crossing his legs. He also smiled, a businessman's smile; Malcolm thought of the Cheshire cat. "Someday, and not in the far distant future, they predict all wars will be fought mainly with machines of this nature."

"The killing will all be mechanized," Malcolm said.

"If you prefer," Adams said. "And the winners will be the ones with the most, and the best, machines."

Malcolm thought of his son John Lincoln, on his way to join the British army. If the French and English were developing these machines, surely the Germans were as well. Perhaps already had them on the plains of the western front. "Why are you showing me this?"

Adams acted as though he hadn't heard; as he spoke, Taylor pointed to the various sections of the drawing with one long slender finger. "Notice how much space is taken up at the rear of the vehicle by the internal combustion engine. To say nothing of all the other mechanisms associated with it, such as the radiator, the flywheel and clutch, the transmission. And right behind the gunner, that large reservoir for gasoline. All that highly volatile fuel inches from the personnel compartment. One high-velocity round and the whole tin can explodes."

"And there are all the fumes inside from the inefficient and, I might add noisy, internal combustion engine," Taylor added, almost gleefully. "Plus there has to be room for the crank to start the engine, with its tendency to backfire and break the arm of the man doing the cranking. Just what you don't want to happen on the battlefield. And the internal combustion engine's well-known habit of stalling out when it encounters an obstacle that the caterpillar treads can't lift the machine over."

Malcolm sat in his high-backed chair, looking at the two men across his desk, one seated, one standing, watching him for his reaction. Surely they're not proposing that Keystone Steam Works gets involved with a project like this, are they? I must be misunderstanding what they're saying, my God, a project like this would bring in millions, millions, we'd be set for life, Gus would be set for life. . . . He looked away, let his eyes roam around his office, at the rows of barrister bookcases containing his father's library, the engineering books and the volumes of company patents that his father had transported here to the steamworks when he moved out of the house, moved here to his office and workshop to devote the end of his life to developing new uses for his steam engines. Malcolm thought they must look impressive to men such as his visitors, must give the impression of being in the presence of a man of learning and expertise, that there was a wealth of engineering knowledge and acumen at hand here at Keystone Steam Works.

But he knew such was not the case, not anymore, not since the death of his father. He knew that he was a mediocre engineer at best; his value to the company was to take the designs and machines his father had developed and market them throughout the world. He had tried his best to keep the manufacturing techniques up-to-date, hoping that would keep the steamworks competitive; but the truth was the company hadn't introduced any new construction or farm machines beyond those his father had developed, they only rehashed existing models, extended this, enlarged that. True, some of his father's original engineers had come up with a way to reduce the size of their steam engines, and developed the forced air induction system, but those men were long gone and no one in the firm now showed the initiative or ability to take the design further. As for Gus, he wasn't even an engineer, having never finished college—he barely started it for that matter, thinking he could learn the business from working in the shop—and his hope to parlay one of his grandfather's designs, the Lylemobile, had gone just about as far as it would go with the company's present-day capabilities. If these government reps were offering what he thought they were offering, it would be the financial salvation of them all.

Taylor was running on, brimming over with excitement. ". . . so the advantages of a steam engine in such a vehicle are obvious. The engine can run on kerosene, which has, as you well know, a much higher flash point than gasoline, so it's safer to handle and less likely to ignite from a munitions round. Plus the mileage is better than gasoline, so the vehicle can run longer without refueling—or for that matter, if supply lines are broken, a steam engine can run on just about anything the crew can find, wood, raw petroleum, coal, whatever. There are fewer moving parts to a steam engine, it's better suited to the speed and torque characteristics of the axle so it doesn't require the bulky and complicated transmission, and it's infinitely quieter!"

Adams couldn't help but smile. "I think Malcolm is quite aware of the qualities of his steam engines, Julian. What we can't emphasize enough, however, is Keystone's ability to incorporate all these qualities of a steam engine into a compact unit that can reach operating speed within a few minutes."

He stood up from his chair and approached the desk again. "Usually, in normal times, you would receive an official request by certified mail or messenger to bid on a project of this size and importance, but these are not normal times. Our entry into the war in Europe seems imminent, and we can't afford to waste time—nor can we take a chance that foreign agents might in some way intercept such transmissions and learn of our intentions. Therefore, on behalf of the United States government, I am authorized to ask you to take on the project of developing a light tank like the one we've shown you, except powered with a steam engine."

"Develop the entire vehicle?" Malcolm said. "Not just the engine for such a vehicle?"

"That's correct," Adams said.

"We'll work closely with you, of course," Taylor said.

"And you said there are no engineering drawings for such a vehicle," Malcolm said. "Only this illustration."

"I'm afraid that's so," Adams said, looking regretful. "Though we're told this is pretty much to scale."

"But making the drawings alone could take months, to say nothing of manufacturing the dies and machines to make such a vehicle. . . ."

"We would expect you to hire the people necessary to complete the project in as little time as possible," Taylor said. "And it's not as if you need to start from scratch, Keystone already produces several caterpillar-driven vehicles—"

"If you're concerned about the cost of development," Adams said, "it's not an issue. We're not asking you to produce such a vehicle on spec or in a bid process. There's no time for that. We know what Keystone Steam Works can do, and we want you to proceed with the project as quickly as possible—"

"Full steam ahead," Taylor said, "so to speak."

Adams glared at him, then looked back at Malcolm. "The first thing I need you to do is to put together a preliminary estimate of what you need to get the project started. How much it will cost to begin hiring people, to begin the mechanical drawings, to begin purchasing materials. At the same time I need a schedule from you as to when you'll have a prototype vehicle ready for testing and review. I'm only looking for approximate figures here, both as to cost and to time, but it's imperative that I have them immediately. The reason is that I'm authorized to write you a check on the spot for what you need to get started. No questions asked, I just need to know the figures. And I need it by end of the day tomorrow."

"On the Fourth?"

"The holiday will mean nothing if we don't have a country with which to celebrate it. We're ticketed on the train that leaves here tomorrow evening. We will be on it; whether or not I write you a check before boarding is up to you."

"You've given me quite a lot to think about," Malcolm said, getting to his feet.

Adams offered his hand across the desk. "I hope the only things to think about are the numbers I've requested. Once you get those to me, I'll ask you to sign a letter of intent, I'll write you a check, and we'll be ready to make history."

Malcolm started to walk around the desk to escort the two men to the door but Taylor stopped him. "You can't just leave that drawing lying out like that."

Malcolm looked at the drawing on his desk, looked at Taylor, an expression on his face as if he thought the other man was joking. "Other people in the company will have to see the drawing, if they're working on the project—"

"I mean it. That's a top secret drawing. You can't just leave it lying around like that." Taylor looked at Adams for support. "If that's the way you're going to treat sensitive material, I don't know. . . ."

Adams shrugged, apparently as surprised as Malcolm that Taylor was making an issue of it. "Yes, I suppose it shouldn't be left lying around. . . ."

Malcolm went back, rolled up the drawing, and placed it in the desk's center drawer, trying not to let the younger man get under his skin. Take it easy, Malcolm, the man has a job to do, he's sent here to protect these things, he doesn't know how we run things around here, get ahold of yourself, the future of the steamworks depends on it. . . . He tried to think of things to say to ease the situation, putting on his own businessman's smile.

"I'm afraid my son isn't back yet with the Lylemobile. Let me call down to the shops and get you a carriage to take you back to your hotel."

"You needn't bother," Adams said. "The walk will do us good. Besides, we have some time to kill before our train tomorrow night."

"Augustus was telling us that there will be quite a celebration in town tomorrow for the Fourth," Taylor said.

"Ah, yes indeed," Malcolm said, pausing in the doorway to the outer office, hoping that Taylor's interest signaled an easing of the tension. "The town goes all out for it every year, it's quite an affair. In the morning is the parade—the town always asks us to display some of our machines, this year we'll be showing one of our new well-drillers."

He pointed to a metal scale model sitting beside the door on top of a stack of barrister bookcases.

"New, you say?" Adams said.

"Yes, in a manner of speaking. It's based on technologies we've used in other machines that we're applying here. The derrick is the tallest we've ever produced, and unlike earlier models that had to be assembled by hand at the drill site, this derrick is articulated and rests on top of the cab until the machine is in position, then the derrick raises and extends by means of hydraulics and is ready to use."

"I'll be looking for it," Adams said.

Taylor had been examining the scale model well-driller; he inadvertently moved the derrick, which fell over onto the cab with a loud metal *Clack!* The three men looked at each other.

"Careful, Julian," Adams said. "We didn't come here to wreck the place, you know."

Taylor was obviously embarrassed but his manner went back to being unpleasant. "I hope the real article isn't that unstable. We'd have to rethink our offer of your services."

Adams laughed, trying to ease the situation. Malcolm laughed as well but he wasn't amused. He tried to think of something else to say.

"After the parade, there will be the dedication of a new park, a block above Main Street. I'd like to invite you to be our guests for that presentation. I'm proud to say my family and Keystone Steam Works are donating the park to the town in honor of my father, Colin Lyle."

"Augustus said something about a statue. . . ," Adams said.

"Yes, my mother will unveil a statue she's donating personally to the city, the figure of a Civil War cavalryman."

"A Union cavalryman, I hope," Taylor said.

The three men laughed, but Malcolm thought if it weren't for the pending contract, the project in the offing, he would have hit him.

13

The crack of sunlight was gone from her bedroom, replaced with only a dull glow in the space at the center of the two drapes, a band of gray light at an angle along the floor. Libby sat again in her rocking chair after the encounter with the three women from the temperance union, rocking slowly back and forth; she started to reach for a sip of her whiskey but thought different of it, too tired at the moment for even that. People and their little concerns, they'll drain the life right out of a body. She studied her left hand resting at the end of the chair arm; it wasn't trembling at the moment as it often did, but her fingers were pulsing as if they wanted to, would have if her hand had been in another position, if it was hanging over the end of the chair arm or suspended in the air without support. Then it would be fluttering with a life of its own, uncontrollably. She hated that, a sure sign of her age; she caught others looking at it, a look on their faces as if they were witnessing a harbinger of death itself. Well, she had one hand that trembled, one that didn't, and the one that didn't was the one charged most times with holding her whiskey glass. There was always something to be thankful for, if you looked hard enough.

At the other end of the floor she could hear Perpetual moving in and out of Mary Lydia's room; she could envision her taking care of Mary Lydia's bedpan, perhaps getting her fresh sheets and changing the bed, coming up and down the stairs with the younger woman's lunch. Perpetual. What would she do without the woman? What would any of them do, and none of the rest realized it. What was her full name? Guadeloupe Heart-of-a-Lion, something-or-other. She just appeared at the front door one morning. That morning. The morning that Colin moved out of the house and down to the steamworks. Sent the dark-skinned young woman to tell me of the new living arrangements of my marriage, and then poor Malcolm was there too, trying his best to organize things and set things right the way he always does, and making more of a mess than ever the way he always does, having no more of an idea what was going on than anyone else. And then the two of them standing there with their mouths open when I went down the front steps and climbed up on one of the wagons and told the driver to take me down to the steamworks or I would kick him off and drive myself, and I would have done it too. I guess that was Perpetual's introduction to what she was getting herself into, what her life was going to be like attached to this family, the look on her face and Malcolm's face equaled only by the look on Colin's face when I walked into his office at the Works.

"Libby, what are you doing here?"

"I think the question is, what are *you* doing here?"

"Didn't the girl tell you?"

"The 'girl,' as you call her, told me something," I said. "But it did nothing to answer the question of what is going on."

Colin was still the tall thin erect man I married, even then into his seventies, the tonsure of hair around his bald pate and his bushy sideburns gray almost to white, but he had never fully recovered from the episode with the war engines and the Rebel infiltrators. He had put so much of himself into those machines, he thought he was finally getting recognized for his designs and the accomplishments of the steamworks, only to discover that the Rebels had tricked him, the government he was working for was the Confederacy. Then he risked his life to blow up the bridge and stop Judson from getting the war engines across the river, even though it meant destroying the engines as well, and in the process permanently damaging his own health, injuring his hip and leg as he escaped the Rebels shooting at him, the rest of his life plagued by constant pain and walking with a limp. There were the other injuries too, of a darker kind, wounds that would not heal and darkened his spirit so at times I barely knew him, he was away somewhere deep within himself and would never speak of those things. Wouldn't speak of them until that day.

"This is for the best, Libby," he said, turning away, unable to look at me. "The best for all of us."

"It's for the best for none of us, you mean," I said, moving closer to him so he had to look at me. "It's not even best for you."

"I just want to be alone now. I just want to work on my designs, to devote the rest of my life to the work we've started here. Don't you realize, I don't have much time left—"

"Which is all the more reason for you not to pull away from me now. I know there's not much time left, that's why we should be together now. . . ."

"You don't understand," Colin said, obviously miserable, his head wagging back and forth as if searching for something lost on the floor. "You never understood."

"What? What didn't I understand?"

"Why didn't you care when it still could have meant something?"

He sat down heavily in his desk chair and we looked at each

other then, perhaps for the first time in years. And I knew what was coming then, I could have told him as well as he was telling me, and it was all beyond speaking, all beyond words.

"Didn't you think I knew what was going on with you and Gene McArtle? Didn't you think I could see what you were doing right in front of my eyes?"

"It was nothing, Colin, he was nothing." I reached to touch his arm but he pulled away. "He was giving me the laudanum, it was the only way I could get it, I thought I had to have it to get through the pain after the last baby and all the confusions, all those women's things, but then I found I didn't need it after all, I stopped it, remember? I stopped the drugs and I stopped Eugene too—"

"You stopped because of Judson Walker." He turned his head away, as if speaking the name was anathema to him. And when he looked at me again, it was up under the shelf of his forehead, up under the weight he had carried all those years. "And didn't you think I could see what was going on with him too?"

There was nothing to say to that. There was no defense for that.

"Oh, I understood, all right," Colin went on. "The dashing bold cavalry officer, he was like something out of a story and you were like something out of a story too, the beautiful maiden caught in his spell. Except you weren't a maiden any longer. You were my wife."

"Colin, I—"

"Why didn't you go with him? Don't tell me he didn't want you to, and don't tell me you didn't think of it, that you two didn't talk about it. And don't tell me it was because of some devotion to me. The time for that is well past."

And I couldn't tell him, I couldn't tell him that the reason I didn't go was because of the laudanum, because I had passed out in my bed and when the time came for me to go with Judson I was in no condition to, that the very drug that Colin condemned McArtle for was the very reason why I didn't leave him, why when the time came I couldn't go with my one true love—but that wasn't true either, because Judson wasn't my one true love, that was what I discovered then, I came to realize the terrible truth that I had two true loves, Colin and Judson, both equal, both forever in my heart, I recognized it in Colin the moment I saw him for the first time on my father's plantation when he came with his steam engines, knew it when he went away back here to Furnass and knew I would follow after him whether he wanted me to or not, in the same way I recognized it in Judson that first night he sat in the kitchen and I bound the wound in his side from a skirmish with the Yankees on his way here, knew who he was and why he had come and why he would never leave me even if he went away and why I would never leave him even if I stayed. And knew then as Colin and I confronted each other and ourselves and our marriage there in his office that there was nothing more to say to him, knew that the price of having two loves was to end up with neither, that to love twice was apparently not to love at all, that love forever after would be in silence and alone.

I left the steamworks then and returned to the wagon waiting for me in the yard, sat on the seat beside the wagoner as we clambered through the passageway beneath the buildings and out into the street, knowing I would never see Colin again, any more than I would ever see Judson again, rode on the wagon up through the streets of Furnass like a condemned woman on the way to the gallows or the guillotine, thinking there would be nothing for me now, thinking my life was over as we entered the drive of the house to see Colin's possessions loaded into wagons ready to be hauled away, entered the house to find my own son trying to take possession of the bedroom that had been mine and Colin's, assuming that he was the master of the house now and he and his wife all too ready to ascribe me to a lesser room, a lesser place in the household, my own son, except for Perpetual, this woman who barely knew me taking my part against them, standing up for me, my new heart's companion, keeping Malcolm at bay from taking my room with a parasol, "You hit him on the head? You hit him with my parasol?" "Yes Mawm, I did, like this, boom boom, oh it was glorious, Mawm, glorious," and recognized that love would be different now from that time forward, that love would take a different form and different meaning now and have a different purpose. . . .

She startled awake; she must have dozed among her reveries; at the end of her arm her left hand was fluttering like a light-crazed moth. Had someone come into the room? "Hello? Perpetual? Is someone there?" She looked about her, listened, but nothing stirred, all was still, there was no one there.

. . . and in the hallway Perpetual stands at Libby's door listening, thinking that as she passed in the hall she had heard Libby whimper and start to call out but decides she must have imagined it, waits a few minutes longer to make sure Libby is all right, that there are no other indications of distress, then continues on along the hallway, her arms full of fresh sheets that she's brought up from the laundry, on around the square of the stairwell that forms the central part of this the original part of the house, before either of the wings were added, quiet as a shadow moving among the noontime shadows, dressed as always in an old-fashioned high-waisted down-to-her-ankles dress the same as her mistress except Perpetual's in the muted multicolored stripes of her island home, to keep her mistress company in her own way as it were, so Libby won't stand out so badly as odd, on around the balustrade past

her own bedroom door and that of a spare bedroom and then around the corner to Mary Lydia's door, slipping inside quietly in case the younger woman is asleep but no, Mary Lydia is sitting up among a stack of pillows as if waiting for her, which she is, acknowledges Perpetual's presence in the room but doesn't smile, it's obvious that she's been crying again as Perpetual comes to the bed and deposits the stack of sheets near Mary Lydia's feet under the covers, "Here we are, my darling, Perpetual will have you changed in no time," and Mary Lydia says, "There's more blood, Perpetual, I looked," and Perpetual sobers but tries not to look concerned, "There, there, my child, I told you there might be, not you be worried now, it's as Perpetual say, it means we have to do as Perpetual told you, I will take care of it, Perpetual is here to take care of you" . . . as downstairs, Missy Lyle, Malcolm's second wife, sits in the living room reading one of her women's magazines just as Libby suspected or knew from experience, having reclaimed her usual place on the sofa, the tiny woman with the close-cropped blond hair as defined in her white lacy peignoirs as Libby and Perpetual are defined in their out-of-fashion dresses, not by design in opposition to the other women of the household but effective nonetheless for setting herself apart from them, hears from upstairs Perpetual talking to Mary Lydia but feels no compunction to go upstairs to see if her daughter is okay, not proud of how she feels but unable to feel differently, vindicated by the doctor's diagnosis that Mary Lydia is pregnant, confirming the dislike she's had of her daughter since she was a little girl, preferring always the girl's twin brother, John Lincoln—Malcolm's son Gus, born of his first marriage, doesn't even figure among her affections, aware the first time she met him that the child was comparing her unfavorably to his birth mother, and besides, as a ten-year-old he was already as tall as Missy, how could she act in her new role of a mother to a boy like that?—

*John Lincoln displaying the qualities she valued in a person—
quiet, undemanding, a good-looking boy too, reflecting well on his
mother, an Adonis—even as a toddler, her disaffection, or rather,
resentment, of the girl all the stronger now that John Lincoln has
disappeared, left her (Missy still doesn't know because no one has
told her about the telegram that said that John Lincoln is sailing
to England to join the war effort against Germany, that in fact
at this very moment he is boarding a troop ship in New York
Harbor preparing to sail in the morning), her outward anger directed at her husband, Malcolm, as it has been almost from the
time she agreed to marry him, and then confirmed soon after the
first and only time they had sexual relations and she ended up
pregnant with what turned out to be the twins, an anger that is
real and seething and always just below the surface, though born
more out of defense now than from any actual grievance—Malcolm is in fact the kindest, most considerate man she's ever
known though admittedly she's known very few—based on the talk
around town she heard most of her life that her husband had
something to do with the death of his first wife, an anxiety on
Missy's part that somehow or other, as the result of his disap-
pointments with her—and they must be legion—he would contrive
to do something of the sort to her, sitting on the sofa in the living
room but always listening for the footsteps coming for her down
the hall, or wherever she is in the house, the shadow of a man
holding a burning lantern . . . while a few hours earlier, Malcolm
sits at his desk at the Keystone Steam Works studying the drawing
left by the government representatives, the schematic of the
Renault FT-17 Mosquito, making notes for himself on a sheet of
foolscap—the caterpillar tread assembly looks similar to the one
used on Keystone's well-driller Model #138, it won't be much of
a trick to adapt it to the tank; and Keystone's latest steam engine
will fit easily in the engine compartment so they can move the*

firewall back six inches at least; but he's concerned about the number of workers he can find with the experience to work on the chassis, he'll need to recruit some from up in Pittsburgh—thinking the requirements for the estimate to get the project started are so loose that he could probably pull numbers out of thin air and they would be sufficient, he won't know until they get deep into the particulars what all they'll need, but there is no question that the project would be profitable for him, no question that war and its preparations are good for business, though taking on the project would end any possibility of pursuing Gus' hope to develop the Lylemobile for production, that would be a blow to his eldest son's already shaky self-confidence, though on the other hand it would give Malcolm the perfect out for not pursuing the Lylemobile, a project he is certain is bound for failure, the use of steam engines in machines such as well-drillers and for heavy construction—and yes, now tanks, machines of war— still up for grabs, the disadvantages of steam engines in general outweighed by their advantages in those applications, but all indications are that the internal combustion engine is the engine of the future as far as personal road vehicles are concerned, the tide is turning against the Stanley and the Locomobile and the Doble, which means the tank project isn't really a matter of preference now for the future of the company, a question of if he should or shouldn't take it, he really has no choice in terms of what's best for the company, if he doesn't take the project some other company will, and Keystone will be left even farther behind their competitors—it is all too depressing for him, this should be a time of celebration for the opportunity and all he can see are pitfalls ahead, he has to get out of here to clear his thoughts—he gets up from his desk and leaving his suit coat behind, in his shirtsleeves and waistcoat, takes the back stairway down to the central yard, ignoring the crew off-loading the dunnage and tie-downs from a lowloader after

*delivering his mother's statue to the new park, shuffling through
the heat and the dust across the yard to a narrow passageway
between the old boiler shop and the warehouse that used to be the
dormitory for resident workers and out the other side, crossing
the railway sidings and the tracks of the trunk line and main line
and down through the tall grass and brush to stand along the bank
of the river, looking back briefly at the* steamworks, *the solid wall
of redbrick buildings like the ramparts of a fort, then facing the
river again, the sandstone and granite bluffs of the valley wall
across the water, thinking his father must have faced a similar
problem when the Confederates posing as Yankees came to him
with the idea of outfitting his road engines with iron plate and
Gatling guns, a purpose totally opposed to the original peaceful
applications his father intended for the machines and yet would
secure the future of the company, and there it was: more or less
the same quandary, history repeating itself: he had the chance to
completely change the direction of the company, from one of
building machines intended for service and the greater good and
the growth of American expansion across the continent, to that
of developing machines that would bring death and terror and
destruction as America established her rightful place among the
other nations of the world, and in the process bring success for
his company, a company that would be worth something in the
future for his son—with the added dilemma that by doing so he
would destroy the future his son wished for the company, Gus'
involvement with the Lylemobile the only time Malcolm could ever
remember his son being excited or even interested in something
in his life—looks downriver to the confluence of the Allehela with
the Ohio River and the bridge across the mouth of the valley, the
bridge built to replace the one his father destroyed as he destroyed
his war engines, wondering what it would take to do something
like that, destroy your work and your future and your passion, to*

risk it all, including your own life, to do what you considered the right thing to do, or for that matter to even know what you considered the right thing to do, the water of the Allehela gurgling and bubbling at his feet bringing him back to the present, the current rolling relentlessly by, saying out loud, looking to nothing in particular, "Help me, Father, I don't know what to do" . . . as in the compound of the steamworks, *Gus pilots his Lylemobile through the passageway under the administration offices, emerging into the yard in a cloud of steam as he parks near the entrance, just missing the sight of his father across the yard disappearing into the passageway between two buildings heading toward the river, Gus hurrying up the stairs and into the administration offices, past the engineers and draftsmen bent over their drawing boards, the rows of accountants and expediters and shipping clerks at their desks, typists pecking away at their typewriters, and into his father's office, hoping that the government reps might still be here so he can drive them back to their hotel, so he can put in a few more good words about the Lylemobile in case that was the reason for their visit, but there is no one here, his father's office is empty, "Damn it," he says to himself and goes over to the windows, looking down into the compound, the crew off-loading the bracing and ropes from the lowloader used to transport the statue his grandmother is dedicating to the new park, the other work going on around the yard, a flatbed truck with a load of pipe heading toward the boiler shop, a derrick unloading sheets of steel plates for the warehouse—he recognized most of the workers from the time he worked in the various shops and gangs, but knew none of their names now, if he ever did, not because he thought he was above them in any way but because people as individuals were simply not that important to him— turned away from the windows and looked around the office with a loud and heartfelt sigh, thinking that one day if things work out the way he wants them to this office will be his, he will carry on the Lyle name as president of the Keystone Steam Works, as his father and grandfather did before him, only now they won't produce only steam-driven heavy equipment, they will be an automobile manufacturer, the Lylemobile up there along with Peerless and Knox and Simplex, that would silence the Elizabeth Quigleys of the world, those who say his family's prominence in town was a thing of the past, the Lylemobile will bring more jobs to the town than anyone ever dreamed of, both for the Keystone Steam Works and for Buchanan Steel as its main supplier right up the river, especially if the government is interested in backing such a project, if that's why the government reps are here, all because he has had the foresight to see the potential of a steam-powered vehicle, that will show all the people all his life who thought him a worthless dreamer—I'll finally be somebody in Lily's eyes, she'll know she was right to marry me, she won't have to be ashamed of me anymore, she'll see I'm somebody in the eyes of the family, not just an afterthought stuck there in a wing at the back of the house, she'll see I am important—smiles to himself as he looks around the office, looks at his father's desk and can't resist, goes over and sits down in the tall-backed chair, swivels to the left and right and pulls forward so his legs are in the well, thinking, Well now, so this is what it feels like, this is what it will feel like—I'll bring Mal here to show him his father's office, this is your dad's office, son, and someday it'll be yours—surveys his father's orderly stacks of papers and ledgers, engineering drawings for approval, letters to be signed and purchase orders to be approved, and directly in front of him a drawing beside a sheet of foolscap with the start of a list of materials and manhours, a drawing of what appears to be a two-man armored vehicle, he's heard talk of armored tanks in the newspapers and guesses this must be one of them, but what is such a drawing doing in his father's office?*

All That Will Remain

Why would his father be working on an estimate for such a vehicle? Is this what the government reps wanted to talk to Keystone about? How long has his father known about this? And why hadn't he mentioned it to Gus before? . . . while a thousand miles away from Furnass, off a dirt road in flatline farm country outside of Wichita, Kansas, Lily Hughes Lyle, Gus' wife, stands on the side porch of the wood farmhouse that serves as the manse, beside the old whitewashed wood church where her father is pastor, watching her father in the expanse of yard behind the two buildings, in a white shirt beneath his suspenders despite the crushing heat, albeit an old white shirt, with a faint red vertical pinstripe running through it, frayed at the collar and cuffs, thin as oilcloth and translucent with his sweat, a battered straw hat sweat-stained halfway up the crown, working with a scythe to cut the tall grass that has grown up since he last cleared it in the spring, her son, eight-year-old Mal, following a safe distance behind wielding a switch, a thin branch from a cottonwood tree, flailing away at the cut grass in imitation of his beloved grandfather, her father in his mid-seventies now but still active, a tall broad-shouldered Scot who came to this country as a boy and whose brogue only seems to grow stronger as he ages, finishes the swath he started and then carries the scythe over his shoulder, cupping the head of his grandson to direct him back toward the house and his mother, the two coming back for some lemonade from the pitcher and three glasses that Lily's mother has left on the porch knowing he would want some sooner or later, Lily pouring them each a glass as her father says, "Doing the Lord's work can be a devil," obviously proud of what to him is a risqué joke, Lily waiting until Mal takes his glass and wanders off toward the chicken house, then says to her father, resting her own glass of lemonade against her cheek, "Have you had time to think about what I asked you?" and her father resets his sweat-stained straw hat, removes the scythe from over his shoulder and stands it on end beside him, the curved blade stretched out like a metal banner, the man transformed now from a weary workman and loving father to a stern psalm-reading Bible-quoting Scots Covenanter preacher, and says, "Daughter, you had time to consider the consequences of marrying the man before you took your vows," and Lily says, "But I didn't know then, there was no way I could have known then, the way his family was going to be," and her father says, "And what is so wrong with Augustus' family? They seemed proper enough when I met them, when I came back to marry you," and Lily takes the sweaty glass away from her cheek and looks away for a moment, watches her son gazing through the chicken wire at the birds pecking at bits of grain or pebbles or sticks or anything else they see on the ground, then looks back at her father, "They're odd, they have these odd ideas about everything, they live in this insular little world of theirs as if there's no one else on earth, his stepmother wanders around in dressing gowns all day long and his grandmother is this black-clothed figure who never talks to anyone except her dark-skinned maid who's got a jungle growing in her room full of all these exotic smelly plants, and Gus' half-sister is this wispy little flower that everybody coddles and thinks she's all sweetness and light and she's anything but, and they all worship her twin brother, John Lincoln, who thinks he's God's gift to—" and her father stops her right there, holds up the half-full, half-empty glass of lemonade in her direction to signify he's heard enough, "I'm sorry, child, no, you canna break your vow to your husband and come back here to live, you are always welcome to visit, of course, we want you to visit because we love you and we want to see our grandson, but I ask you, how would it look for the pastor's own daughter to forsake her promise to God to love, honor, and obey her husband simply because his family's a little soft in the head, no, girl, you

*made that vow to God and now you must live it" . . . while four
hundred miles in the opposite direction from Furnass, on a dock
in New York Harbor, John Lincoln walks up the gangplank to a
makeshift troop ship, an old tramp steamer unfit for other service
pressed into duty to get American volunteers to the war in Europe, a tall strapping upright young man, with the high cheekbones
and protruding Adam's apple of his namesake, the very picture
of the American self-evident ideals of life, liberty, and the pursuit
of happiness, ready to defend those God-given inalienable rights
on the fields of Flanders, his recently purchased (because it looked
more military than his tweed-covered suitcase) duffel bag balanced on his shoulder, follows the direction of a sergeant from an
army he doesn't recognize through an oval doorway and then
down an impossibly steep set of stairs, down and down to come
finally to a room full of bunks and other young men staking out
their territories for the journey, John Lincoln settling for an upper bunk near the bulkhead under a stack of leaky and drippy
pipes, leaves his duffel bag there and against the stream of other
volunteers coming down goes back up the numerous sets of stairs
to the deck again, this time to the side of the vessel away from
the dock and the commotions of people coming on board and the
preparations for sailing the first thing in the morning, stands at
the railing looking out toward the open water and the distant
shore of New Jersey and the figure of the Statue of Liberty rising
above all, thinking, We were always so close growing up, it seemed
there was nothing that could come between us, each one the missing half of the other, her body was my body and mine hers, we
used to kid around back in high school when she was going to take
a bath, or rather I used to kid around, I'm not sure now whether
she liked it or not, I doubt if she knew whether she liked it or not,
I used to try to snatch the towel from her when she walked without
her clothes, to the bathroom but she never waited to get undressed*

until she was in the bathroom either, and there was a crack in the frame beside the door so I could peer in at her as she removed the towel or when she got out of the bathtub and dried herself, she would call, You better not be peeping at me, but I never lost the feeling that she knew I was there, somehow wanted me to be there, those thin slices of her naked body forming once and forever what I thought a girl's naked body should be, but now that's gone forever, I will lift up mine eyes unto the hills from whence cometh my help, she betrayed all that we were and ever could, she let that happen to her, she let somebody else touch her, she should have known better, known this would happen if she wasn't careful, if she went ahead and tried to do something on her own, without me, tried to have thoughts and feelings without me, I would have taken care of her, now and forever, she didn't need anything beyond me, outside of who we were together, that's what real love is, isn't it? but now the world will never be the same, can never be the same, the Lord shall preserve thy going out and thy coming in from this time forth, and even for evermore, I couldn't stay to see what would become of her, if she did something like that with no thought of me or what would become of us why should I care about the dreadful situation she brought upon herself, but that's all behind me now, it no longer exists now, she no longer exists for me, there is only now and there is only me and I've left all that far behind me, and to celebrate his new freedom and his new life away from Furnass and his family and his wayward lost twin self, John Lincoln climbs up on the railing surrounding the deck, standing on the middle rail with his shins braced against the top rail so he can be as tall as he can be, so he can be as open to the sky and the day and the world as he possibly can be, spreading his arms wide to embrace all that is and all that his new life will hold . . . as in Furnass, in her room in Sycamore House, Mary Lydia lies in her bed in a tangle of covers, listening for Perpetual

*on the stairs, hoping she'll come soon, not that she's lacking
anything or is in need, what she needs is the woman's company,
her only friend now it seems, the only one to understand, her
mind flooded with memories today, images of the past she can't
shake, the day of a picnic a few months earlier, at the end of
April, on the hillside of the valley across the river from the town,
across the river from the college, the annual outing of the students
of Covenant College to paint the giant C laid out with stones near
the top of the bluffs, the first picnic of the year, the only reason
she signed up for it because he did, it sounded like a fun time
with all her friends from the college, all the friends she had
made over the year, but it ended up just the two of them, just the
two. . . .*

14

The tall grass tickled my face, tickled my ears, crackled as I lay
there, as if the blades of grass were reaching for me, welcoming
me, touching me with their love.

It was a tradition at Covenant College: as soon as the weather
was warm enough, usually around mid-April, that a group of un-
derclassmen, both men and women, would rent a half dozen wagons and teams from local farmers and make the journey across
the river and up into the hills on the other side of the valley, to
the clearing on the wooded slope opposite the college with the
large *C* laid out in white-painted rocks—the letter placed there
in celebration of the college by one of its first graduating classes
in the late 1800s—the yearly outing to clear away debris from
the past fall and winter and repaint the rocks a sure sign of
spring, the first of the social festivities—May Day, Founder's
Day, Graduation—that marked the end of the school year.

It never occurred to Mary Lydia that he might sit with her in the wagon; he never paid any attention to her when others were around, barely acted as if he knew her at all. It was expected that he would sit with the other leaders of the outing, in one of the first wagons; Mary Lydia was content to sit with some of the other girls of her class. But even so it was a special day for her. She was wearing her new picnic dress that Perpetual had made her for just such outings. Peachy-pink, as Perpetual called it, in the newest fashion she found in a magazine, light and airy, with its three-quarter-length overblouse, the dress itself with a natural waistline and slim skirt just hitting the ankles. She knew she stood out among the other girls, but that was the point, wasn't it? And it was a fine, fine day, warm enough that she didn't need a coat to spoil the effect of her dress, a harbinger of warmer days, summer days to come, the sky as blue as the blue of his eyes.

As the little procession rolled out of the campus and down long Orchard Avenue, past the trim brick houses of college professors and supervisors from the mills and merchants who wanted to live in a better part of town, Mary Lydia perched on a bale of hay in the back of the wagon, surrounded by the other girls like her attendants, feeling like a fairy princess being paraded through the streets on her way to her royal wedding.

After the little caravan crossed the Twenty-sixth Street Bridge over the Allehela, everyone got down from the wagons and walked beside them to help the horses up the grade of Drumlins Road to the top of the valley wall. To keep up their spirits through the long climb, they sang songs, part of the tradition, starting out with religious and patriotic themes, "Onward Christian Soldiers" and "The Battle Hymn of the Republic," but soon turned to some of the popular songs of the day, "There's a Long, Long Trail a'Winding" and "By the Beautiful Sea." So it was a surprise when halfway up the grade he left the friends he was walking with ahead and dropped back beside her, walking with her as they sang,

By the sea, by the sea,
By the beautiful sea,
You and I, you and I,
Oh, how happy we'll be. . . .

Mary Lydia was as happy as any day she could remember, she was so proud to be seen with him—he was dressed in a tweed Norfolk jacket and tweed pants with heavy wool socks pulled up to his knees over his trouser legs as might befit an English gentleman on the hunt; she knew they looked spectacular together, like they belonged together, she knew the other girls were so jealous of her—their hands almost touching as they swung along, though there was no question of letting that happen, that would have been totally inappropriate, no matter what the circumstances. Then at the top of the hill he was gone again, back with his friends in the front wagon, and Mary Lydia was by herself again. Only now her heart was priming with joy, he had walked with her, he had showed them all that he wanted to be with her—he was with me, I was with him—such a beautiful day, forever a day like no other.

Overhead the few clouds streamed by like the banners torn from approaching armies, the trees still bare from winter but with a hint of green from the first buds. I raised up, resting my weight on my elbow so I could see the view. From this height on the slope of the valley, the town across the river was spread before me, as if just for me, my realm; beyond the town, higher up the slope of the valley, I could see Sycamore House, the Lyle House, my house, solitary among the black trees. He sat on the grass a little ways from me, his knees drawn up, looking at the view as well, like the biblical stranger in a strange land, the proverbial lost figure in a landscape. Then, as if he could feel me looking at him, he turned and gazed at me as if he knew my mind, knew what I was thinking.

In a mile or so along the ridgeline, they stopped beside a farmer's field, the horses unable to get them any closer to their destination, and all got out of the wagons. For a while Mary Lydia lost track of him in the confusion of helping to unload the wagons and dividing up the equipment to be carried to the site, buckets of whitewash, brushes, rakes, and brooms to clear away a year's worth of undergrowth. Then they followed a trail beside the field and into the trees down the slope of the hill, the group strung out in a long line, everyone chattering and laughing about their great adventure. And then he was beside her again, walking with her as if it were the most natural thing in the world. Partway down the slope one of their number took out a Kodak Brownie, and the two of them joined the group posing in the grass. As they headed down the trail again Mary Lydia started to say something to him, but he put his finger to his lips, as if they shared a secret, then nodded to her, slowing his pace to let the others behind them pass by until they were last in the procession, the two of them making a game of it, matching their strides slower and slower until the others in front of them had disappeared into the trees down the slope.

Then he dropped the shovel he was carrying into the tall grass beside the path, took the rake she was carrying and tossed it there as well and grabbed her hand and led her into the brush across the face of the hillside, clearing a path for her through the sumac and chokecherry and tangleberry, the two of them laughing, Mary Lydia already out of breath and struggling to keep up with him, the others totally out of sight now, crashing and stumbling and giggling through the brush till they came to a small clearing among the trees. He dropped her hand then. They looked at each other, sober now, and walked slowly into the clearing, Mary Lydia a few steps behind.

"Did you know this spot was here?"

"How could I?" he said, in his best accent. "This is not my country."

"What if the others miss us?"

"They won't." He glanced at her over his shoulder, then away again, suddenly shy. "They're too busy doing God's work white-washing stones."

She swished her foot back and forth among the grass, pointing her toe like a dancer. "They do take themselves seriously, don't they?"

"He who has an ear, let him hear what the Spirit says," he said, raising his finger like a preacher. "To him who overcomes I will give a white stone, that I painted myself, with a new name written on it that nobody else can read. Or something of the sort from Revelations."

She giggled.

He gave a little nod of appreciation, obviously playing to her as audience. "For you shall be in league with the stones of the field, and the beasts of the field shall be at peace with you, especially if you use enough whitewash."

With that he plopped himself down in the grass as if weary of it all. She stood there a moment longer, then sat down and leaned back, into the tall grass, pressing it flat around her, resting her arm across her forehead to shield her eyes from the sun.

He looked almost sad as he gazed at me, the deep melancholy that seemed so much of his life. Then his long beautiful sculptured face broke into his mischievous grin, a little boy looking for trouble. He rolled over onto his hands and knees and started toward me through the tall grass, slowly, stealthily, now like a stalking panther, intent on its prey, a Greek god come down to earth intent upon a lover, I was Leda to his Zeus the swan, Europa to his Zeus the bull. I leaned back again into the tickling prickling crinkling grass and his sad long beautiful face slid across the sky above me, blanking out the sun and the clouds and the day itself.

He leaned over her, playful, teasing almost, as if it were all a game between them, then it was no game, for either one. She opened her arms and reached up and embraced him, her arms around his neck, not pulling him closer to her but obviously not pushing him away either, willing for whatever was going to happen next, and he leaned down and kissed her full on the mouth, then harder, his tongue forcing open her lips as he started fumbling with her dress with his free hand, reaching up under her long skirt and petticoat until he found the soft warm cotton mound of her short-legged panties, sticking two fingers under the edge into the hair and the skin and moisture. Then there was no question what was going to happen, he broke away from her arms and straightened up on his knees between her legs so he could take care of logistics, wadded her skirt and petticoat up around her waist and pulled her panties down, Mary Lydia arching her back to help him, the cloth momentarily hanging up around her knees and he finally just ripped them apart and threw them into the grass beside them; then he was fumbling with his own pants, pulled them and his underpants down freeing his penis pulsing like a metronome, frantic now to get it inside her as quickly as possible and dropping down on top of her again, poking and prodding his erection into her crotch trying to find where it was supposed to go. When the head unexpectedly slipped inside her, there was a look of amazement and surprise on his face that quickly turned to befuddlement as she cried out in pain when he rammed it into her as far as it would go, but her reaction only made him hurry the more, lost in his own concerns, frantically pumping his hips but he only did so three times before exploding inside her, his face registering ecstasy and joy and total release. Then he realized she was crying harder, he had obviously hurt her, and he leaned back on his knees as he pulled out of her and found his penis streaked with blood. He grabbed the torn panties from the grass and wiped the blood and ooze off his penis and started to back away from her but she was crying now in a different way, saying, "Wait, don't go away, stay in me," and the look on his face said he realized he had to get away from there as fast as he could. He struggled to his feet, pulling up his pants as he looked down at her lying in the grass, she was like a discarded thing and reached for him but he turned and ran back through the grass toward the trees, ignoring her pleas not to leave her.

And then he was gone, it was over, almost before it began, before I knew what was happening. After all the years of waiting and wanting and trying to imagine what it would be like when it finally happened, it had happened, then was now and back to then again, once and for all time. I raised up on my elbows but he was running across the field, afraid I suppose of what he had done, what we had become, that things would never be the same between us. That it would ultimately drive him away from me, as far from me as he could get, across the ocean to a foreign land that I could barely imagine, a world away and time, never to return.

"Wait! Come back! Stay with me! Don't leave me!" Mary Lydia sat up in the grass, calling after him but he was already gone, disappeared into the trees, back the way they had come.

She was crying from the pain and the shock and everything that had happened. Then she became aware she was half-naked, her skirt pulled up around her waist, the warm air and sunlight on her exposed thighs and crotch. Worse, there was blood on the grass between her legs though it seemed to have stopped dribbling out of her. She reached for her underpants where he had thrown them but they were already soaked with blood and semen. She scooted on her bum back away from the blood on the grass and pulled down her petticoat far enough that she could tear a piece of cloth from along the hem and used it to clean herself the best she could. Her beautiful picnic dress was ruined, grass stained and dirty though luckily there was no blood on it. She dabbed at the blood on the matted grass but to no avail, anyone who happened along could see what happened here, she was so ashamed, so ashamed. She started to cry all over again.

Then she stopped. Froze. Thought she heard something. What if there was someone watching her now? A man hidden among the trees. She looked around wildly. There were men standing just beyond the treeline, some had guns, they saw what he did to her and now were waiting their turn at her, they were coming for her. She hurriedly got to her feet, pulling her dress and the remains of her petticoat down into place, started to walk toward the trees. Then she was running, into the trees, frantic now, trying to get away, the bushes snagging at her clothes, hands reaching for her, someone trying to trip her, to get her back on the ground again, running, running, gasping for breath, then she was free, back on the path again down to the *C* on the hillside, already hearing the others laughing and talking as they worked, she could see them now scattered along the hillside. And he was among them, working with the others. As if nothing had happened.

Afterward, after he hurried back to the others, I found my

way back to the trail and followed it down the hillside to the clearing with the *C*. They were busy with their work, he was among them, with his jacket off working in his shirtsleeves, they had cleared away the brush and dead leaves and started to burn the debris in a bonfire. As they raked the debris onto the flames, they danced around the fire like celebrants at a sacrifice, some pagan rite. Others had begun painting the stones, the *C* coming into prominence again against the dirt of the hillside. But I sat at the edge of the clearing, my knees drawn up under my chin, my arms embracing my legs, watching the others in their mean-ingless talk and laughter, the smoke from the bonfire drifting down the hillside and out over the river, the college and the town spread out on the hills on the other side of the valley, watching it all with new eyes. Aware that I was different now, that nothing would ever be the same for me now, and you were there, flitting in and out among the work groups, the heavy work not your style as you would say, always the dilettante, part of your charm you thought and maybe it was, there and not there as was your wont, and I wanted to tell you what had happened, the difference I was feeling about myself, share it with you so you could join in with my happiness, but then I thought why should I, it happened to me not to you, suspecting you wouldn't appreciate the import, I was a woman now, rocking back and forth in my own embrace, full of the secrets of love, full of secrets. . . .

She woke with a start, Perpetual's face leaning over her, filling her vision. The dark woman's face breaking into a smile as she saw Mary Lydia stir. In her hands she held a tray for dinner.

"Well, there you are, child. Perpetual was beginning to wonder about you. You were whimpering in your sleep."

"I'm fine. How long was I asleep?"

"It can't be very long. You were sitting there, lost in your thoughts, when Perpetual went down to the kitchen to get your dinner. Now, scoot up there, child, let me set this tray down on your lap and get you fixed so you don't spill it all over yourself."

Perpetual set about arranging Mary Lydia on the bed, fixing the sheet over her legs, fluffing up the pillows behind her.

"Perpetual, my picnic dress. . . ."

"What about your dress?"

"Were you able to get the grass stains out of it?"

"Perpetual took care of it, didn't I tell you I would? You can't tell there were ever any stains there at all. Silly girl, wear a pretty dress like that to a work party."

"I know, I know. I should have known better. It's just that I love it so, I couldn't wait to wear it. And I was so afraid it was ruined, I don't want anything to ever happen to it. It's so important to me." She hugged herself as she sat there on the bed.

"Perpetual will make sure nothing happens to it. Just like Perpetual takes care of you. Now, eat your dinner. You'll need all the strength you can muster for what we're going to do. . . ."

15

After dinner, in Malcolm's study, instead of his usual seat behind his desk, Malcolm settled into the twin leather wing-back chair beside his son in front of his desk, ignoring the look of surprise on Gus' face but enjoying it nonetheless. Gus watched as his father lit his cigar, obviously having trouble containing himself. Finally, he couldn't stand it any longer.

"So. Are you going to tell me how the meeting with the government reps went? Or is it a secret?"

Why am I doing this? Malcolm thought as he watched the stream of smoke curl around the green-shaded lamp on his desk. Why am I keeping him dangling like this? Well, the boy has to

learn to hide his feelings better if he's going to succeed in business. Not be so transparent. Though he's not a boy, is he, he's a
grown man. And I know why I didn't want to tell him, why I'm
stalling. . . .

"It's no secret. I didn't want to tell you at dinner because none
of it concerns Missy or your grandmother. In fact the less your
grandmother knows about what's going on the better, she'll only
want to have a say." Malcolm shifted in his chair, crossed and
uncrossed his legs. "Besides, I didn't want to get anyone's hopes
up."

"So it went well."

"It went about as expected. And as for keeping something
from you, I could say the same to you. You haven't said a word
about what you learned about Mary Lydia's possible boyfriends
up at the college."

Malcolm let out another column of smoke. That was good,
throw it back at him. He has to learn to hold his own, we'll see
if he even remembers his original question. He rested the cigar in
his ashtray, watching the smoke gather and stabilize into a gray
pillar, watching it sway slowly back and forth with the unseen
currents of air in the room. Scratched idly at the scars on the
backs of his hands.

"Well, as I thought beforehand, the place was pretty much
deserted at this time of year. But I did manage to speak with an
Elizabeth Quigley. She's the dean of students."

Malcolm shook his head. "I don't know her."

"She knows us. Or at least she thinks she does."

"The way you said that doesn't sound as if she has a very good
impression of us."

"She doesn't, believe me."

"What have we ever done to Elizabeth Quigley?"

"It's more of a case of not doing enough, at least in Elizabeth Quigley's eyes."

"Did you remind her of the steeple on Old Main? And the bell?"

"She was unimpressed. Seems that's too far in the past. Though her gripe appears to be against the family in general. She had good things to say about Mary Lydia. And of course John Lincoln. Couldn't say enough good things about John Lincoln."

Which would irk the blazes out of my oldest son. The competition between them, which is really no competition at all, unfortunately. But all Malcolm said out loud was, "Hmm."

"She did mention that she thought there was one young man that Mary Lydia appeared to be sweet on. But it turns out he's Greek and has left the country to return home."

"Is there some way we can contact him in Greece?"

"Well, actually he's from Turkey."

"I thought you said he was Greek."

"He *is* Greek. But he lives in Turkey, his family lives in Turkey."

"I don't understand."

"He and his family are Greek Covenanters who live in Constantinople."

"There are such things as Greek Covenanters?"

"Apparently."

Malcolm shook his head. "Well then, when will he be back at school?"

"Elizabeth Quigley isn't sure he is coming back. His family is being persecuted by the Turks and he'll probably have to stay there to help them."

Gus, Gus, Gus, Malcolm thought, inhaling again on his cigar. You're always too willing to accept the first answer that comes along. There must be some way to contact this Turkish Greek.

Though it doesn't sound as if Elizabeth Quigley would be any more forthcoming from a second visit, he seems to have worn out his welcome very quickly. I should have gone to the college myself, but of course that was impossible with meeting the government reps. "It's too bad John Lincoln isn't here, he would probably know who she was referring to."

"Maybe the fact that he did know is why he chose to disappear."

"Meaning?"

"Maybe John Lincoln knows who got her pregnant and that's why he went away. He was always too sensitive about her. Maybe he couldn't stand the thought of whoever it was touching his sainted sister."

"Don't talk nonsense," Malcolm said, flicking half an inch of ash into an ashtray, spoiling what he hoped would grow longer. Then he regretted his harshness. Aware that he didn't like to hear Gus talking disparagingly about John Lincoln. Aware as well that it had occurred to him there might be another darker reason why John Lincoln might disappear when it became known his sister was pregnant. His sainted son. From the expression on Gus' face, Malcolm wondered if he was alone in his suspicions, his fears.

"So. That's *my* news," Gus said, settling back in his chair.

Which means, obviously, what's *your* news? Good for him, to throw it back to me again. Except now I have to tell him. Something he doesn't want to hear.

"As I said, the meeting went about as I expected it would. Adams and Taylor are on a fact-finding mission, to talk about capabilities. And they're very well versed in the capabilities of Keystone Steam Works. They know our history and what all we've accomplished in the past—"

"Are they aware that we've never produced a tank before? I think that's what they call them: tanks—"

"How did you find out about that?" Malcolm broke in. "That information is top secret, no one is to know the government is even considering building such a vehicle."

"Then I suggest in the future you don't leave the schematic and estimate lying around on your desk."

He went poking around my office when I wasn't there. But I know he often goes in there when I'm away, to leave something on my desk, I can't very well start locking the door. But he's right, I should have put that material away, if Adams and Taylor found out I left it lying around the project's over before it begins. . . .

Gus was watching him, waiting. When he couldn't stand it any longer, he said, "So is that why you didn't want to tell me about the meeting?"

"Yes. No. I don't know. Yes, I should have told you as soon as I learned what it was about, I wanted to. But nothing's definite, nothing's been decided."

"It would certainly be a defining moment for the Keystone Steam Works. As big as anything that's ever happened to it."

"Bigger," Malcolm said. "It would assure the future of the company for decades."

"So why are we hesitating? Why aren't we jumping at the chance?"

I'm surprised, he's actually excited about it. Maybe I've been reading him wrong all this time, maybe he cares that much about the company, the good of the company, what's best. "There's a lot of things to be considered. We can't just rush into it before we know what we're getting into."

"I'm sure we've got the resources and expertise to do it."

"A deciding factor was the smaller steam engine you've had developed for the Lylemobile."

"So that's why they were asking so many questions about it. When I brought them up from the hotel."

"They were quite impressed, I must say. I just have to make sure the figures work before I respond to them."

Gus' excitement was growing, he could hardly sit still, clasping his hands together at the prospects. "And it will give us the capital to develop the Lylemobile."

So that's it. That's why he's not upset about the tank project. He only sees it as a way to develop his steam car project. He has no more understanding of the business than he ever did.

"You're overestimating our capabilities, and underestimating the ramifications of this project. If we take it on, and if we're successful, it will lead inevitably to other projects. Not only changes to the original vehicle from what we learn of its performance in the field, but entirely new vehicles, larger tanks with whole new technologies. Just to put this first tank into production will take everything we have, we'll need to be thinking expansion of our facilities, additional buildings and storage facilities, where to put the production lines, we'll have to get loans—"

"What you're telling me is that it's an either-or situation as far as the Lylemobile is concerned. Either we produce the steam tank, or the steam car. Not both."

This is the perfect opportunity, to let him know once and for all. But how can I tell him that I've never been convinced he could successfully bring the car into production, even if we could find a market for it. How can I tell him that he's simply not the man to accomplish that, neither the engineer nor the entrepreneur nor the businessman. That he's simply not smart enough. . . .

Gus didn't wait for his father's response. "Then I don't see much of a discussion. I know what you'll do. I guess what you have to do."

"As I said, I need to run the figures. . . ."

Gus got up from the chair, looked down at his father, his lips sucked in as if he would swallow his face, before turning and leaving the room.

Malcolm continued to sit where he was for a while, occasionally taking a long pull on his cigar, but mainly just sitting there, feeling drained, wasted, his mind a blank. Then leaving the cigar on the edge of the ashtray, a column of smoke rising from it into the shadows like a kind of incense, he got up and walked around behind his desk, standing in the shallow bay window, looking out into the night.

Down the black hillside, the town was laid out in squares of streetlights leading down to the river, with an occasional lighted window like a small vision of domesticity; along the river, the furnaces of Buchanan Steel flared orange and red, pulsing against the bluffs on the opposite wall of the valley. Gus, Gus, Gus. He fretted for his firstborn, felt sorry for him, but knew there was nothing he could do for him; he couldn't make him different than he was. Malcolm knew the boy had never recovered from seeing his mother burned alive in the trench on their front lawn when he was six years old, looking down from his parents' bedroom window, stealing into their bedroom because he was that anxious to see his mother return, only to witness the horror of her death. And the ultimate failure of his father, not only to save his mother from burning alive, but making sure that she would, could never recover from the burns.

Lydia. Oh Lydia. The love of his life. No matter that he burned his hands severely trying to save her, laid up for months afterwards unsure if his hands could be saved, the trauma of the unending pain. He traced the lines of those scars now as one might finger the beads of a rosary. No matter that he would have changed places with her gladly in the trench, willingly given his life for her. No matter, he would always be to Gus the man who killed his mother. Whether Gus could admit it or not, whether his son even realized it or not. How could he have made such a mistake? A question he asked himself at least once a day, every day since.

And then Missy. He had no illusions about his marriage to her. A woman as different as possible from Lydia. He understood why he married her. He did want more children, and she was from a prominent Furnass family, it seemed the thing to do. And she was appealing—cute, petite. He had never loved her, any more than she had loved him, that was the given between them. And after the initial act one night and the begetting of the twins, sex for either one of them was never part of the equation. She kept the house, or went through the motions of it, under the watchful eye of his mother—and probably more to the point, under the watchful eye of Perpetual. Nothing seemed to escape the notice of Libby's Caribbean maid. To the betterment of them all, he had to admit; but sometimes it seemed that rather than a woman brought in to aid his aging mother, Perpetual was the center point of the house around which the family revolved.

But no matter now. Nothing much mattered now. Quite by accident or fate or coincidence, the Great Whatever, he had been given the opportunity to secure the future of the company. His legacy would be complete. And his family would be taken care of, Gus would be taken care of, whether his son wanted it or not. Malcolm would be thought of as a success, not of the caliber that people thought of his father, Colin, but a success nonetheless. No matter how he felt about himself, no matter how aware he was of his failings; but that was the way of these things, wasn't it? That was the way the world worked, things looked one way, and the truth was something else entirely. Your measure was how well you could thread your way between the two, never putting too much stock in either one. He turned away from the window, back to the room. Cigar smoke filled the upper reaches of the room in layers, striations of gray. He stubbed out the cigar in the ashtray and left the room, heading for bed, the end of a long and determining day, his passage leaving swirls and eddies in the smoke.

PART THREE

TUESDAY, JULY 4, 1916

16

The five little animals—Mole Rat, Hedgehog, Rabbit, Turtle, and Fox—realized the bird was singing to herself, a loud raucous song full of cries like the sound of the universe laughing at itself, as she kicked her way back and forth across the clearing, sending the fallen leaves flying like particolored decorations. When The Crow saw the others approaching, she stopped her pacing, gave a tilt of her black head, and regarded them with a curious eye.

"Well now, what have we here? A delegation?"

"We've come seeking wisdom from The Crow," Mole Rat said. Unfortunately she was looking off forty-five degrees to the left and Hedgehog had to set her straight.

"Hmm. I don't know about *The* Crow," said the black bird, ruffling its tail feathers. "But I'm certainly *A* Crow. Ashley Crow, to be exact. How can I help you?"

"We've come to ask you why we are the way we are," Mole Rat said. "Why am I blind and have to live underground where it's cold and dirty and the sun never shines?"

And Hedgehog said, "I want to know why I'm covered with these spines so no one can get close to me."

And Rabbit said, "I want to know why everybody always chases me and all I can do is run away."

And Turtle said, "I want to know why I can neither defend myself nor run away, all I can do is hide."

And Fox said, "I want to know why everybody sees me only as a wily, bloodthirsty killer who no one can trust."

"Good grief," said A. Crow. "That's quite a list of grievances."

"Mole Rat heard some humans say that you were the wisest creature in the forest," Rabbit said.

"We're hoping you can enlighten us as to the ways of the world," Turtle said.

"Personally," Fox said under her breath, "I'm curious why you think anything this bird has to say is worth crowing about."

"What?" said Hedgehog.

Meanwhile A. Crow had ducked her head under her wing and was aggressively pecking at a tick. When she straightened up again, the bird clicked her beak a couple of times, ruffled her feathers, and cocked her head.

"Well, those are certainly the big questions, all right. But I want you to consider something. Mole Rat, because you do live underground, you might as well be blind because it's too dark down there to see anything. And as it is, you can't tell whether the sun is shining or not, so, as sad as it is to say, it doesn't make a whole lot difference whether it's pretty or not where you live."

"Hmm," said Mole Rat, "I guess that's true enough. . . ."

"And as for you, Hedgehog," Crow went on, "you're just so darn cute that if you weren't covered with those spines you wouldn't have a moment's rest without someone either trying to hug you or make a meal out of you so you'd never have a life of your own."

"Well, I suppose. . . ."

"And you, Rabbit, yes, you get chased all the time, but isn't that only the way it should be because you're so fast? It wouldn't be right for someone to be chased all the time if they were slow, would it?"

"No, I guess not. . . ."

"And you, Turtle. You feel bad because all you can

is hide when you face adversity. But others spend their entire lives looking for the comfort and safety of a home, and you always carry yours with you. And you, Fox. Yes, you have a reputation for being sly, and deservedly so. But you have to be in order to compete with much larger, and deadlier animals in the food chain. Besides, whoever heard of being sly as a skunk?"

The animals all looked at each other as they considered what A. Crow said, nodding in agreement. But Mole Rat, for once looking in the right direction directly at the crow, rolled its blind eyes. "But why? That's what we want to know. Everything you say is true, of course. It's how we live in the day-to-day. But that still doesn't answer the question of the big why? Why are we the way we are?"

"Oh that," A. Crow said. "Don't be silly. Nobody knows the answer to that. Total mystery. If you ever find the answer to that one, please let me know. Now, you'll have to excuse me, I have a bone to pick."

And with that A. Crow flew up over the trees and away, cawing raucously in the call that sounded like a cosmic laugh.

"Wait a minute," Rabbit said. "We've been seeking spiritual guidance from a bird that goes around picking fights?"

"Er, no," Fox said. "When Crow said she had a bone to pick, she means she really has a bone to pick. A whole skeleton, most likely, a rotting corpse somewhere. She is a carrion bird, after all."

"So, that's that, then," Turtle said. "We came all this way to find out we not only don't know why our lives are the way they are, we don't even know how to ask about it."

"Much less to who," Rabbit said.

"To whom," said the Fox, combing out her tail. Shrugged. "What?"

"Doesn't sound like much to build a life on," Turtle said.

"It better be enough," Hedgehog said, feeling prickly.

"It seems that what we have is all we're going to get."

17

Gus left the Lylemobile on the steep side street, front wheels cranked to the curb, rear wheels braced with wood chocks he got from the shop, and headed into the alley, pulling his lopsided crumpled fedora down over his forehead as if that would keep him from being recognized, staying close to the stables and sheds along the side, and let himself in the gate of the garden wall, glad to find it was still left unlatched. For me? he wondered. Does she keep it unlatched on the chance I might decide to come back some early morning? Or maybe for somebody else. I guess I better get myself prepared for that. He continued down the flat stone walk noting her gardens were flourishing, as always, the woman had a knack for making things grow. He thought of picking a bouquet of dahlias and cornflowers but decided that would be pushing it. As he neared the back of the house he could see her moving in the kitchen. Anyone with her? I guess I'm in luck. If that's what you want to call it. When she saw him approaching she stopped what she was doing and waited while he came up the steps across the back porch, standing beside the drainboard, coffee pot poised above her cup as he came through the back door.

"Yes, please," he said, closing the door behind him.

Emma Edgeworth stood where she was for a moment looking at him, then a slight wry smile came over her face as she put down the pot, got another cup and saucer from the cupboard.

"Only because you said please."

She poured both cups and handed him one, nodding for him to sit at the table while she remained standing, her hip resting against the side of the drainboard. She took a sip, then said, "If I knew you were coming I would have baked some cornbread. I remember you always liked cornbread in the mornings."

"I didn't know I was coming myself. Until last evening," he said, taking off his hat and putting it on the chair beside him.

"So, this is a surprise for both of us." She shrugged and took another sip, glancing out into the garden, as if to make sure there weren't any more surprises coming her way, and looked back at him. Not really smiling but not unfriendly either.

She was naked under her nightdress, a long white sheer wrapper that did little to hide her heavy breasts, the soft roll of her puff belly, her thick bare legs. She had put on weight since the last time he was with her, over a year ago—he guessed it was closer to two years now—but he found he had trouble keeping his eyes from her thighs, the patch of hair between her legs, it didn't seem all that long ago. He was aware that she was aware where his eyes kept falling. She was still a good-looking woman, there was something about her that still got to him though twenty years his senior. On her head was a bell-shaped white lace cap that barely contained her thick red hair.

She put her coffee cup and saucer down on the drainboard and turned back to him, her arms folded under her breasts as if barely able to contain a cornucopia of delights. "So, if this is a surprise visit for both of us, what brings you here? Does Lily know you're out and about at this hour of the morning?"

"Lily's in Kansas. At her parents'."

"Did she take little Mal with her?"

"Yes."

"That doesn't sound good."

"She hadn't been back there since we've been married. She said she thought her parents should see their grandson."

"Still doesn't sound good," Emma said.

"I'm sure she just wanted to go for a visit," Gus said, suddenly not so sure at all. It did seem that she took a lot of clothes with her. . . .

"So you decided you'd start your Independence Day celebration early," she said, taking off her lace nightcap and shaking out her hair.

"Actually I've got a lot to do today. There's the parade this morning, they asked me to drive one of the new well-drillers. And then Grandmother's donating her statue for the park around noon—." He stopped cold. She's not talking about that at all, is she? What a fool. I never could read the signs. . . . .

Emma Edgeworth looked at him a moment, as if thinking the same thing. She gave her hair an added shake, freeing it off the back of her neck. "Is that why you're here, then? About your grandmother?"

"What about my grandmother?"

"I thought maybe because we went to see her yesterday, the ladies of the temperance union. I was with them."

"No, I didn't hear anything about it. What on earth would the temperance ladies want with my grandmother?"

"It was Mrs. Whitticom's idea, I tried my best to stop it but she was full of herself. She wants your grandmother to make a temperance appeal during her speech today."

"My grandmother? With her endless glass of rye? She didn't say she'd do it, did she?"

"Oddly enough she did. At least we think she did. Mrs. Whitticom thinks she did, and that's good enough for Mrs. Whitticom."

"Well, it's all news to me, but no, that's not why I'm here. I came to ask a favor."

"A favor," Emma said, then became coquettish. "You never called it that before."

Careful, careful. She's going to get the wrong idea entirely. "Heh heh. No, I mean a true favor. I need you to ask your son Anthony if he will finance the development of the Lylemobile. Not ask him *if* he will, ask him *to* finance its development."

She studied him a moment as if to make sure he was serious. Then turned and retrieved her coffee cup and saucer from the counter. "And why would I do a thing like that?"

The sunlight coming through the kitchen windows behind her shone through her red hair, creating sparks of copper highlights, outlined her shoulders in the sheer wrapper. He remembered she always had a rumpled air about her, but rather than making her less appealing, it tended to make her the more. "Keystone Steam Works isn't in a position right now to find the financing for the project. So I'm hoping Buchanan Steel will pick it up."

"As I said. Why would I do that?"

"It's a good business proposition for Buchanan to finance such a venture. Once the Lylemobile is in production, there will be a steady demand for steel, a demand that'll last for years to come."

"Evidently the prospect isn't enough to convince your father to put money into it."

I can't tell her about the tank, I can't. "Let's just say he has other irons in the fire right now."

"Your father always struck me as an astute businessman. So did my husband before he died. So if your father's not interested in a project, I'm certainly not going to drag my son into it."

"It's not that my father isn't interested in the Lylemobile. He is. He's as much as told me so. It's just that he can't right now. The company doesn't have the capital on hand to make that kind of investment. But the time is right for a steam car. People are undecided about whether they favor the internal combustion engine or steam. And now that we've solved the delay in getting a steam car up and running, I'm certain the virtues of the Lyle-mobile will build a whole new following for steam. We'll be ahead of the curve. I'm sure of it."

Emma took another sip of coffee, obviously thinking of something, then returned the cup and saucer to the counter. She turned and looked out the window, the sunlight streaming through the folds of her wrapper creating a glow about her body, her perfectly rounded buttocks. "Well, that would be quite a favor, on my part. To ask my son to do something like that."

"I know, I know," Gus said, looking away from her, trying not to look at her. "And I wouldn't ask you such a thing if I thought there was any other way. And I truly do believe it would be a good investment for Anthony and Buchanan."

"Well, you make a convincing argument." Emma continued to look out the window a minute longer. Then looked back over her shoulder at him. Turned to face him again.

"And I could see me asking my son such a thing. For someone who was close to me. Who I believed in. Who I believed I could trust. Who held my affections."

Uh-oh.

"You know, Gus, you really hurt me. Just cutting it off between us the way you did. With no warning or anything."

"But we had talked about it. How things weren't as good as they used to be."

"We talked about how to make things better again. The way they were when we first started."

"And I just didn't think it was fair to Lily and all. Me sneaking around like that. Suppose someone put two and two together and told her? It would have devastated her."

"It doesn't sound like that's a problem anymore," Emma said, walking over to him, standing in front of him.

He could smell her, all those woman smells that Lily never had; his wife's were briny and bitter, he didn't like them on his fingers, but Emma's were different. I can smell the bed on her, the way the bed smells after we've rolled in it. Oh God. . . . He stood up to confront her but she embraced him and then they were kissing, he was holding her, all the flesh of her through the sheer wrapper, she was reaching down for his penis, she got it out before he even knew how she did it and he started to bend her over the table, Emma chanting, "Oh yes, my love, my love. . . .

He pulled up the sheer wrapper, pushing it up around her shoulders and stroked the flesh of her broad back, her white white skin tinged red, grabbed her fleshy buttocks—and couldn't do it. No. No, no, no, no, no. . . . He backed away from her, looking at her bent over in front of him, stuffing his penis back in his pants and buttoning up again, then started out the door before remembering his hat. He snatched it off the chair and headed out the door again, across the back porch and into the garden, ignoring her calls after him. Then for a moment as he hurried out the gate he could swear her calls had turned to laughter.

18

Malcolm Hayes Lyle confronted himself in the mirror over the bathroom sink. A fine figure of a man, he thought, if I do say so myself. Especially at the age of sixty-one years. I could be mistaken for ten years younger, maybe fifteen. Okay, maybe a dozen years younger. At most. But still. Unfortunately I'm more suited to an age maybe twenty years, maybe thirty years ago. A relic of a time past. A fossil. Certainly not someone in step with the modern age. He watched as he raised his fingertips to the line of his salt-and-pepper mustache over his upper lip, the extension of his bushy muttonchop sideburns, traced the curve of hair down across his face and up to his hairline in front of his ear. At one

time his pride and joy. His trademark, a distinguishing charac-
teristic, his meticulously trimmed muttonchops a sign of prosperity and position and self-fulfillment. Well, no matter. There was
no help for it now. Nothing else to do. He was a man of decision,
and he had just made one.

From the narrow bureau beside the claw-foot bathtub he took
the precision barber's scissors he had bought specially for his
daily grooming. But this morning, instead of tracking down the
ends of wayward hair, he began to trim away all the hair of his
mustache, tentatively at first, then with real gusto, really getting
into the activity, snip-snip-snipping away, the hair drifting like
autumn leaves down into the sink, chasing the hair on both sides
of his face until mustache and sideburns were only a shadow of
themselves, trimming them so they were fashionably level with
the tops of his ears. Then he took his shaving mug with its goat
milk soap and worked up a lather with his badger hair shaving
brush; stropped his Sheffield steel bone-handled straight razor on
the strap hanging on the back of the door, first on the linen side,
then on the leather side to finish it; and proceeded to shave the
remaining traces of his muttonchop sideburns from his face.
There. He splashed water on his face and toweled away the remains of the soap. A new Malcolm. A fine figure of a man if ever
he saw one.

Except he hadn't figured on the whiteness of his skin where
the hair had been removed—though it was red and blotchy now
from scrapes with the blade—the contrast with the tanned and
weathered skin of the rest of his face. His head looked as if it were
divided in two along the lines of where his mustache and sideburns had been, that you could access his brain by simply tilting
back the lid. So be it. There was nothing he could do about it
now. The rawness of skin would be assimilated soon enough, just
as everything else in this world is assimilated, if you just give it

time. The way of the world. He put away his shaving things, splashed some witch hazel on his face and throat, and headed back to the bedroom.

Missy was still asleep in their bed, the top of her close-cropped blond hair peeking out from the edge of the covers like a stain on the pillow, but he knew there was no danger of waking her; early on in their marriage he named her One of the Great Sleepers of the Western World. It was only a little after seven now and she wouldn't waken much before ten, no matter if the front of the house fell off. He put on his white shirt for the day; adjusted the removable collar; tied a four-in-hand knot in his recently pur chased Windsor American Batter Up red necktie with the pictures of baseball players and American flags—he thought it appropriate for the Fourth of July —; pulled up his braces where they draped around his hips and strapped them over his shoulders; took his brown tweed suitcoat, from one of three brown tweed suits he kept in rotation, from his wardrobe; and, ready to face his day, headed downstairs.

The house was still dark at this hour of the morning, the sun behind the hills behind the house, though as he descended the steps he caught glimpses of the day through the windows at the front of the house, the sidelights and fanlight over the front door, of sunlight on the town farther down the slope of the valley, on the bluffs of the hills across the river. His thoughts were already filled with what all he had to do today, despite or in addition to the holiday. He had to finish the estimate and proposal for the armored tank and, though it seemed like a foregone conclusion at this point, make sure the necessary documents were in the hands of Adams and Taylor before they caught their train this evening. Plus there were the arrangements for the steamworks' role in the Fourth of July parade later this morning, he needed to get down to the shop as soon as possible to make sure the units they were contributing were in good order, especially the new well-driller that Gus was going to drive. And later there was his mother's dedication of her statue for the new park, he'd never hear the end of it if he wasn't there for that. His mind was immersed in all of this when he rounded the newel-post at the bottom of the steps and nearly ran into Perpetual standing in the shadows, hand on her hip, wrist folded under, her head cocked to one side.

"*Bonté divine*! What did you do to Mr. Malcolm?"

"Perpetual! What the blazes—"

Before he realized what she was doing, she reached up and traced with two fingers the line of where his sideburns had been. He juked away from her touch as if shocked from an electric current.

"Perpetual!" He brushed past her and headed down the corridor toward the dining room.

The woman giggled as she started to follow him.

Malcolm stopped and turned around, Perpetual almost bumping into him.

"What's so amusing?"

"Perpetual thought Mr. Malcolm cut himself shaving. Cut himself so badly, he almost take his head off."

"What's so amusing about that?"

"Nothing at all amusing about that. Perpetual's just happy that white line isn't a scar. Like the ones on Mr. Malcolm's hands."

Malcolm looked down at the scars on his hands as if mildly surprised to see them there; though the event that caused them never left him, he rarely consciously thought of the scars themselves, they were simply facts of life. Perpetual took the opportunity to walk past him to lead the way toward the dining room.

Did she just say that so she could get ahead of me? I wouldn't put it past her. . . . Malcolm harrumphed and followed her, the woman a muted particolored shadow among shadows. In the dining room Margaret the cook was just finishing bringing in the plates of food—ham and grits, baked eggs, and cornbread. Malcolm looked around uncomfortably.

"Isn't anyone else coming?"

Perpetual was amused as she took her place ninety degrees from him. "Well, I thought Mrs. Libby needed her sleep, seeing as it's her big day with the statue. And Mary Lydia, as you know, is still upstairs in her bed taking care of her baby-to-be. Mrs. Lily and Little Mal are in Kansas. Your own Mrs. Missy is never awake at this hour. And Mr. Gus, well, he's up to his old tricks of disappearing early in the mornings on Mr. Gus Business. So I guess for once it's just you and Perpetual. Isn't that a marvel, though?"

Malcolm remained standing behind his chair. "What do you mean, 'Gus Business?' He's driving one of the machines today in the parade. I would think he's probably down at the shop already, checking things out."

"Oooh, Perpetual would agree that Mr. Gus surely does like to check things out in the early mornings," she said, helping herself to the cornbread.

"What are you implying?"

"Perpetual never implied a thing in her life. Wouldn't even know how. What Perpetual does know is that a while back Mr. Gus would sneak out of here early in the mornings before he thought anybody was awake and go to see a lady friend. And Perpetual knows this because one morning she went and followed to see where he was going on his tomcattin'. The sad thing being that Mr. Gus quit his tomcattin' before Mrs. Lily got fed up and took herself and Little Mal back home to Kansas."

"I won't listen to this," Malcolm said, but found himself sitting down regardless.

"Won't or can't," Perpetual said. Taking a ladylike portion of baked eggs from the cast-iron skillet. Then looked at him.

She's waiting for me to respond. Like she's playing a kind of racquet game, my serve. It's like she's always been playing some game with us, like she knows some secret about us that keeps her distant from us. Keeps her amused with us. Like we're the subjects of her study.

"You've never liked me much, have you, Perpetual? Never liked me at all." He shook his head when Perpetual offered to pass him the ham.

"It's not Perpetual's job to like anybody. It's my job to take care of Mrs. Libby. And Perpetual does that."

"We got off on the wrong foot. I've always felt badly about that. Since that first day, when you conked me on the head with my mother's parasol." He smiled at the memory, despite himself.

Perpetual between bites gave a little sideways smile in acknowledgment. "Perpetual had to do what she had to do. To protect Mrs. Libby. What Mrs. Libby's husband, Mr. Colin, your daddy, told me to do."

"No, I'm glad you did. I've thought about it since, I was out of line that day. I let myself get carried away with the prospects of Father moving out of the house and my new role in the household. I'm glad you stepped in, it's my mother's place to have the master bedroom."

Perpetual put down her fork and studied him a moment. "Perpetual knows that Mr. Malcolm wears a worrycoat of pain."

"A worry-what?"

"Perpetual knows. Perpetual can see it."

"What are you talking about?"

"Perpetual knows Mr. Malcolm has never forgiven himself for what he did to Mrs. Lydia."

"What are you saying?" What does she know? "Of course I've

never forgiven myself for what happened to Lydia."

Perpetual was shaking her head. "No. It isn't just what happened to Mrs. Lydia. It's that Mr. Malcolm thinks he killed Mrs. Lydia. Perpetual knows. Perpetual can see it."

"You can see nothing. You don't know what you're talking about."

"But you should never blame yourself. Mrs. Lydia doesn't blame you. She said she doesn't. She has nothing but love for you. And sympathy for you having to put up with Mrs. Missy."

"What do you mean, 'She said she doesn't'? How could you—?"

"Perpetual knows because Perpetual's talked to Mrs. Lydia."

Malcolm looked at her dumbfounded. She's a crazy woman, crazy.

"I talked to her here. In this house. She's here sometimes. She comes to tell you herself but you can never see her. But Perpetual can see her."

"What do you mean she comes to tell me? What does she come to tell me?"

"She knows you think you caused what happened to her, but she comes to tell you that she knows it wasn't your fault. It was nobody's fault. She knows you think you caused her all that pain, but she wants you to know the pain was never that much, it was nothing she couldn't bear, the pain was greater seeing the pain you were in, thinking you caused her pain. She wants you to know that she knows you didn't mean it, that it was nobody's fault what happened, that it was just supposed to be. And it was."

Malcolm was sinking inside. Like he was falling, collapsing into himself, the sides of a dark well giving way, falling away forever. "You can't see her. . . ," he said feebly.

Perpetual looked at him with the deepest sadness. "Perpetual wishes you could. Oh, if only you could. . . ."

Malcolm pushed away from the table, sending his chair tumbling backward, hurried from the room, almost running into Margaret who was coming to see what the commotion was about, in a blind fury, hurrying out the door and down the driveway. I have to get away from here. What does she mean she can see Lydia? Of course she can't see Lydia. Lydia is dead. And I'm the one who killed her. She can't see her, nobody can see her, Lydia is gone. As he walked along he looked down at his hands. Perpetual said she thought at first the white lines on my face were like the scars on my hands. What does she see? What does she know? He had reached the end of the drive and looked back at the house. But suppose Perpetual could see Lydia? Suppose she does come here sometimes? He could imagine what it would be like to see her standing in a window on the second floor, looking back at him. And for an instant he thought he did see someone, a woman standing in the window. I've got to get away from here, I can't start thinking like this, I can't let Perpetual work her island voodoo bunkum into my thoughts. He turned and hurried on, down the road and into the streets of the town, toward the river, heading to the safety of his office at the steamworks.

19

Libby stood at the French doors in her bedroom, watching as the line of sunlight crept slowly up the hillside toward her, as if a blanket were being rolled up to reveal the town one street at a time, when her son Malcolm appeared below in front of the house, in the driveway beyond the edge of the balcony over the porch, seemingly in a huff about something. When he got to the road he looked back at the house; Libby waved but apparently he didn't see her, or didn't want to let on that he had seen her—What was the matter with his face? From this height and angle it looked all webbed like he had walked into something—but he turned away abruptly and continued down the road toward the town.

She had spent a lifetime—well, his lifetime—standing here at these doors looking down at her son, playing soldier in the front yard, a child lying in the grass beside his father as Colin swung in the hammock reading technical papers, a young man arriving home from the steamworks as he tried to learn all his father wanted to teach him. Most of the time when the Rebels were there she kept the children at a neighbor's, but Malcolm had come home one day and in the evening she stood at these doors to check on him, he must have been on the front porch or sitting on the steps out of Libby's view as Captain Walker rode up the hill from the works and, instead of passing on by the house to the stables, saw the boy and rode into the front yard, Malcolm appearing beyond the edge of the balcony over the porch to talk to him. Even from here she could tell he was pestering Judson to give him a ride; Libby started to open the doors to tell the boy to leave the captain alone, but before she could do so Judson leaned down and picked him up under the arms and placed the boy onto the saddle in front of him. Malcolm looked as happy as she'd ever seen him, his face one big grin as Judson eased the big roan forward, holding on to the boy, taking a turn around the driveway and then across the field beside the house, never faster than a walk, out of her line of sight for a few minutes then appearing again, breaking into a slow canter briefly as they pulled up in front of the house again. Then Colin was there, she hadn't seen him coming up the hill, coming into the driveway and telling Malcolm, "That's enough now. Get down." The boy wanted to stay where he was and Judson started to explain but Colin would have none of it. "I said get down now, and I mean get down *now!*" Judson carefully lifted the boy off the saddle and leaned down to place him on the ground again, Malcolm starting to cry as he ran into the house beneath the edge of the balcony. Judson started to say something to Colin but Colin disappeared into the house after his son. For a moment Judson looked after them, then looked up at Libby—had he known she was there the whole time? He must have. . .—before nudging the horse forward and disappearing around the side of the house toward the stables.

She turned away from the doors and, steadying herself with an outstretched hand to the wall beside the tintype portraits of her parents, to the top of the bureau avoiding the mirror, over to the floor lamp and then the back of the chair, sat down in the rocker. She took a sip of the whiskey from the water glass on the stand beside the chair before starting her slow rhythm, back and forth, back and forth. Poor Malcolm. She hated to think of her only son in such terms, but that was the way of it. He was one of those people for whom things never quite work out. She knew that about him, it broke her heart but there was no denying it; there was no way around it either.

He had always been misfortunate, star-crossed, even as a child, a boy whose pets—and he tried everything: a dog, cat, turtle, goldfish—died soon after he got them, whose ventures such as building a tree house resulted in broken bones, whose attempt to use the rope swing at the swimming hole like all the other boys almost got him drowned. It was a trait of his son's character that didn't go unnoticed by his father.

"Does he try to do things badly?" Colin said once, pacing around this very bedroom as Libby sat at the vanity, watching him in the mirror as she brushed her hair. "Doesn't he try to do things right? What is it with the boy?"

"Give him time, Colin. He's doing the best he can. Things just happen—"

"But that's the point, Libby. There isn't time. Responsibilities are going to come to him before he knows it. And I'm not sure when they come along that he can handle them."

She turned and looked at him then. "The child is aware that he's expected to fill some very big shoes—"

"Nonsense," Colin said, waving his hand as if brushing aside a pesky fly. "That has nothing to do with it."

As it turned out, when the responsibilities did come, when his father finally relinquished control of the company in the early 1880s and turned the company over to his son, Malcolm did surprisingly well for a number of years; the company grew as it never had under Colin's management when it was more concerned with innovation rather than selling machines. Malcolm changed that, he had some skill at marketing and merchandizing, he was lauded as a successful businessman in town—Keystone Steam Works well-drillers, construction rollers, and steam-powered shovels were known the world over. Though Libby knew, as she knew Malcolm knew, that his success was built on very little of his own accomplishments, he was only putting into production the ideas that his father had developed in his workshop, most of those ideas from his last years after he moved out of the house and into the works. The same that Libby knew, as she knew Malcolm was beginning to suspect, that the real test was upon him now that steam-powered vehicles were being challenged by the internal combustion engine.

Colin had indeed turned over control of the company to his son, but that didn't mean he thought his son was capable or worthy of holding it. Libby hated to think that the transfer of power was meant to show that Colin was right about his son's shortcomings, but it seemed a possibility, the way Colin hovered over Malcolm's every move. And then the terrible night of the fire. Both Colin and Libby had been impressed with Malcolm's choice of a bride in Lydia, she was from a good family in town, they had met at Covenant College so she was of sound moral fiber, she was pretty and vivacious and sociable enough for the two of them—she and Malcolm seemed the ideal couple. But it all came to a horrific end that night when Lydia fell into the trench beside the front walk.

"I saw it, Libby," Colin said later that night when they got back from the hospital. "I witnessed the whole thing, I was standing in the window of my study as they got out of the carriage and started up the walk. I saw her fall into the trench and the oil from the lantern she was carrying spill over her, I watched her go up in flames. And I saw Malcolm, at first just stand there, then run to the porch and—"

"I'm sure he did what he could," she said feebly. Libby stared at her hands, sitting at the dining room table, his words like blows about her head.

"I saw him do it, Libby. I saw him faced with a life-and-death choice and he panicked. He couldn't handle it. I've turned the company over to him, and he's lived up to every fear and doubt I ever had about him. How is he going to manage a company when he can't even make the right decision to save his wife's life?"

She had no answer for her husband that night, any more than she had an answer now. Malcolm had lived up to every fear she had for him as well, long before the night of Lydia's accident, but she wasn't as ready to blame her son for his lacks as Colin was. She would always wonder if her own lacks and shortcomings had contributed to those of her son: her years in a drug-induced stupor, her lack of proper attention to her husband, her foolish conduct with the good doctor McArtle. And, of course, Judson Walker. How much did her lack as a parent carry over to her son? How much did her personal distractions contribute to her distracted son? As for Colin, she didn't know how much he blamed himself—or her, for that matter—but she knew he had taken it upon himself to keep as close an eye as possible on Malcolm's management of the company, as well as provide him with as many ideas for its future as he could come up with in his closing years. When he moved from the house to the steamworks, she made up fantasies that his leaving had to do with her earlier associations with McArtle and then Captain Walker—particularly Captain Walker—that she had been unfaithful to him, in thought if not in deed, and that had been the reason to drive him away for his closing years. But she knew such fantasies were just that, storytelling to herself, because they were easier to bear than the real reason for his leaving: that he cared more for his work and the steamworks than he did for her; that underneath the pretense of keeping an eye on Malcolm's handling of the company was his inability to let go of what he had spent his life building up; that his real love had always been for something other than her. She thought Colin might see Judson as a rival for her affections, as well he should have; but the truth was the idea of a rival never entered into his thinking. She had been the one to force the issue of the union with Colin; she had been the one to follow Colin to Furnass, he hadn't returned to South Carolina to claim her. As far as he was concerned whatever attraction they felt for each other during his time on her father's plantation could dwindle away and die, left to his own devices he wouldn't do a thing to stop it. He wouldn't because he couldn't, it wasn't in his nature. As far as a rival was concerned, she learned it was she who had had the rival all along, in competition for his affections with a brick compound of buildings called the Keystone Steam Works. Colin's one and only true love.

She took another sip of whiskey, continuing her slow journey back and forth. Back and forth. Thinking: To have a great love in your life. How many people could say that? You were larger than life, there on my father's plantation with your steam tractor huffing and puffing away, the massive pistons snapping back and forth, the engine that you brought from so far away as if from some magical kingdom, standing there astride it as you explained all the levers and gauges, steam and smoke billowing about you like you had descended from the clouds to offer me a new life, new hope . . . you stood in our kitchen with the smells of leather and horses and worn wool about you, you filled the room with your presence as if the room and the house and our lives had shrunk about you so that nothing about us, about me, could ever contain you and yet you needed me too, you were injured and bleeding when I eased the makeshift bandage from the gaping wound and I felt my knees give way and thought I'd faint but knew I couldn't, I wouldn't have another chance in my life, I cleaned the wound and wrapped you and felt the strength and power of your body, your muscles moving beneath your skin like the driving pistons of some great engine that you had designed and forged with your own hands, one love but no love at all because there was never any difference between you because you were all one and I could never tell the difference. . . .

She woke to find Perpetual's face in front of her, filling her vision, as if too close to a mirror, her companion's dark-skinned face like the negative image of a tintype before the backing was applied.

"*Bonjour* in there," Perpetual said, smiling. "Welcome back."

"Was my mouth open?" Libby said, shaking her head, stalling for time as she struggled to remember where she was, what day it was, what time. "I hate it when my mouth is open when I sleep."

"Yes, Mawm, your mouth was wide open. A terrible sight it was too. Perpetual is told that people were talking about it all the way up in Pittsburgh."

"Oh, get on with you," Libby said, looking around for her

cane. As if she read her mind Perpetual retrieved the cane from beside the bed and gave it to her. But Libby didn't get up right away. "Were you ever married, Perpetual?"

"Do say," Perpetual said. She stopped straightening the things on top of the dresser and looked at Libby, elbow crooked, hand folded under on her hip.

"It's *Do tell*, as you know very well. I don't know why I bother."

"Regardless, that be a good one, Mawm. When is Perpetual going to have time to take care of a man when she has to take care of all of you?"

"I guess you're right. We haven't given you much chance to have a life of your own, have we?"

"Perpetual likes her life just fine, *merci*, Mawm. What made you ask that?"

"I don't know. Maybe it was a dream I was having. I just got to thinking and realized I really don't know that much about you."

"Truth be told, Mawm, Perpetual is married and keeps her husband stashed away under her bed. After thirty years, I'm surprised you haven't caught us before now."

"Posh," Libby said, taking another sip of whiskey. "I don't know why I put up with you."

"Because you love me, Mawm. Perpetual knows that. You couldn't live without me."

"Well, that's certainly true. But you know what I meant, when I asked if you were ever married."

"Yes, matter of fact Perpetual does. You want to know if I was ever with a man."

"Well, I didn't mean that exactly. . . ."

"Matter of fact, Perpetual was with a man once. Back on my island. Perpetual got herself pregnant too."

"You have a child? Where is it now, back with your family?"

Perpetual looked at her, straight-on, under her eyebrows. "Perpetual said she got herself pregnant. Perpetual didn't say anything about a child."

"You're right. I'm sorry. I shouldn't have presumed—"

"Just so. It's all right, Mawm. As long as we understand each other. Perpetual is experienced in such matters as surprise babies."

"Of course, of course—"

Perpetual was her friendly self again, all smiles and busywork, bustling about setting things in order, straightening Libby's bed, hanging up her nightclothes. "And Perpetual knows your real question is if Perpetual ever misses being with a man. The answer is no, Mawm, I don't. Love with a man is messy business, it gets all over you and leaves stains you can't wash out easy. Perpetual she doesn't need any more pain in her life. Love means something else to her now."

Libby took another sip of her whiskey and started to get up. Perpetual hurried over and helped the older woman to her feet, her firm grip on Libby's flaccid underarm.

"Steady on?" Perpetual said.

"Steady on," Libby said.

Assured in their private code that the older woman was stable enough to be left on her own, Perpetual went back to straightening up the room. Libby stood there a moment, braced with her cane, weaving slightly in place as she built up steam, then headed toward the door.

"So, how is Mary Lydia today? I heard you earlier in and out of her room."

"She be fine." When Perpetual saw Libby in motion, she followed up behind her. "Later on when everybody's gone I'll help her with the baby. Like we talked."

Libby stopped midway down the corridor and looked over her

shoulder. "That's right. You're not going to the ceremony."

"No, Mawm. Perpetual already seen the statue once. Don't need to see it again." The two women smiled at each other as if they shared a secret.

"Well, you have things to take care of here. And Malcolm said he would escort me so someone will be around to pick me up if I fall over." She continued down the corridor to the top of the steps. "Lord knows I'm certainly not looking forward to this today."

"Don't forget the notes the temperance ladies gave you."

Libby stopped at the head of the stairs and looked at Perpetual as she stood beside the banister, straight on from under her eyebrows, her version of the look Perpetual gave her earlier. "Oh, don't you worry about that. I intend to do the temperance ladies proud."

20

When Malcolm got to the steamworks, he found the machines that were participating in the parade—one of their recent KSW Model 90 steam tractors; a 12-ton Model DMX dirt excavator; and the pride of the company, its most recent accomplishment, a KSW Model T40 Well-Driller, featuring a newly developed upright flue boiler and the much heralded articulated derrick—lined up in the quadrangle going through their final maintenance checks, the engines chuffing away. Next year at this time, Malcolm thought, we'll be able to show off our new Mosquito Tank, that will raise a few eyebrows in town, that'll show the good people of Furnass that the Keystone Steam Works is still a major industry in town, that other industries are dependent on us, not the other way around . . . and it should stop the talk once and for all that all I ever did was recycle my father's ideas. . . . But Gus was nowhere about. When he asked MacIninch, the foreman from the Boiler Shop who was supervising the preparations, if he had seen Gus, the small wiry man gave his best Scottish "Nooo" with a sad shake of his head. "We hae no seen the young master this morning. Should I be thinking aboot one of the other lads to drive the well-driller?"

"I wanted Gus to drive it, so people would get used to associating the steamworks with him."

"Oh aye, Mr. Lyle, I think they doo that well enough already," MacIninch said, nodding as he looked across the yard.

Coming through the entrance to the quadrangle, chuffing through the covered passageway under the administration offices, was the Lylemobile, decorated with small American flags flying from each corner of the roof and patriotic bunting draped across the sides, Gus sitting proudly in the driver's seat. He took a turn around the yard in the vehicle, tooting the whistle and waving his rumpled fedora to the workmen. For a moment it looked as if he considered doing a second lap, then thought better of it; he pulled up in front of his father and MacIninch in a cloud of steam and smoke, the dust he stirred up settling around them, and climbed down, pulling off the leather sleeves he used to protect the sleeves of his suit coat, obviously proud of himself.

"What's all this about?" Malcolm said to his son.

"I had a great idea. We'll run the Lylemobile in the parade instead of the well-driller."

"Why would we do that?"

"It'll show the town our latest vehicle. And it will demonstrate to those government reps that we're committed to the development of steam automobiles."

Malcolm shook his head. "First of all, everybody in town has already seen the Lylemobile because you drive it around everywhere. And second of all, we haven't made that kind of commitment to its development as yet."

"Well, okay then," Gus said. "We'll run the Lylemobile

along with the well-driller."

"No, we won't," Malcolm said. "Either you drive the well-driller as we discussed, or I'll get someone else to drive it. And either way, we're not including the Lylemobile."

"Aye, I'll leave you two gentlemen to your wee discussion," MacIninch said, nodding to both. "You let me know what you need from me, Mr. Lyle."

"Thank you," father and son said in unison, then glared at each other.

As the bandy-legged Scot walked back to the machines, Gus said, "All right, all right. I said I'd drive the well-driller and I will."

"Then you better get yourself ready. You should have been here before this, checking out the machine for yourself. Making sure you actually know how to drive this driller, some of the controls have changed, you know. . . ."

"That's pretty funny, you telling me about changes on this driller. Remember, I'm the one down in the shop most of the time while you're tucked away up in your office."

Malcolm had turned to leave, ready to leave things as they were, but he came back, incensed that his son would take that attitude with him. "When they told me at the house that you had left before breakfast, I assumed you were down here at the shop taking care of your responsibilities."

"I had something else to do."

"I'll bet you did. The same kind of *things* you used to sneak out of the house early in the mornings to take care of."

Gus blushed and turned a few degrees away. "That's none of your business."

Malcolm stepped back into his son's line of sight. "I'll say it's my business. You're my son, you've got a position in this town— you're a married man, for heaven's sake. You can't go playing around with other men's wives."

"She's not married, now."

"Oh, so that *is* what you've been doing. I was just taking a shot in the dark, hoping it wasn't true. What about Lily? Is that why she took Mal and went back home to Kansas?"

"No," Gus said, kicking at a small piece of slag in the dirt near his shoe. "At least I don't think so. I don't think she knows anything about it. She never said anything, if she did. . . ."

Gus, Gus, Gus, Malcolm thought as he turned away again, looked around the yard, the brick facades that lined the quadrangle. Where did such behavior come from? How could Gus allow such a thing to happen to himself? How could he allow himself to give in to the baser instincts and risk everything, his home, his marriage, the respect of his community? No wonder Malcolm didn't trust him with more responsibility, no wonder Malcolm didn't give the go-ahead with the Lylemobile. And he had to admit that learning this now about his son certainly made it easier to choose whether to sink the company's assets into the Lylemobile or the Mosquito Tank.

"We'll need to talk about all this later," Malcolm said, turning back to his son. "But for now we need to deal with the business at hand. Get MacIninch back here to check out the driller and go over those controls with you."

"You just don't grasp it, do you Father?"

"Grasp what?"

"Exactly." Gus in his turn started to walk away, then stopped. "You'll never give me the benefit of the doubt. You'll always think the worst of me. You always have. If you ever have the choice to think good or ill of me, you will always choose the ill. Always choose the ill."

Because you give me no choice, Malcolm thought. Because you will always make the bad choice, always make the mistake if there's one to be made. Don't you think I want to think good of you?

Gus stared at him for a moment as if waiting for something. What? What?

When Malcolm couldn't think of anything further to say, Gus readjusted his crumpled hat on his head and headed over to the well-driller and climbed up on the rear platform. When MacIninch saw him and started toward him, Gus motioned him away.

And Malcolm had a terrible thought. Always makes the bad choice. That's what everyone has always said about me.

21

The afternoon sunlight slanted down through the branches of the sycamore trees in the yard, creating shifting patterns of light and dark across the screen door as the warm breeze touched the leaves of the trees, light and shadows passing over the bunny tail of cotton tied on the outside of the screen to discourage the flies and mosquitos and moths that liked to rest there on the mesh hoping for their chance to get inside. From down the hill in the town came the occasional sound of a brass band or a calliope, the faint roar and applause of an audience reacting to a feat of daring or strength, the swell of appreciation for the horse races or the fire-men's water battles, the background murmur of the crowds along the promenade of booths and displays for the Old Home Days celebration filling the main street of town. As I watched I caught glimpses through the trees of a multicolored balloon, gaily striped like Joseph's coat of many colors, lifting slowly above the town, above the rim of the valley's hills into the blue blue summer sky, Professor D'Angelus' Balloon Ascension according to the adver-tisements, its tether like a pencil line drawn to earth.

Your long soft fingers covered my eyes and I didn't even flinch, knowing it was you before knowing it was you.

"I saw you leave with the others," I said, placing my fingers over the fingers that covered my eyes.

"I decided to sneak away and come back," you said, spreading your fingers so I could see slices of the day again. "It wasn't any fun without you there."

"And I didn't want to be there if we had to be with the others."

"I know," you said and lifted your hands away. Though I still didn't turn to look at you, the two of us standing there looking out the screen door at the town below in the valley, you standing close enough behind me that I could feel your breath in my hair.

"You must have really snuck," I giggled. "I never saw you coming up the road."

"I came up Nineteenth Street and then across through Black Town."

"Weren't you scared? A white boy in Black Town?"

"Nah. They all know where I live. I think Perpetual and Margaret feed half the families over there on the hill, though no one in the family is supposed to know about it."

"I'll bet Grandmother does," I said, turning my head to see you over my shoulder.

"Yes, you're probably right. I wouldn't be surprised if she was the one who told Perpetual to start feeding them in the first place. Wouldn't Father have a fit if he knew?"

I turned all the way round to look at you. What were we, thirteen, fourteen at that time? We were close to the same height then, you were maybe only an inch or two taller than me, not like later when you were a whole head taller; looking at you then was like looking back at me, your face the mirror of my face.

"Have you looked in Perpetual's room lately?" you went on. "It's like a real jungle in there."

"I'm afraid to," I said and shivered. "It's like something might be hiding in there to get me."

"Come on," you said, taking my hand and pulling me towards the staircase. "I'll protect you."

Up we ran to the second floor and around the banister, giggling like the children we were. Perpetual's room was at the end of that side of the hall, next to Grandmother's room at the front of the house. We stopped in front of her door.

"Wait," I said. "We can't go in there."

"Sure we can," you said. "All you have to do is turn the handle. See?"

We giggled again, then became solemn as acolytes entering the holy of holies as we stepped in the door, closing it behind us. It was an L-shaped room, the short end with a door that led to Grandmother's room, the long wall taken up with a bay window filled with Perpetual's plants—there were mason jars with plants hanging from ropes from the ceiling, pots of plants along the windowsill and lining the baseboard, more plants placed on stands and tables on that side of the room.

"I knew she had a lot of plants. . . ," I said, leaving the rest of the sentence unfinished. "Where did they all come from?"

"She brought the first ones with her from Martinique and the rest just grew."

"But what does she do with them all?"

You stood there batting at a tendril dangling in front of your face. "Don't you know? She grinds them up into powders and potions and she and Margaret sell them out the back door, mostly to people from over in Black Town. That's another reason why I never have to worry walking through there. Everybody knows about Perpetual and her cures."

I walked among the hanging leaves and stems, letting them drift over me, tangling in my hair, caressing my eyes. My vision was full of jars of brownish brackish water tangled with roots and tendrils, spiny hairs and tubers, the dark dank water full of the smells of growing things and decay.

"We shouldn't be here. Suppose Perpetual caught us."

"She might turn us into toads," you said. We laughed but I wasn't sure it was funny. You started to poke around her desk; to distract you I went over to the front window where I could see the multistriped balloon through the branches of the sycamores start to be pulled back to earth.

"Oh, I wish we could go for a balloon ride," I said.

"Why can't we?" you said, coming over to stand behind me at the window.

"I told Mother I didn't feel like going to the festival. Suppose she saw me there now? Or Father or someone?"

"Wait," you said, your face all alight. You grabbed my hand and led me out of the room again, careful to close the door behind us, then led me back down the hall to your room where you positioned me beside the bed, then went to your wardrobe and, after giving the clothes inside careful consideration, pulled out a brown tweed suit and held it up against me.

"Yes, this will do fine," you said, handing the hanger of clothes to me, then reached in again for a tattersall dress shirt. "Here, put these on."

"I can't wear these," I exclaimed.

"Whyever not?"

"They're boys' clothes. Your clothes."

"So?"

I giggled at the idea, but you were serious. "No, you're right. Bring them along."

Before I could say anything more, you were out the door and down the hall. I found you in my room going through my wardrobe.

"Now what are you looking for?"

"I'll know it when I see it," you said, snapping the clothes hangers along the pole one after the other. I was wearing a plain high-waisted blue check dress, but you pulled out my best party dress, white muslin with puffy sleeves and a layered skirt.

"You want me to wear that?"

"Hold on a minute."

You draped the dress over the foot of my bed and ran back down the hall to your room. When you returned a moment later you were carrying one of your white cotton sleeveless undershirts and a pair of white cotton briefs.

"Here, you have to put these on under my suit."

"Why am I wearing your suit?"

You picked up the dress from the foot of the bed and held it up in front of you. "Because I'm wearing *your* dress! We are going to the festival incognito!"

"But that's ridiculous," I laughed. "We're twins. People will recognize us anyway."

"Nonsense," you said, brushing away the idea like a pesky bug. "You'll see. We're not identical twins, we don't look that much alike. It's just what people get used to seeing. Now, where do you keep your undergarments? Go on, start taking off your clothes, I will too."

"But why do we have to put on each other's undergarments too?"

"Because if we're going to do this, we have to do it all the way. Right down to the foundations."

Before I knew what was happening you had kicked off your shoes, pulled off your socks, and were taking off your pants and shirt. When I just stood there, you gave me a look as if to say, What are you waiting for? and I started to undress as well. We hadn't seen each other without our clothes since Perpetual used to bathe us when we were babies, but now, seeing each other naked there in my bedroom, the afternoon sunlight washing over us, it seemed the most natural thing in the world, as if your long white body was already engraved in my being, in the same way that my body felt an extension of your body, joined in some other sphere or lifetime. I put on your coarse white underthings, feeling boyish, as I watched you pull on my split drawers, my undershirt, garter and stockings, my chemise. Then you pranced around the room pointing your toes, and I pretended to hit a baseball, the two of us dissolving in laughter.

"You look charming, my dear," I said in a pretend gruff voice. "Simply charming."

You raised your pinky finger to trace the line of an eyebrow, then curtsied. "And you look smashing. Simply smashing."

I marveled at the weight of your suit of clothes, the stiff coarse cloth against my skin, it was like a protective shell that you could put on every day, a carapace to carry with you against the world, no wonder boys were so sure of themselves, able to do everything without hesitation or doubt. I wondered what you felt as you pulled my dress on over your head, though the weight of my garments was in their accumulation, the individual layers light and diaphanous but taken together in their overlap, the maze of seams and openings, the strata that went together to make up how a girl or woman presented herself to the world, an unexpected weight and burden, but you didn't say anything. When we were finished putting on each other's clothes, we stood side by side in front of my dresser mirror. I put my arm around you in brotherly fashion; you rested your head on my shoulder, then straightened up.

"We have to do something about your hair," you said.

"And the fact that you don't have any," I giggled. In a bureau drawer I found a white bonnet that I put over your head and tied it under your chin.

"Fetching," you said as we checked how it looked in the mirror. "I've got an idea what we can do with your tresses."

You again led me out the door and down the hall, but this time into the Nearer Wing where Gus and Lily had their rooms.

"Wait!" I said, pulling my hand free of yours. "How do we know they're not here?"

You stopped in the middle of their upstairs hall and looked back at me as if surprised to see I could speak. "Because, silly, I saw both of them downstreet with Mother and Father. Besides, this is our house as well as theirs."

"But not this new wing. It's supposed to be only for them—"

"Oh piffle," you said and flounced the skirt of my dress you were wearing. "Us girls can go anywhere we like. All we have to do is look cute and appealing and we can always get our way."

With that you fingered an imagery dimple in your chin, curtsied, and sashayed on down the hall and into Gus and Lily's bedroom. I giggled in spite of myself and followed.

I hadn't been on the second floor of the new wing since it was built, much less in their bedroom; more than that, I had never been in a newlywed couple's bedroom before. The room was decorated in pinks and whites, full of flower prints and frills; if something could have a ruffle it had three.

"It's their love nest," I said, visions of romantic love dancing in my head.

"Kiss me, my darling," you said, clasping your hands underneath your chin.

"Yes, my darling," I said, taking you in my arms and bending you back in a movie embrace. Our lips barely touched and you bounced up again, going over to the wardrobe and rummaging through the top shelf.

"Here we go," you said, pulling out one of Gus' old fedoras from the tangle of scarves and wraps. "I was pretty sure big brother kept his old hats around somewhere or other."

You held up the hat like a crumpled trophy, then reached inside the crown and beat it back into a semblance of its original shape. After admiring your handiwork, you placed it on my head, tucking my hair up underneath it. Then you spun me around so I could see myself in the bureau mirror, standing in front of you, your hands gripping my shoulders proprietarily like some perverted version of Pygmalion and Galatea. In front of me on the bureau top were Lily's sterling silver hairbrush and comb and mirror set, along with the small milk glass pots for foundation, powder, eyelid paste, and rouge for her cheeks and a stain on the mouth for the bitten-lip effect—all the cosmetics she bought at Gus' insistence when they were first married, he said they would help break her free of her strict Covenanter mold, but after she tried them once she never used them again. Before you knew what was happening I grabbed the puff from the jar of powder, turned around, and dusted both of your cheeks with it.

"What the—?!"

I giggled at your surprised expression and whirled back around to the bureau, delighted that I could contribute a fun idea to our masquerade. I got some rouge on my finger and turned back to you but you grabbed my wrist, your face wrenched in anger, your eyes reduced to slits.

"What are you doing?"

"This'll be fun. And I'll draw a pencil mustache on my face—"

"You stupid, stupid girl!" You dropped my wrist and pushed me away, heading out of the room. "You always go too far, you always spoil everything. . . ."

You left me there, the rouge still on my finger like a wound, facing the image in front of me in the bureau mirror, this hapless bereft creature neither one thing nor the other, part girl part boy part child part adult, part all those things and none of them. And

I knew you were right, like you were always right, I always spoiled everything, I could never do things right to please you. I sat on the edge of the bed and took off Gus' hat, buried my face in my hands and started to cry, our beautiful fun day together turned to ashes, all because of me. When I had run out of tears I decided there was nothing to do but go to my room and get out of your clothes and go back to being just me. But when I left Gus and Lily's room and started down the corridor back to the main part of the house, I found you sitting at the top of the stairs to the first floor like nothing had happened.

"There you are!" you said, all smiles, getting to your feet and straightening your dress. "It's about time, we have to get going if we're going up in the balloon. What did you do to Gus' hat? Here, let me fix it again. . . ."

And you fussed around me, tucking my hair back under the hat and straightening my tie, then took my arm like you were my best girl and down the stairs and out the front door we went, arm in arm, into the heat of the summer afternoon, skipping through the dust, down the road from our house to the city streets below.

The main street, Seventh Avenue, was blocked off, with the attractions for Old Home Days—"For Thee and Me"—strung out from Ninth to Fifteenth Street. There were tents and pavilions where ladies' auxiliaries cooked sausages and corn on the cob, while men poured beers and cups of coffee; Nelson's Slide for Life at Fourteenth Street; Doctor LaRosa's Feats of Strength at Thirteenth Street; boxing contests near Twelfth Street; poultry exhibits; Monsieur Monsuela on the high wire across the intersection at Eleventh Street; a dog show on the steps of the new Carnegie Library; a bandstand near the Farmer's Bank where the volunteer firemen's brass band pumped out marches and waltzes; and rising above it all, anchored at the end of the arcade just beyond the dogleg of the main drag before Tenth Street—like a great multistriped bubble, the colors of Araby, like something you'd see in the Arabian nights, at home with minarets and dome roofs and flying carpets, tugging at its tether as if in anticipation of its flight—Professor D'Angelus' Balloon Ascension.

We had gone barely half a block when we ran into Gus coming from a refreshment stand.

"What are you two doing dressed like that?" he said, his face suddenly as red as his Italian ice cone. "Is that my hat? Who told you you could have my hat?"

"It's just one of your old ones," you said.

"I don't care," Gus said as he tried to snatch it off my head. "How did you get it?"

I ducked away to one side, you ducked away to the other, and we ran past him laughing as he stood there twisting back and forth grabbing at air.

"Oh hurry, hurry!" I said, as we ran through the crowds. I wanted to fly away with you to somewhere far away, just the two of us—I could see us lifting off, rising over the town, looking down at the little houses and the people like specks of dirt along the sidewalks, the smelly mills and the automobiles and horse and wagons along the layers of streets and the church steeples and all the places that constrained us and held us back from who we were and who we wanted to be, that never allowed us to be ourselves, reaching for the clouds. But you were having too much fun to hurry, you flounced along, waving to everyone we met along the arcade, tootling your fingers, flirting with the men, pretending to be the hussy, your idea of what it was to be a girl. It was all in good fun until we encountered a group of boys, from high school or a little older, standing around on the sidewalk smoking near the Buchanan Steel Mercantile Store. You skipped right into the middle of them, bold as you please, puckering your lips to one, tugging on the shirt front of another, taking one's cigarette from his fingers and pretending to take a drag then flicking it away toward the curb.

"Hey, what the hell—"

"Get back here!"

You grabbed my hand and off we ran again, through the crowds along the arcade. The boys started to chase us but we lost them when we joined the audience in front of the Strongman Exhibition—on the stage men in tights lifting barbells and swinging Indian clubs—ducking down, running hunched over, threading our way in and out through the spectators, giggling the whole time until we popped out into the clear on the other side, continuing down the street. Ahead of us the great balloon rose above the rooftops of the buildings that lined the street, fitting like the stopper to a bottle. But when we reached the gate we found the ride was closed for the day, there was no one in the ticket booth, the area around the basket was deserted. Overhead the balloon nudged against its tether, the particolored stripes blocking out the day, everything in shadow underneath it.

"Hey cutie, what's your hurry?"

The half dozen boys were coming up the street behind us, and the grins on their faces weren't meant to be friendly. Their leader was the one whose cigarette you tossed away, a stringy guy a few years older than the others, maybe in his early twenties, with a mouse-colored cloth cap pushed back on his head. They shoved me aside and surrounded you, Mouse Cap planted in front of you, close enough that I couldn't tell if he was going to hit you or kiss you.

"Whatcha run away for, sweet cheeks? You and me have some unfinished business."

At first you tried to carry off your flirty girl routine. "Oh please, kind sir. What could you ever want with little ol' me?"

"Don't give me that crap. You're going to pay me back for throwing away my cigarette." He punctuated his words by punching you in the shoulder.

"Ow!" you said, in your own voice now. "That hurt!"

"Oh, poor little thing. Did the big bad bully hurt you? Tell you what, let's take a look to see if there's a bruise."

And with that Mouse Cap grabbed the material on the front of the dress and pulled it down off your shoulders.

"Yay!" another one laughed. "Let's strip her!"

"Strip her!" another one cried, and they were all grabbing at your clothes then, you doubled over trying to protect yourself but to no avail, they were pulling the dress off you and then had you down on the ground, your legs in the air, their voices full of a terrible joy that I had never heard before, a sound I never knew boys could make, and then Gus was there, out of nowhere, pulling the boys off you and tossing them aside, but Mouse Cap grabbed him along with several of the others and they had both you and Gus on the ground, all of you rolling around and flailing at each other and I tried to help and drag the boys away but they kicked at me and I couldn't grab ahold of anyone and I didn't know what to do, I did the only thing I could think to do, I thought maybe I could divert them, I ran over to where the balloon was tethered to a stake in the ground and untied the rope, the knot coming loose surprisingly easy, for a moment the rope hanging free, dragging in the dust like the curl of a snake, the balloon as if unaware as yet that it was set free, and then it slowly began to rise, the rope following obediently after, slowly, tentatively at first, then faster, the great circle of cloth overhead lifting above the line of the rooftops, the sky suddenly cracking open above us like a lid lifted above the street, the sunlight slicing across the dirt-covered pavement where the bodies twisted and flailed at each other, the combatants on the ground stopping abruptly as they were revealed, looking around, wondering what was happening, then all of them at once aware that the balloon was no longer above them, that the crowds along the arcade were starting to cry out as people became aware the balloon was loose, a figure in a frock coat and stovepipe hat who everyone knew was Professor D'Angelus running through the crowd and into the area where the balloon was once anchored, leaping to try to reach the dangling end of the rope as it bounced over the top of the ticket booth and then across the front of a nearby ring-toss game, the good professor tripping and falling over the makeshift fence around what had been the balloon launch area, and all those on the ground, you and Gus and Mouse Cap and his gang, realizing at the same time that no matter who was responsible for releasing the balloon they were bound to get the blame for it, all scampering to their feet and scattering through the crowd. You and Gus started to run as well but Gus stopped and ran back and grabbed my hand and the three of us slipped between the rows of tents up Tenth Street and then into Cherry Alley, running parallel to the tents and booths along main street to Thirteenth Street and then back down to the midway again, joining the crowds that stood looking up at the balloon as it grew smaller drifting toward the end of the valley, joining Grandmother and Perpetual and Mother and Lily as if we had been there all long, you and me and Gus breaking into laughter then for the first time since we made our escape, Gus helping you pull the remains of the dress back up around your shoulders as Mother stared in disbelief.

"What on earth are you doing in those clothes?" she said, looking from you to me and back to you again. "Is this for some kind of show or something?"

"Exactly, Mother," you said, and gave one more mince of your hand though it was obvious your heart was no longer in it.

"It's probably better not to ask a question you don't

want the answer to," Perpetual said.

She looked at Grandmother, who raised her eyebrows in response.

"I've always found it's better to listen to Perpetual about these things." Grandmother shifted her cane to her right hand and started toward the car. "But if anyone asks, we say they were with us the entire time. Understood?" She stopped and looked back at Mother, who shrugged her agreement. Perpetual nodded and we all headed to the car to return home.

I remember Gus was driving one of his early Lylemobiles; we all piled in and after he stoked up the boiler we were off, chuffing back up the steep streets away from the center of town, up the slope of the valley and into the trees toward home, the sounds of the festival trailing away behind us, the balloon only a distant speck, barely a memory. The tilt of the car up the steep grade pushed you and me together against the back seat, but we were no longer laughing, we were aware that something serious and enduring and irreparable had happened though we were too young to know what it was or how it might change our lives, we only knew it would, that the world for two children would never be the same, and then Perpetual was there, standing beside the bed, her kind dark face staring into my eyes, in her hands a small glass beaker of greenish-blackish liquid, saying, "It's time to wake up, Miss Mary Lydia, most everybody's downstreet at the parade so nobody will bother us, time to take the medicine, like we talked about. . . ."

. . . *and Perpetual stands beside the bed and watches as Mary Lydia chokes down the glass of foul-smelling greenish-blackish liquid that Perpetual has made for her, the potion she's ground together from plants she's grown in her room, cooing her sympathy and encouragement, aware of how terrible it tastes but making sure Mary Lydia drinks all of it regardless, thinking, This is my family, this is the closest to a real family that I've ever known, I came here to America looking for a job and a way of life different than what I had known in the islands, a way of life different than the one charted out for me from birth, and instead found myself tied irreparably to the fate of this family, this collection of diverse souls and personalities, tied inextricably to their matriarch and therefore inevitably with all of their lives, found herself woven into the fabric of their lives more than she ever was to her family on Martinique, barely able now to remember any of her dozen brothers and sisters and cousins all jammed together in the stucco hut, just vague impressions here and there, the one indelible memory that of her father coming home in the evenings from the fields, his machete on his shoulder from another day cutting sugar cane, Perpetual at his feet on the stoop of their hut as he tried to gather his strength enough to go inside for the meal of goat stew and hominy bread, and after he had eaten, what she supposed was his only joy in life, before going to sleep mounting her mother even though they were visible in the semi-darkness to all the children in the room, Perpetual's introduction to the wonders of love and what would be expected of her when her time came, a lesson she learned so thoroughly that after husbands were found for her older sisters and she was next on the block Perpetual convinced her father to sell her instead to an agent in Fort-de-France who was looking for young women to transport to America as maids— as an added incentive to her father promising to send half her pay home each month, which she continues to do to this day— chosen by Colin Lyle through letters sight unseen to be his wife's attendant and having settled into that role never wishing to be anywhere or with anyone else for the rest of her days, having found with time that the term family as it applies to the heart has nothing to do with bloodlines or obligations or birth orders or anything else for that matter that you could quantify or put your finger on, she only has to look to her own heart to know this is true—Gunshots! she flinches then relaxes again as she realizes it's only fireworks, coming from down the hill in town, the Fourth of July celebration getting underway, the parade that Gus will be part of, and later Libby's dedication of the statue in the park, an event she would like to see if only to be part of Libby's involvement though she knows she's most needed here with Mary Lydia, that Libby is counting on her to take care of this, and when Mary Lydia is finished drinking the liquid Perpetual takes the glass from her and helps the young woman get settled once again in the bed, "Everything will be fine now, Mary Lydia, you just lie here and rest and let Perpetual's drink work its magic, all will be well for you now, you'll see," and checking once more that the young woman is comfortable, leaves the room and returns downstairs, down through the house empty today with everyone except Mary Lydia's mother, Missy, at the celebration down in the town (and with Missy there it's the same as if she's not there, the diminutive blond-haired woman floating through her days in her nightgown, tucked into a corner of the sofa in the living room with her choc-olates and women's magazines), for all intents and purposes just Perpetual and Mary Lydia and the spirits that only Perpetual can see but are real nonetheless occupying the big frame house on the slope of the valley . . . as across the country America begins to celebrate its birthday, the decided-upon-date of the birth of the Union, the grandest experiment in self-government that the world has ever known, the fragile jointure of dissimilar peoples and in-tentions and activities melded into a makeshift family of supposed equals, small and large towns from sea to shining sea waking this day to set off fireworks and join in picnics and parades in honor of the day and, without them always knowing it, celebrate them-selves . . . as in Guerneville, California, the day's festivities start off with the annual tug-of-war contest in the dirt on the main street of town between two teams in a tradition that no one can remember how it started much less how the teams are decided upon . . . while in Tulsa, Oklahoma, buckboards and farm wagons and carriages gather at a local field to watch a baseball game between chapters of the Rotary and Kiwanis Clubs, a game that will proceed as soon as a few runaway pigs are cleared off the diamond . . . as in Dekalb, Illinois little Billy Wilson, dressed as a miniature Uncle Sam, fights to keep his balance and maintain his salute, the pose his mother instructed him to hold as she tows him around the municipal park standing on a small wooden wagon decorated with red, white, and blue bunting under a poster that reads* DECLARATION OF INDEPENDENCE CONGRESS 1776, *Mrs. Wilson determined to win this year's Best in Show over those uppity society women and their expensive flag-draped baby buggies . . . as on the National Mall in Washington, D.C., two women dressed in bedsheets, one woman in a sheet dyed green to match her spiked headdress holding an upraised torch to represent Lady Liberty, the other woman with long flowing tresses, a metal breastplate, and a laurel-bedecked metal helmet, holding a staff crested with a rampant eagle as she represents Columbia the Gem of the Ocean, both representations at this time the embodiment of America, icons that within a few years will fall out of usage in favor of Uncle Sam, when America starts to see itself as masculine rather than feminine, a change of viewpoint that coincides, interestingly enough, with women taking a more prominent role in society with the right to vote . . . as in New York City, at the climax of the Preparedness Day celebration—a movement to get the country prepared for entry into the war in Europe, although no kind of patriotic fervor could prepare anyone for the kind of war happening at that very moment in the opening days of what will come to be known as the Battle of the Somme, a battle that is to last one hundred forty days, kill or maim one million men, and demonstrate the importance of air power and the introduction of the tank—Fifth Avenue is bedecked with what is called "The Greatest Display of the American Flag Ever Seen in New York," including a parade led by an enormous ninety-five-foot flag, a display immortalized in a series of flag pictures by American impressionist Childe Hassam . . . but this is Furnass, where the decorations are considerably more modest, consisting mainly of strings of pleated fan bunting hanging across the parade route on Seventh and Eighth Avenues, with flags angled out from the light poles, all of which are now forty years old and much the worst for wear, dedicated to the city by Buchanan Steel for the one hundredth anniversary of the signing of the Declaration of Independence and never replaced—or updated for that matter, eleven states (and stars to the flag) added since then, namely Colorado, North Dakota, South Dakota, Montana, Washington, Idaho, Wyoming, Utah, Oklahoma, New Mexico, and Arizona— the strings of decorations rather droopy and more than a little faded by this time, but once they're put away each year no one thinks about their shabby condition until the next year when they're unpacked again . . . and again this year no one is paying attention to the decorations as the various units leave the staging area among the grassy traffic islands in the middle of upper Seventh Avenue and begin the parade through the business district along the main street, led by the band of the Volunteer Firemen's Association, the twenty or so musicians in their military-style blue uniforms and kepis who are not so much marching down the street as ambling along together in a semblance of keeping step as they pump their way through the few marches by John Philip Sousa that they know how to play, "Stars and Stripes Forever," "Hands Across the Sea," "The Washington Post," the spectators along the curbs less interested in the music than in seeing who*

they recognize among the players—"Oh look, there's Mr. Keller
tootling his flute," "Wave to Jim Jenson pounding his drum,"
"Better he pounds that than something else"—followed by the
city's three horse-drawn hose wagons, soon to be replaced by an
American-LaFrance chemical truck and a 460 GPM Pumper
when the city hires its first full-time firemen . . . then various
civic organizations: the Furnass Athletic Association with its
rank-and-file members swinging Indian clubs, along with one particularly athletic young woman who can apparently turn cart-
wheels ad infinitum; a cluster of grade school children each
waving a small American flag; the local chapter of the Women's
Christian Temperance Union, a half dozen middle-aged women
dressed in white with severe expressions carrying signs that read
FOR GOD, HOME, AND HUMANITY and LIPS THAT TOUCH
LIQUOR WILL NEVER TOUCH MINE . . . a series of floats constructed on horse-drawn farm wagons, including one portraying
Betsy Ross sitting in a rocking chair sewing a thirteen-star American flag; a diorama of the founding of the town with a simulated
iron furnace spewing paper cutout flames with real smoke from a
charcoal brazier inside the chimney alongside a papier-mâché falls
in a tissue paper river; a group of bare-chested high school boys
bedecked with feathers and tomahawks portraying chief Colonel
Berry and the tribe of Onagona Indians who originally inhabited
the region . . . and then a contingent of motorized vehicles, their
principal attraction being that they demonstrate that the individual or company who owns them is progressive and "modern"
enough to have the latest equipment, such as Hap Taylor driving
his new Cadillac Touring Car and Charles Miller with his Pack-
ard Twin Six Town Car, the R. V. Cunningham Funeral Home's
new Buick Model D-4 3/4 Ton Hearse, the Model T delivery van
of Furnass Screw and Bolt (commonly known in town as
"Furnass Diddle and Duck"), and Buchanan Steel's Reo Heavy

Duty Reliable Speed Wagon . . . and leading them all, Gus Lyle at the helm of a Keystone Steam Works Model T40 Well-Driller, a box-like machine built on an open framework—looking something like a large circus wagon with the boiler and pulleys and gears inside where the lions and tigers and bears might be—with the extendable derrick resting on the roof of the framework and the controls on a stand-up platform at the rear, the controls themselves consisting of close to a dozen levers and valves and regulators with attending gauges and a large metal wheel for steering; as Gus leaves the staging area among the traffic islands and enters the business district along Seventh Avenue, after seeing all the gasoline-powered automobiles in the parade, he's kicking himself for not standing up to his father to let him drive the Lylemobile in the parade, it would have been the perfect opportunity to show the town the company's commitment to the vehicle, thinking, I always give up too easily, it's the story of my life, every time I've wanted something for myself I let somebody talk me out of it, no wonder no one takes me seriously, I'm a fool, I'm a fool . . . but passing into the second block of stores as the crowds get thicker along the sidewalks he starts to feel a little better about himself seeing people in the crowds he recognizes who wave to him and he waves back, as well as people he doesn't even know applauding as he drives by and he considers that as a matter of fact this well-driller is an impressive piece of machinery in its own right, such as the ridged steel wheels that give it a lot of maneuverability, which he decides to demonstrate by weaving back and forth as he continues down the avenue, heading toward first one curb and then the other, getting quite fancy with it, and the crowds love it, cheering him on—as he passes the Farmer's Bank Building he sees Emma Edgeworth standing among the crowd, all in white with her large-brimmed white hat, the uniform of the temperance union ladies, and Gus assumes that Emma completed her role in the parade and has come down to Seventh Avenue to see him (an incorrect assumption, incidentally: Emma is there to wave to Bert Featherstone, driver of the Reo Heavy Duty Reliable Speed Wagon), poor thing just can't get enough of me—so he changes course and steams straight toward her then as he steers away tips his crumpled fedora to her, eliciting a wry smile from her which is good enough for him, all of which is enough to convince him that he's a pretty splendid fellow despite what his father thinks of him . . . following the unit in front of him up Tenth Street, a float drawn by two white horses sponsored by the local chapter of the DAR depicting a young George Washington with an axe after cutting down a cherry tree being confronted by his father, up the hill to Eighth Avenue where the parade route doubles back on itself, back up through the town toward the reviewing stand in front of the park between Thirteenth and Fourteenth Streets, though Eighth Avenue is very different than the main drag, a tree-lined street with apartments and small office buildings on the downhill side, large homes set back on terraced lawns on the uphill side, the patriotic bunting sagging over the street through the branches of sycamores and maples, the crowds even denser here because of the reviewing stand with many of the folks who viewed family or friends in the parade on Seventh Avenue walking up the hill to see them again on Eighth, Gus once again weaving back and forth as he chuffs along when he sees in the crowds a block before the reviewing stand the two government reps, Adams and Taylor, and Gus buoyed by the attention of the crowd and feeling better about himself than he has in who knows when aims toward the two men like he did with Emma Edgeworth except he decides he wants to do something more to impress them, something special, that if he can't show the government reps his Lylemobile at least he can show them what's superior about the Keystone Steam Works Model T40 Well-Driller, and as he heads toward them pulls the levers and regulators that will raise the front end of the derrick lying on top of the machine, his plan to raise it a few feet and then lower it again, showing off the engineering involved, except Gus, though he spends much of his days on the fabricating floor of the steamworks so that he's aware of a lot of what's going on with the various machines, only pays strict attention to those machines he's most interested in, which means most of the time lately his own project, the Lylemobile, so that he knows a little bit about the controls of the Model T40 Well-Driller but he doesn't know a whole lot, for instance he doesn't know or remember that when he raises the front end of the derrick off the roof he also starts the telescoping sections of the derrick to begin their extension, the brilliance of the machine in the gearing that as the front of the derrick rises the various stacked sections move forward and snap into place so that in one motion the derrick stands fully assembled at the front of the machine a full twenty feet tall, which means that Gus knows the controls to start raising the derrick but he's not sure of the controls to stop and retract it, a rather critical omission at this point with the front end of the derrick some six feet off the front of the roof now and extending six feet in front of the machine, and getting taller all the time, an omission of which Gus becomes aware at the same time that he realizes the front end of the derrick is about to hit a branch of a sycamore tree near where the government reps are standing and for that matter has already hit a string of the saggy patriotic bunting and whereas he might choose to stop the well-driller before things get any worse he chooses to instead turn away from that side of the street and head toward the other side but it's too late, he's already knocked down the branch of the tree, scattering the crowd for cover—fortunately no one is hit—and pulled the string of bunting free from its anchor on a light pole and as he keeps on going he tries frantically to remember which levers control the retraction, the Model T40 Well-Driller by this time closing in on the trees on the other side of the street as the derrick is even higher now and further ahead of the rest of the machine, the crowds on that side of the street having seen what happened on the other side of the street running for cover as the machine tears into the branches of a maple tree and rips another string of bunting loose from its mooring, this time however also ripping into the electrical and telephone wires that run along the street as Gus still unable to stop the derrick from rising further turns back toward the center of the street, the derrick now carrying with it the strings of bunting and a collection of overhead wires along with assorted tree branches, Gus at least having the presence of mind that he needs to warn people of what's happening and he blows the steam whistle that sends its shriek along the avenue terrifying the horses pulling the float of George Washington and the cherry tree in front of him, the horses raising up on their hind legs in their traces and deciding all this noise and kerfuffle is enough for them, taking off up the street at a gallop and scaring the horses pulling the float in front of them and the horses pulling the float in front of them as Gus and the shrieking well-driller approach the reviewing stand . . . where Gus' father, Malcolm, is there to support his mother when Libby dedicates her statue in the park behind them, the two of them standing there beside the mayor and the six councilmen and the fire and police chiefs, watching a fife and drum corps march by, the shrill penny-whistle keen of the fifes inevitably bringing to mind the painting of "The Spirit of '76," thoughts of patriotism and devotion and "My country 'tis of thee," remembering that this morning his son John Lincoln, even though he knows his family would be against him doing such a thing—why else would he just sneak away like he did without telling anybody, not even his beloved twin sister; why   indeed?—is on a ship leaving New York Harbor bound for

England to join the fight against the German aggressors, that John Lincoln is actually doing what other people just talk about, standing up for his country and its beliefs in life, liberty, and the pursuit of happiness, and for a moment Malcolm is full of pride for his youngest son, no matter how angry he was at the boy earlier for disappearing and whatever other reasons he might have for his flight, John Lincoln's going off to war the kind of action he would like to think endemic from a son of his, showing him to be a Lyle to the core, carrying on the Lyle family tradition, men of action where others hold back, a reflection of the family's lineage and upbringing and yes, their very blood . . . his thoughts interrupted, however, by some commotion down the street and he turns and looks where everyone else on the reviewing stand is looking to see what is going on, what appears to be some disruption in the parade a block or so down the street, all of them watching in wonder as the next unit approaching the reviewing stand, a contingent of the Knights of Columbus, resplendent in their robes and plumed helmets and decorative swords, takes one look behind them and abruptly breaks ranks and flees to the curbs on either side as thundering up the street toward them comes first a horse-drawn float carrying Betsy Ross rocking furiously as she's propelled forward with her thirteen-starred flag flopped over her head followed by another float with an iron furnace that appears to be genuinely on fire and then a float with a bunch of bare-chested high school boys whooping like Indians as they hold on enjoying the ride, all of them pursued by the team of horses pulling the DAR float with young George Washington on his knees clasping the stub of his cherry tree like a shipwrecked sailor in a storm, then, after a telling distance, trundling along on its own, the Keystone Steam Works Model T40 Well-Driller, the derrick on top of the machine half-erect decorated with a tangle of tree branches and dragging on either side the remains of half dozen strings of bunting and electrical and telephone wires the ends of which drag along the sidewalks causing the remaining spectators, those who haven't fled along with the panicked parade units, to hop, skip, and jump over the bouncing wires, with Gus still at the controls of the well-driller looking as though it's all as much of a surprise to him as to everyone else, who looks over and sees his father on the reviewing stand and, with a sheepish look on his face, shrugs, to which in response all Malcolm can do is laugh. . . .

22

"Well, that didn't go as expected, did it?" Libby said. She and Malcolm were the last people on the reviewing stand, sitting alone on the row of wooden chairs where the dignitaries had been, watching what was left of the crowd milling about on the empty street. "Do you think Gus did it on purpose, or did it just happen that way?"

"Knowing Gus," Malcolm said, "I'm sure it just happened. The way things always just happen to Gus." As a group of musicians from the Volunteer Firemen's Association band passed by, a trumpet player, obviously drunk, let out a resounding *Bla-a-a-at!*

"My sentiments exactly," Libby said. She reached in her purse and took out a flask of whiskey. "I say we celebrate with a wee dram, will you join me?"

"Mother!" Malcolm said, half-shocked, half-laughing. "What are you doing?"

"I think it high time that I had drink with my son. And what better time than to celebrate your son's and my grandson's total disruption of the town's Fourth of July parade." She handed the flask to Malcolm.

Malcolm looked at it as if she had handed him a grenade. "Why do you have a flask of whiskey with you? I didn't even know you had such a thing."

"Don't pretend you didn't know that I have my daily ration of rye. And it stands to reason that I'd need something to carry me through those occasions when I might be away from home for any length of time. But today I brought the flask with me"—she stopped and motioned for Malcolm to take a swallow, which Malcolm did, surprised at how good it tasted after the initial burn— "as part of my speech, though I'm sure I would have regretted including it after the fact. And we're toasting Gus' disruption of the parade because he kept me from going through with my regrettable plan."

Malcolm took another swallow before handing the flask back to his mother. "And what were you going to do that you thought you might regret?"

"The good though misguided ladies of the temperance union wanted me to include in my speech some remarks regarding the evils of demon liquor. And I indicated to them that I would indeed acknowledge their agenda, but in fact my plan was to take out my flask, salute them and their cause, and then take a long and healthy swallow in front of the entire town. I thought that would put those high-minded busybodies in their place. But it's undoubtedly best that it never came to pass, wouldn't you say? Nothing good ever comes from bitterness. Besides, it's best to keep such pleasures to ourselves." Libby tilted back her head and had several good swallows of the whiskey before lowering the flask again; she pumped her eyebrows at her son, and said, "Ah!"

After his initial shock, Malcolm tried not to be too surprised at his mother's antics; he was more concerned that as time went on the world in general was beginning to be a bit fuzzy. He wasn't a stranger to alcohol—an occasional glass of wine at dinner with a client, a sometime celebratory glass of sherry or port at someone else's special occasion— but rye whiskey in the morning was a new experience. "Still, it's a shame you didn't get a chance to dedicate the statue and all. . . ."

"Nonsense," Libby said, offering the flask to Malcolm again—Malcolm respectfully declined, though a part of him desperately wanted another couple of swallows—before tucking it away again in her purse and folding her hands primly in her lap. "What was there to say about it anyway? Here's a statue, I hope you like it. From today on, it will sit here totally ignored except as a designated meeting place—'I'll meet you at the statue in the park'—and as a target for every pigeon in town. I really had nothing to say beyond my salute to the temperance ladies, I was hoping something would occur to me as I stood there with everybody looking at me."

"Even so . . . ."

Coming toward them along the reviewing stand, sidestepping along the row of empty chairs, was Dr. McArtle. When he reached them Libby offered her hand; Malcolm kept his hand to himself, but then relented when the doctor presented his hand to him.

"I saw you two still sitting here and wondered if everything is all right," McArtle said.

"Everything is fine, Doctor," Libby said. "But it's nice of you to be concerned."

"That was a pretty stressful morning, if you ask me," McArtle said. "Not your typical Fourth of July parade."

"It was certainly exciting," Libby said, looking to Malcolm for confirmation. The doctor looked at Malcolm as well, but Malcolm remained noncommittal, his attention wandering a bit in his alcoholic haze.

Malcolm didn't like the doctor, though he knew it had little to do with the man himself, it was about the man's father. He remembered all too well as he was growing up the attention the elder Dr. McArtle had lavished on his mother; the way the doctor would show up whenever Malcolm's father was away, or at least it seemed that way; the way he arrived at the house every Sunday morning in his surrey to take his mother to church, waiting for her until after the service, then the two of them going for a ride for several hours before he brought her home again. And Malcolm remembered all too well the way his mother phased out whenever she took the special medicine the doctor gave her; remembered that after the trouble when the soldiers came to town and his father was injured destroying the war engines he helped make for the Confederates, his mother returned to the way she used to be—without the spells of locking herself in her room for days at a time, and when she did come out walking around distracted as if listening to something only she could hear; she was his mother again—remembered afterward that Dr. McArtle was no longer welcome in the house and eventually moved away and that the family was back to normal again, at least for a while.

"We're waiting for Gus to come back with the car to give us a ride home," Malcolm said, after an awkward silence. "If, indeed, he intends to come back."

"Otherwise, if he doesn't come, we'll have to try to hitch a ride with somebody," Libby said, looking at McArtle and fluttering her eyelashes.

"I'll be glad to take you," the doctor said, speaking right up. "It would be an honor. My car is just down the street. I'll go get it, it doesn't seem like Gus is coming anytime soon."

"That's very good of you, kind sir," Libby said, the coquette. "It is getting a bit warmish with the sun and all."

Look at her, Malcolm thought as the doctor hurried away. She was flirting with him, eighty-nine years of age and flirting with him. Maybe the whiskey had something to do with it but I don't think so. Regardless, he fell for it hook, line, and sinker. Off he runs. The same look I'd see her give his father back then to get him to do what she wanted. Turn him inside out with just a glance, a little smile. They must be born with it, it must be part of being female, come with the equipment. But I guess what else can they do? Born into a world of men, made by men for the use of men. . . .

In a few moments McArtle was back, sidestepping along the empty row, then helping Libby to her feet and holding on to her elbow as they returned down the aisle to the end of the reviewing stand and the doctor's waiting car, a Model T Runabout.

"I thought maybe you'd have a horse-drawn surrey like your father used to drive," Malcolm said, coming along behind. Aware that the whiskey was making him a bit pushy.

As he helped Libby into the car, McArtle glanced at Malcolm, a look both questioning and knowing, but waited to say anything until she was settled in the passenger seat.

"So you remember my father's surrey? I heard him talk about it, but this seems more appropriate for a town with this many hills."

"Yes, of course, I was just saying. . . ."

"I'd offer you a ride too, but . . . ," McArtle said, looking apologetically to the car's lack of a rear seat.

"No, no . . . ," Malcolm said, feeling surprisingly awkward. "I'll walk. Like I usually do."

"So maybe we'll see you at the house," the doctor said, closing Libby's door and going around to the front of the car. He adjusted the choke near the right fender, took the crank and gave it a quarter turn to prime the carburetor. Then he climbed in behind the wheel, turned the key, set the magneto, adjusted the timing stalk, set the throttle stalk downward for idling, and pulled back on the hand brake, which also put the car in neutral. Returning to the front of the car, he used his left arm to give the crank a vigorous half turn—if the engine backfired and the level swung counterclockwise, the left arm was less likely to break. This time the engine caught and McArtle returned to the driver's seat. Watching someone go to all the trouble—and hazard—of starting an internal combustion engine made Malcolm appreciate all the more what Gus had accomplished with the Lylemobile.

As McArtle got settled behind the wheel, Libby said, "You know, Doctor, when your father used to pick me up from church, we'd take a little drive around town. Would you mind if we did that now? I haven't seen some of those places in years."

"Well, certainly," McArtle said. "You just tell me where."

Libby gave McArtle her special smile, then fluttered her fingers to Malcolm as they drove away.

23

Did she do that just to irk me? Malcolm thought as he started walking, across the street past Holy Innocents Church and up Eighth Avenue. Ask him to take her for the same ride that his father used to? I wouldn't put it past her, just to remind me of— what? Well, I don't know what, but I wouldn't put it past her. He continued along the block, past Holy Innocents school and nunnery and the parsonage on the corner, then turned up Fifteenth Street, starting the climb that would take him home. For the first couple of blocks the houses were large and well-kept, set back from the street on manicured terraced lawns following the slope of the hill, Victorian-era homes from when the town grew and prospered after the Civil War, Buchanan Steel and Keystone Steam Works the largest employers in town, the homes of managers and executives, along with the owners of other business attracted to the town because of the success of its leading industries, manufacturers of gauges and controls and specialty steels, Strathmore Coin Bag and Furnass Screw and Bolt and Onagona Coal and Fuel Company, and merchants as well, Berkman Department Store and Matthews Clothing and Seneca Mercantile.

Along the sidewalk the roots of the sycamore and maple and elm trees planted in the parkings were just beginning to unsettle the paving, cracking the concrete and creating its own lumpy topography. Farther on, the houses became leaner and meaner, small frame houses that looked ready to slide down the hill with a strong wind, pressed hard against the sidewalks, the sidewalks here merely dirt trails beside the unpaved streets, the tree roots exposed across his path like tangles of snakes. A lumpy middle-aged woman in a short white housedress—it might be her slip or undergarment—stood at the railing of her porch, close enough that he could have touched her as he passed, eating from a bowl; she looked at him with recognition but no friendliness, and Malcolm was the one who was embarrassed.

But what else can they do? he thought, remembering his earlier comments to himself about his mother's manipulations of McArtle. Born into a world of men. Work their wiles to get what they want; more than that, to get what they need. A world that sees them as less than a person, even here in this supposedly civilized country, I can't even imagine what it must be like for women in other parts of the world. The Lesser Sex, as they're sometimes called. The Distaff Side, as opposed to the Spear Side. Good for holding spun wool but not for real action. But who am I to talk? I have a pregnant daughter at home and I've not thought once about what she must be going through, how scared she must be, alone even with us all around her. Maybe because of us all around her. All I've cared about is the name of the guy at the college who is responsible and what his intentions are. If I'm honest with myself, to make sure that there was a guy at the college, or somewhere else, that it wasn't something darker, closer to home. But that's what men always do, isn't it? Look for someone to blame, someone other than themselves, what we force on the women around us. The suffragettes have a point, and it has to do with more than just voting: men don't see women the same way they see other men, we only see them on scales of pretty or usefulness, if we ever see them at all.

Maybe it was the remains of the alcohol buzzing around in his system; or his recognition earlier that the things he criticized in Gus were the same things people criticized in himself; maybe it was his talk with his mother on the reviewing stand, the first time they had ever talked in that manner, like equals somehow, the way you would talk to a friend; or maybe it was watching his eighty-nine-year-old mother flirting with the son of a once-upon-a-time lover. Whatever, thoughts occurred to him that had never occurred before.

He walked on, up the gradually steepening slope, the houses thinning out now, more like shacks set back from the road than proper houses. He remembered the summer evening he was walking home, it must be ten years ago, the twins were only eleven or twelve, and he was worrying that John Lincoln didn't seem interested enough in boy things; John Lincoln liked to stay in the house and read and listen to records on their Victrola rather than be outside playing, rolling hoops and flying kites and climbing trees. Malcolm was afraid the boy wasn't going to grow into a proper man unless he started paying attention to the things that boys always did. Then something was coming toward him, low and fast, at ground level, through the tall grass in the field beside him; his first thoughts were a rabid raccoon, a snake—but it turned out to be a baseball, rolling into the path in front of him, a teenage boy coming over the rise in pursuit. Malcolm picked up the ball and threw it to him.

"Thanks, Mr. Lyle," the boy said, coming over to him. "It didn't hit you or anything, did it?"

"No, didn't come close." He recognized the boy from his walks home, Malcolm was sure he lived nearby, that his father worked at Buchanan Steel. Coming up over the rise and through the field were half a dozen other boys to see what was going on, one carrying a bat over his shoulder, the others with a ragtag collection of old baseball gloves.

"You boys have a field for baseball?"

"Not really. There's an area down the hill there we use sometimes—"

"You got to be careful of the all the rocks and stuff," another of the boys piped up. "But it's okay."

"I've got an idea," Malcolm said. "Why don't you boys come up to the house? There's the backyard between the house and the garages. It would make a pretty good diamond and it was just mowed."

The boys looked at one another, unsure whether they should accept or not. Everyone in town knew Sycamore House, of course, the Lyle House, the boys could see it now from where they stood, halfway up the slope of the valley's hill, the white frame facade between the trees.

"At least come up and take a look at it," Malcolm said, starting to walk on. "I'll have Margaret make us some lemonade. I've been wanting my family to have some backyard baseball games. This way we'll have enough players to make it fun."

The boys looked at one another and shrugged, why not? Malcolm continued along the path with the boys trailing after him as if he were some kind of pied piper, through the covered bridge over Walnut Bottom Run and on up the slope to the house. He led them up the driveway past the house and showed them the backyard; the boys took one look at the wide, level expanse and started throwing their ball around, deciding where home plate and the bases would be, and dividing up into teams. Malcolm, grinning broadly, headed in the back door into the kitchen where Libby, Missy, Margaret, Perpetual, and Mary

Lydia were standing at the window.

"What's all this?" Missy said.

"This is an opportunity to get John Lincoln involved with some real boy activity," Malcolm said. "Where is he?"

"He's up in his room," Missy said. "Suppose he doesn't want to play baseball?"

"What red-blooded American boy doesn't like to play baseball?" Malcolm said.

"Can I play too?" Mary Lydia said.

Malcolm continued on through the kitchen to the front of the house. Malcolm had to admit that when he thought of the family playing baseball, he was thinking only of himself and Gus and John Lincoln, not any of the rest of the family—meaning none of the women of the household—though he was aware that the three males weren't enough to do more than just toss the ball around, which was why he never got around to trying to organize it. But the solution to that quandary was here in the backyard. Now all he had to do was round up John Lincoln, it didn't matter whether Gus was around or not, in fact, considering Gus' lack of coordination, it was probably better that he wasn't included. Malcolm started calling halfway up the stairs.

"John Lincoln! Come on, son! We've got a baseball game starting in the backyard!"

Malcolm hurried down the hall and burst into his son's room. John Lincoln was sitting on the bed, propped up on pillows with his back against the headboard, a sketchpad on his lap, copying the picture of a castle from a magazine. He looked up at his father, obviously displeased with the interruption.

"Didn't you hear me? We've got a baseball game starting in the backyard. Come on."

"Why would I care about that?" John Lincoln said, checking something on the picture in the magazine before returning to his drawing.

"Come on," Malcolm said, finding his son's reaction hard to understand. "We're all going to play, the whole family."

"Mother too? Grandmother? Perpetual?"

"No, you know what I mean. You, me, Gus if he's around. . . ."

"That's hardly enough for a game of baseball," John Lincoln said, focused on his drawing.

"And there's some boys from down below. I invited them to play too."

John Lincoln looked up at him then. "What do you mean from down below?"

"Some of the boys who live at the foot of the hill. I suppose some of them live in those . . . cabins, on the other side of the bridge—"

"They're here? In the backyard?" John Lincoln said, sitting up straighter. "Those guys hate me. They try to beat me up every time they see me. Father!"

"Why would they hate you?" Malcolm said, suddenly uneasy. "They didn't say anything when I invited them up—"

"You invited them here? They hate me because I live up here in this house and they live down there in a bunch of shacks. And most of them are older than I am, I don't have a chance around them. They chase me home every chance they get. . . ."

"I didn't know," Malcolm said, going over to the window and looking down on the backyard. Now that he thought about it, the boys were three or four years older than John Lincoln, why didn't that occur to him before? "Maybe if you came out now and we all played a game they'd take it easy on you in the future—"

"And maybe not. And what, you're going to play too? What, to try to keep me safe from them? They're not going to want you to play, you're an old man. Were you thinking of having Mother and Grandmother play too? Oh wonderful, just wonderful!"

Malcolm was confused and conflicted. On the one hand, he

was furious that these boys would pick on a son of his; on the other hand, he was just as upset that his son wouldn't stand up to these bullies, even though they were older and he was outnumbered. Malcolm was tempted to go down there and teach them a lesson himself, but then thought better of it—how would that look, a grown man slapping around some teenage boys. Then, too, a couple of them were rather large, and there were half a dozen of them, he might find himself the one getting beat up. What was he going to do, he even promised them lemonade!

He left John Lincoln sitting on his bed looking miserable and headed back downstairs. When he went back into the kitchen, all five women turned from the window to look at him.

"Can I play too?" Mary Lydia said.

"Nobody's going to play," Malcolm said. "Margaret, go out there and tell those boys to go home."

"Me?" Margaret said. "Why would I tell those boys to leave? I didn't invite them there in the first place."

"Because I want you to, that's why," Malcolm said

Margaret folded her hands in her apron and retreated to the corner of the kitchen. "No bunch of white boys going to listen to an old fat black woman, that's for sure," she muttered, her head down.

Malcolm wondered himself why he asked her, she was right, there was no way the boys would listen to her. But he certainly couldn't do it himself, not after being the one to invite them. Maybe if they just ignored them they'd go away. . . .

"I'll go tell them they can't stay," Perpetual said, and started toward the back door.

"If they're not going to listen to Margaret, why do you think they'll listen to you?" Malcolm said. And regretted it the moment he said it. Perpetual looked at him with eyes that could have burned right through him, though her voice was as soft and lilting in a kind of Caribbean patois.

"Why, Mr. Lyle, Perpetual deh yah, yuh know? Everything criss. Dees boys, nuh romp wid mi, Perpetual soon cum bock, yuh know?"

Malcolm told himself he should have learned by this time not to question what Perpetual could or couldn't do. With a deadly little smile on her face, she loosened several of the top buttons of her long multicolored dress and reached inside, pulling out what appeared to be some sort of amulet hung on a leather thong around her neck and lifting it over her head. Then she stepped out the back door and down the wood steps into the backyard, swinging the amulet in front of her like a thurible as she started to crisscross the yard in a diagonal checkerboard pattern. At first the boys ignored her, tossing the ball around her or waiting for her to pass before running a base, but then stopped and watched her, Perpetual's face without expression, walking past the boys as if they weren't there, the boys growing increasingly uncomfortable with every pass. Finally the boy Malcolm first talked to said, "Let's get out of here," and another one said, "Yeah, she's scary," and the boys headed back around the side of the house, looking over their shoulders to make sure Perpetual wasn't following them.

Malcolm looked questioningly at the women. "But what did she do?"

Margaret, who had joined the others at the window, went back to her corner. "Everybody in town is scared of Miss Perpetual." She looked at Malcolm: "Everybody should be, too."

The boys never came back after that evening, nor did Malcolm ever encounter them on his walks to and from the steamworks. But for a year afterward, when he walked past the shacks at the foot of the hill, occasionally a crabapple or piece of rotten fruit would come winging at him from out of nowhere. Nor did he ever speak to John Lincoln about the events of that evening or if his son was still having trouble with the older boys; as much as he wanted to help his son, Malcolm had to admit he really didn't want to know because he didn't know what he could do for him. But thinking about that evening now, in light of his earlier thoughts of ignoring Mary Lydia as she was growing up, he realized there was another aspect of that evening that he'd never considered before. He always thought that evening was about John Lincoln; but Mary Lydia was part of it too, or should have been. Malcolm totally ignored the girl's desire to play baseball with the rest of them; he brushed it aside when she mentioned it because it seemed ridiculous at the time, girls didn't do such things, they shouldn't want to because they didn't do them well. He never considered that she might want to regardless, wanted to because she thought it might be fun. He remembered that later that evening he happened to look out the back window and saw Mary Lydia and Perpetual in the backyard; Perpetual was teaching Mary Lydia how to hit a ball, how to hold the bat on her shoulder and swing, and later, how to catch, keep her eye on the ball all the way into the glove, how to throw overhand. He watched until they had to stop because it had grown too dark to see. He remembered that at the time all he wondered about was where on earth Perpetual got the ball and gloves and bat.

Coming from behind him, from below in the town, were the distant sounds of fireworks, the crackle of firecrackers, the whistle of skyrockets, the festivities for the Fourth starting up again after the debacle at the end of the parade. And the sound of a Flivver coming up the road from town, a Bouncing Betty, a Leaping Lena, a Tin Lizzie. McArtle and Libby went sailing past him, each with an arm raised in salute; the Model T continued up the road the quarter mile or so and turned into the driveway to Sycamore House. Did Gus really think the Lylemobile could compete with those? Henry Ford was turning out gasoline-fueled cars every three minutes, so they said—at best, the Keystone Steam Works might be able to turn out three Lylemobiles a day. More to the point, despite the rigmarole of starting a gas-fueled car— and the talk was that they were developing an electric starter that would eliminate the crank—the time for the steam engine to compete with the internal combustion engine for automobiles was past, regardless how much safer, fuel efficient, and environmentally friendly the steam engine was over its rival. The vox populi had spoken, as misguided and driven by the wrong concerns, the easy wants and false hungers, as usual. There might be a place for steam with heavier vehicles, but in automobiles it certainly seemed a lost cause.

The shadows of the sycamores in the yard laced across the front of the house, vague and unsettled. This is my father's world, a voice sang in Malcolm's thoughts, he shines in all that's fair. Malcolm was proud of Sycamore House, the distinctive architecture of the white frame structure, a classic example of what was called Carpenter Gothic, though with a number of individual touches, the veranda extending the width of the house, the twin high-peaked gabled windows on the second floor flanking the balcony over the double front doors and the wide front steps. But he was aware as always that he hadn't been the one to build it, it wasn't his house originally, he had inherited it, though he had left his mark on it, the addition of the two wings, one on each end, to provide living space for his children as they got older and had their own families. As he walked up the drive he wondered what his father thought about each night when he walked home as he approached the house. Did Colin wonder about his children, if he was doing what was best for them? His father certainly had done no better than Malcolm with his own daughter; Malcolm's sister Anna fled Furnass when she was eighteen to become an actress in New York and had never returned, rarely even wrote to tell them she was still alive. The truth was his father's first priority wasn't raising his children, his first concern was to develop his business, the Keystone Steam Works; his father might claim that building the business was to leave a legacy for his children, but Malcolm knew better, the man would have devoted his life to the steamworks regardless.

But Malcolm couldn't claim to have done much better, for all his trying. His relationship with Gus was ill-fated—how could the boy have any respect or trust in his father after what he had done to his mother? But Malcolm knew he had done nothing afterward to reach out to the boy. The truth was Gus reminded him too much of his first wife, Lydia, his first love; since the accident and her subsequent death, Malcolm not only didn't approach his firstborn son, he actively avoided him. By the time the twins came along, the management of the steamworks demanded all of his time; he tried to keep tabs on their upbringing—he could see now he was mainly interested in John Lincoln's upbringing—but asking about them was about the extent of his involvement. For better or worse, he left raising the children to his wife, Missy, though he suspected that much of the actual hands-on child-rearing was done by Perpetual and Margaret under the watchful eye of their grandmother.

When he reached the house and climbed the front steps, he found the double doors standing open—because they knew he was coming, or just hadn't gotten around to closing them?—and Libby and McArtle in the front hallway, his mother recounting the day's events to Missy, Perpetual, and Margaret.

". . . and here comes Gus in the well-driller, the derrick half-up after ripping down all the decorations over the street and dragging them behind him and all the people along the curbs having to play jump rope not to get knocked over. . . ."

He would have stayed to listen to her version of the events but the phone was ringing in his study and he went to answer it.

24

Missy watched her husband come through the foyer into the house and down the hallway to join the little group in front of the stairs—Margaret from the kitchen; Perpetual on the last step coming from the second floor; Missy herself from the living room—listening to Libby tell the story of Gus and the well-driller ripping down the decorations over the street and scattering the spectators in his wake. The way Libby told the story had Margaret and Perpetual and Dr McArtle laughing, though Missy didn't think it was so funny. Apparently neither did Malcolm, but Missy knew that look on his face all too well; she knew he was barely listening, he never really listened to anything that didn't directly concern him, or concern the business, which was the same thing. When the phone rang in his study, he hurried away from the others to answer it, relief written all over his face.

Malcolm, Malcolm, Malcolm. This wasn't the way she thought their life would be at all. Her life. She thought that she was marrying into a family of prominence and prestige, a family whose social position bested her own—she was the only daughter of the first chairman of the History Department at Covenant College—an upper level of the town's social strata that, until the age of twenty-nine, she had never encountered firsthand and considered unattainable. The Lyles along with two or three other families in town, the old-money families, owners of the industries and banks upon which the town was founded and which kept the town alive, seemed to exist on another level of reality, a higher level of existence, up there in the social stratosphere, viewable from down below perhaps with the everyday folk, but unreachable, beyond knowing. Then the next thing she knew she was the wife of

Malcolm Lyle, honored and celebrated as if, with one simple ceremony, she had been lifted up on wings of glory. But within a few months of taking her wedding vows, she found the Lyles were all too human, all too knowable, all too much like everybody else; she found she had fallen into what she considered a collection of fools, a family whose values were based on pretense and delusion, self-deception and ignorance, a family who lacked true refinement and intelligence beyond how lever A moved gear B. The worst part was that she couldn't even blame Malcolm for getting her into the situation, that he had somehow misrepresented himself and how their life would be together. She did it to herself, with her eyes wide open, albeit with eyes full of star-stuff, fairy powder, seeing in front of her a man who never existed in the first place.

In fact, she realized that before they were married she never saw the whole man at all; she saw only his hands. It was his hands she first noticed, first paid attention to, his hands that she fell in love with. She knew who Malcolm Lyle was, of course, from growing up in Furnass, but she actually met him for the first time at the dedication of the new steeple and bell for the administration building at Covenant College, the steeple and bell donated by the Lyle family and the Keystone Steam Works. She had been on the dais with her father during the ceremony. Afterward, Malcolm preceded her off the platform, then turned and offered his hand to help her down the steps. His hand covered with scars and burned skin.

She hesitated only a second, an involuntary recoil at the sight of the ruined flesh, but it was enough, and she knew Malcolm was aware of her hesitation. No, it was stronger than that: her revulsion. It wasn't as if she hadn't been aware of his affliction beforehand, she just never expected the burns to look that . . . ugly. Hideous, even. For as long as she was aware that there was an individual in town named Malcolm Lyle, she had heard the stories of his wife being burned in a trench and his terrible mistake—some called it a tragedy; some called it stupidity; some made jokes about chicken-fried wife and a floury divorce—but to her the real story was in his attempts to beat out the flames with his bare hands and the wounds he suffered. She felt terrible that she acted the way she did at the sight of his hands, but there was nothing she could do about it once it happened. At the reception on the lawn after the dedication she did everything she could to avoid the man so she wouldn't have to face him again, so she wouldn't add to his embarrassment, and hers.

Then while she was at the refreshment table getting a refill of the fruit punch, Malcolm came over and stood beside her, close enough that she couldn't get away without appearing rude.

"Excuse me, you're Missy Sarver, aren't you? Professor Sarver's daughter?"

He wasn't an exceptionally tall man, but she was rather short, and it required her to lean back slightly to address him. "And you're Malcolm Lyle."

"I am indeed," he said, with a smile that seemed to infuse even his eyes. "I would offer to shake your hand but I believe you already noticed my condition."

Without hesitating she reached over and took his hand in hers. "I did. I hope this doesn't hurt you."

"On the contrary," Malcolm said. "My hand has never felt better."

She expected he'd go away as soon as the pleasantries were over, but he didn't; they ended up spending the rest of the afternoon together, strolling along the crisscross walks of the campus, talking about one thing and another; afterward, she couldn't have told you what they talked about, she only knew that he fascinated her, she was fascinated that apparently he was fascinated with her. She had reached an age—she would be thirty the following year—when she was beginning to think that romance and marriage were things that were never going to happen for her, not from a lack of offers, but because none of her would-be suitors ever came close to meeting her standards. The importance she placed on "measuring up" was not from the awareness of her own lack of stature, though the fact that she was shorter than normal certainly had an effect on her viewpoint of the world. She had spent her adult life at a child's level, a world of belt buckles and elbows, a crowd of any size a cause for panic, the threat of literally being trampled or pushed aside; she had learned to do the pushing first, to elbow her way through uncomfortable situations, and by like measure, to judge people by their levels of learning and refinement, the connection in her mind being that such people would be less crude and less likely to walk all over her, either literally or figuratively. Yet here was this older man who was not particularly noteworthy in either learning or refinement—and though not particularly tall was large enough it seemed to make two of her—but for whom the measuring sticks evidently didn't apply in light of Missy's inability to stop smiling as they walked around the campus. It was a further surprise when a week after the dedication Malcolm turned up at the Sarver house on Orchard Hill, hat in scarred hand, to see her.

Her mother greeted him at the door and showed him into the parlor before going to get Missy, upstairs in her room. Missy had never thought their house particularly small, but Malcolm, when he stood up as she entered the room, seemed to fill it, absorb the furniture and walls into himself—he didn't have to duck to keep from hitting his head on the ceiling but it wouldn't have surprised her if he did.

"I hope you don't object to me just turning up this way. I probably should have telephoned beforehand, but I thought. . . ."

He let his thought dwindle away.

"No, it's fine," she said, wishing more than anything that she had put on her new crepe dress with the little red poppies this morning as she was originally going to, instead of this old gray thing she was wearing, but there was nothing to do about it now. "It's nice to see you. But I'll admit I'm a bit puzzled. Are you sure you're not here to see my father?"

"Why would I want to see your father?"

"About the changes at the college."

Malcolm shook his head, laughed deprecatingly. "Well, now I'm the one who's puzzled. I don't know anything about changes at the college. . . ."

Missy looked around; she could hear her mother in the dining room, she supposed her father was in his study if he was home at all, but one of them could walk in on them at any time. "Let me get a sweater and we can go outside in the yard. It's a little chilly today but it's still sunny—don't want to waste a nice day before the snow comes."

She hurriedly got her camel cardigan from the hall coat closet—it didn't go with her gray dress but it would have to do— and led him back out the front door and around the side of the house to the large back yard. It was a gray stone cottage built in the English style, with a high-peaked, steeply pitched roof and cross-gables, a broad stone chimney facing the street, and tall narrow multi-paned windows, surrounded by shrubs pressing up from the foundation. The large lot was on the back side of Orchard Hill, the backyard sloping slightly toward the edge of the hillside. Their footfalls crunched in the leaves of the syca- mores and maples as she led him to a bench at the end of the yard overlooking Walnut Bottom Run.

"Is something wrong?" Malcolm said, sitting beside her. "You seem concerned—"

"No, no, it's nothing really," Missy said, patting her cloche-like blond hair into place, aware of how the way she was acting must look to him. "I just didn't want my father to overhear . . . anything. . . ."

"Why did you think I wanted to talk to your father about changes at the college?"

"I was just being silly," Missy said wagging her shoulders from side to side. "Silly ol' me. I know you're involved with the college, that's where I saw you the other day, and I made the wrong assumption. It didn't occur to me that you'd be here to see me."

"Well, I did come to see you. But now you've got me curious. What are these changes at the college, and what do they have to do with your father?"

Missy sighed, readjusted her hands in her lap. "There's been talk about folding the History Department, of which my father is the chairman, into the Theology Department. He would still hold his professorship of course, he's tenured, but he would no longer be the chairman, and it would destroy everything he's work so hard to build up for the department."

"I can see how having History subservient to Theology would fit the viewpoint of the more conservative members of the board of trustees. But that certainly doesn't seem the best curriculum for students to get a balanced education."

"The rationale they're giving for the change is economic. They're saying that with the current level of enrollment the college can't afford the administration expenses of two separate departments. But Father is sure it's political. He's made it into a first-rate history department, one that can hold its own with the bigger universities, but he did so by having his students question the established histories; he insists that they go back to the primary sources and draw their own conclusions."

"It certainly sounds heretical to me," Malcolm said, grinning.

"And something the college would want to get under control if possible. We certainly can't have college students thinking for themselves, now, can we?"

Missy had to smile in spite of herself. It was the first time she had encountered Malcolm's ability to take a difficult situation and extend it out to its absurdity, stretch an attitude or opinion until it was easy to poke holes in it, defuse a conflict by appearing to deal with it when in fact he deftly sidestepped it as the issue went charging by like a bull after a red cloth. Her disenchantment with how Malcolm handled situations, domestic and otherwise, would come later; for now she was charmed beyond measure.

They spent that autumn afternoon getting to know each other, or rather, getting to know that part of themselves each wanted the other to know, the first of many afternoon get-togethers that took place at first at her parents' home on Orchard Hill, then became long rides in the country bundled up in Malcolm's glassine-windowed surrey. Later came a sleigh ride to cut down pine trees for both the Lyle's and Sarver's Christmas, and attendance at a candlelight service where the pastor standing at the door afterward made a point to say that it was an occasion to see Malcolm at church, it certainly wasn't something that happened very often. As she got to know him better over the span of months, she couldn't understand how anyone in town could think ill of him; she especially couldn't understand how anyone could think him less than a hero for trying to save his wife as she lay burning in the trench. His hands, the scarred and ravaged skin, became the symbol of the man to her, emblematic of his courage and strength and devotion to those he loved; she held his hands whenever she could, and as they became more intimate, raised them to her lips, traced the ridges of the scars with her tongue, rested her cheek against the husk-like flesh.

Then it was her turn to appear at his door unannounced. It

took her three different trolleys to get there, but one morning in early spring she presented herself at the offices of the Keystone Steam Works and asked for Malcolm Lyle. The look on his face when she walked through the door of his office was itself worth all the effort to get there.

"Missy! What on earth are you doing here?" He started to bend over to kiss her, holding on to her shoulders like handlebars, but realized the secretaries and clerks in the outer office could see them. He ended up just patting her shoulders as if molding her and escorted her inside his office, getting her settled in one of the tall leather wing-back chairs and then hustling around to his side of his desk. "What brings you all the way down here? Why didn't you tell me you were coming?"

"We've had some good news," she said, sitting forward in the chair, taking off her gloves and clasping her bare hands in her lap. "And I wanted to tell you in person."

"Excellent, excellent. What is your good news?"

"Well, my father just learned that there will be no more talk of merging the History Department with the Theology Department."

"Really," Malcolm said, sitting back in his chair as if retreating to a corner, pushing away from the desk far enough so he could cross his legs. "That certainly is good news. Your father must be very relieved."

"Oh, he is, he is. But there's more. It seems that the reason they won't be merging the departments is that there's been an anonymous donation to the college, the establishment of an endowed chair in History for the college. It's to be called the Duncan MacMurchie Chair in History. And it seems one of the stipulations of the endowment is that the History Department remains autonomous."

"Really," Malcolm said.

"Really," Missy said. "And the other stipulation is that my

father is the first to hold the Duncan MacMurchie Chair in History, and retain his position as head of the department."

Malcolm was looking at his hands, tracing one of the scars over the hills and valleys of the bones.

"It took him some research to find out who exactly Duncan MacMurchie is, or was. It seems that Duncan MacMurchie owned or at least took care of the land where the original iron furnace was constructed close to the Allehela, the furnace around which the town of Furnass grew. He was the father-in-law of the founder of that furnace, a man named Malcolm Lyle. Your namesake, I assume. Your grandfather. So Duncan MacMurchie would be your great-grandfather."

"Well, your father is a historian. And a good one. I shouldn't be surprised that he discovered the origins."

"You didn't have to do that, Malcolm."

"In a way, I did. It needed to be done. The college is important to this town, it raises us above being just another mill town. So we need the college to be the best it can be. We can't have a conservative faction holding back the quality of education that's offered. Lord knows—no pun intended, though maybe there is— being a Covenanter college, it's hard enough to—"

"Malcolm," Missy said for the third time, and Malcolm finally got the message and stopped talking. "What I meant was that you didn't have to do that for me. I'm impressed enough with you as it is."

Malcolm got to his feet and came around the desk, and Missy rose to meet him, wrapping her arms around his middle while he more or less hugged her head.

He called her his Pocket Love, and later, after they were married, his Pocket Wife. A name she liked in the beginning because she thought it originated with the time she told him that she wished he could carry her around in his pocket so she'd be with him all the time, hear what he heard, see what he saw. Later, though, she came to realize that the name must have come from other sources, other connections in his mind. It was after they made love one night, the first time they did so after close to a year of marriage—what turned out to be the only time they made love—when they were lying side-by-side in the tangle of night-clothes and bedsheets, when he traced his finger down the length of her body, starting with her shoulder and running down to her knee, and said, "You're like a miniature of a woman."

She looked at him questioningly. "Meaning?"

"You're like a detailed scale model of. . . ." He let the thought trail off.

"A detailed scale model of a real woman? Is that what you're trying to say?"

"No, that's not . . . you know what I mean. . . ."

Unfortunately, she was getting a good idea what he meant. The real woman she was being compared to wasn't real at all, it was the ghost of his first wife, Lydia, a ghost in what seemed a house of ghosts, or spirits of some kind. Thinking back, she realized that her life at home on Orchard Hill had been idyllic, all things considered. After graduating from Covenant College, she tried teaching, she even found a position at the grade school downtown in Furnass, but she left in tears after a few months and never tried it again. For one thing, she learned she didn't like children all that much; for another she learned they didn't like her. Because she was not that much taller than some of her students, they had little or no respect for her, particularly the boys, the sons of mill hands and laborers; the truth was that children scared her, facing forty or fifty of the little devils at a time. After that she occupied herself with some charity work at the hospital, and helped her father with research at the college library, sometimes traveling to Pittsburgh to visit libraries for him there. But most of the time she spent at home, idling around the house—her mother wouldn't let her help with the cleaning or laundry or cooking, having staked out these duties for her own sense of self—crocheting and embroidering and reading anything that came her way, from romance novels to Emerson.

So she wasn't at all prepared for the life she was expected to lead in Sycamore House. There was the fact that she was stepping into an established household where the responsibilities and duties were already defined. How could she be expected to supervise or even collaborate with Margaret the cook and housekeeper when Missy herself couldn't cook and had never kept house? Moreover, how could she be expected to interrelate with Perpetual when, first of all, Perpetual was said to be her mother-in-law's personal attendant and untouchable as far as anyone else in the household was concerned; and second of all, Missy had never dealt with domestics of any kind. Because, personal attendant or no, Perpetual ran the household, nothing happened in the house that Perpetual wasn't at least aware of and usually had a hand in. And she did so with Libby's unspoken authority. The old woman's presence was felt throughout the house, and Libby and Perpetual moved through the rooms and hallways in their old-fashioned ankle-to-neck dresses like twin hallucinations, one black, one multicolored, specters of another age or world. How was Missy expected to be the woman of the house in the presence of all that?

Then there was Malcolm, or the lack of same. As soon as they were married and Missy had moved into the house, her husband all but disappeared. He said it was because of his work, that his responsibilities at the steamworks demanded that he be on-site for long hours, seven days a week; he said she should have known this about him. The little time he was home, he barricaded himself in his study at the front of the house, appearing only for meals and to go to bed. He made it clear, nevertheless, that he expected the house to continue its already established routines, routines Missy learned that were established by Malcolm's first wife, Lydia. Meals were late, at eight or nine in the evening, because Lydia thought they were more elegant that way; the menus of what dishes were prepared—a soup course, whether one wanted it or not, usually a clear broth or occasionally with lentils or beans; always two kinds of meat, beef or lamb, and chicken or ham, never fish; three vegetable dishes, including at least one of potatoes, all in heavy sauce; a simple salad of lettuce and tomatoes and carrots, always carrots; dessert was one of Margaret's fruit pies or an angel food cake—and how they were served according to Lydia's tastes. If nothing else Missy worried about the waste of the food left over from such extravagant meals; but it turned out that Margaret took the remains with her when she left the house each night and walked down the dirt road across the slope of the valley to her home and distributed the food to those in need in Black Town.

The chores for the days of the week—Monday-washing; Tuesday-ironing; Wednesday-mending; Thursday-marketing; Friday-baking; Saturday-cleaning—were kept not because they were traditional but because Lydia always kept them that way, a rule of order that Missy found was sacrosanct when she tried to have Margaret do the marketing on Wednesday instead of Thursday; Margaret quit on the spot and walked out of the house, Perpetual had to go herself to Black Town and ask the older woman to come back on the promise that things would go back to the way they were. As for being a mother Missy learned early on that her stepson, Augustus, wanted nothing to do with her, the saving grace being that the boy apparently didn't want anything to do with anyone, staying most of the time in his room playing with his collection of toy soldiers. When the twins, John

Lincoln and Mary Lydia, came along, Missy figured she had had enough of them after carting them around for nine months and then suffering the pain of childbirth. She willingly gave their care over to Perpetual and Margaret, having already learned she was no good with children; plus it was apparent the two women were hell-bent on raising the children their way regardless, which meant the way Lydia would have raised them. It took a few years from the time Missy came to join the family, but soon enough whatever ideas and hopes she had for being the mistress of Sycamore House were snuffed out under the collective weight of the house's ghosts and spirits, living and dead.

But the deadliest ghost of all was the shade of what the family once meant to the town, and how the family perceived itself now that it no longer held that position. The family was haunted by its former prominence; its former prestige was a spirit that lived on in the household but was suffering a slow death, that refused to die. To help keep it alive, the family, whether aware of it or not, maintained a self-appointed grandeur, an attitude of fundamentally being better than anyone else, smarter and more knowing, a pretense that particularly rankled Missy, having grown up around truly educated people. Rankled her enough that one day she finally had enough. Something within her snapped. Broke. Gave up. That morning she only got out of bed long enough to change her nightdress for her best white gauzy peignoir, then climbed back into bed and spent the day luxuriating at the idea that in fact she didn't have to do anything today, she actually didn't have anything to do ever, that the household could run along just fine without her, that her presence wouldn't make any difference regardless; she was content to lie in bed and wiggle her toes at her newfound sense of freedom, watching out the window where the leaves of the sycamores in the side yard waved to her occasionally. When she hadn't appeared for breakfast or lunch,

Perpetual, as if she knew intuitively what was going on with Missy, knocked on the bedroom door and came in carrying a tray with tomato soup, an egg salad sandwich—the crusts removed and cut into triangles the way Missy liked—and a cup of tea. After getting Missy propped up on pillows and the tray secure in her lap, Perpetual said, "Well then, do you have everything you need?"

"Well, now that you ask," Missy said, "I left some magazines in the living room yesterday, if you could get them for me. Please." She was particularly proud of the "Please," she thought it added just the right tone of graciousness.

Perpetual cocked her head at her, nodded, and left the room. Returning in a few minutes with the stack of magazines.

"Thank you, Perpetual. I appreciate it. And this lunch is just wonderful. Very thoughtful, indeed."

"Is there anything else?"

"No, no, I can't think of anything at the moment. Perhaps we can rig up a bell arrangement if I think of something later. . . ."

Perpetual had started to turn away from the bed. But she came back now, one hand clasping the other across her diaphragm as if she were about to sing an aria, a look on her face that wasn't unfriendly but that said, Don't trifle with me.

"I know what you're doing, Mrs. Lyle. Missy. And I can't say I blame you. Not in the least. I don't know how you've put up with it as long as you have. Perpetual's all in favor of conversing with the dead but only if it helps understand the living. Keeping them around just to keep them around, Perpetual has no truck with that. The idea, using her hair for his watch fob—"

"What?"

"Mr. Malcolm's watch fob. You never saw what it is? It's Mrs. Lydia's braid, he had it cut off after she was fried in the trench and uses it to hang his watch on. That's powerful medicine, that.

No wonder the woman won't stay in her grave and wanders around."

"Do you see her, Perpetual? Walking around here? I just know she's here, I can feel her." Missy hugged herself as if she felt a chill.

Perpetual thought of something for a moment, then decided against it, shook her head, focused back on Missy. "That there is nobody's business. But what is my business is that Perpetual knows what you're doing. And Perpetual will go along with it today. But that's the end of it. Tomorrow you're on your own. Perpetual don't care if you don't get dressed or you walk around the house in your bare nudities, it makes no never mind to Perpetual. But as for Mrs. Missy, you'll need to fend for yourself, Perpetual isn't going to wait on you, no ma'am. That day is only this day and this day is over tomorrow."

Missy rarely got dressed after that day. A few times a year she put on street clothes to visit her parents on Orchard Hill, but they were standoffish now that she had become a Lyle, as if she had an affliction and they were afraid it might be catching. Otherwise, except for an occasional shopping trip to Pittsburgh, she stayed at home, dressed in her growing collection of peignoirs and gauzy wrappers, joining the others for meals and such, sometimes making a pretense of supervising Margaret in the kitchen or the girls that Margaret brought in from Black Town to do the laundry and cleaning and straightening up, a parody of what a true mistress of the house would do, but that was the extent of her involvement with the world; she spent most of her days camped out in the living room going through her supply of magazines— *Red Book* and *The Saturday Evening Post, The Ladies World* and *Good Housekeeping, Vogue* and *Vanity Fair* and *Harper's Bazaar*—and eating chocolate-covered bonbons. All spirit, all initiative, life itself for all intents and purposes was drained out of her. And Malcolm never said a word. True, he was never around that much to comment one way or the other; he left early for the steamworks long before Missy was up, and when he returned in the evenings he retreated to his study after dinner and she was usually asleep when he eventually came to bed. For that matter, she wasn't even sure that he noticed the change that had come over her.

She was an outsider in her own family, a fact that was apparent all over again as she stood in the hallway listening to her mother-in-law and Dr. McArtle relate the events of the Fourth of July parade. Libby's telling of the story was directed to Perpetual and Margaret, the domestics as it were—to Perpetual only, if the truth be known—it didn't include Missy; Libby didn't look her direction, smile her direction, gesture in her direction; it was as if Missy wasn't there at all. After a few minutes Missy turned and walked away from the others, went back into the living room where she had left her latest copy of *Movie Pictorial*. From here, standing beside the couch looking out into the hallway, the little group at the foot of the stairs looked like its own silent picture, a dumb show of familiar but unsympathetic characters. It was complete when Gus, her stepson, came in the front door, joining in the muted hilarity for a moment until Malcolm appeared from his study, a grave look on his face that sobered the others, the group frozen in a kind of dread. Then the scream.

25

Gus was mortified. He wanted to get the well-driller with its collection of ripped-away banners and tree branches off the main street as soon as he could—he wanted to go hide somewhere, crawl in a corner and curl into a ball and bury his head—but even though the horses he frightened had scattered the closing units of the parade, the curbs were still crowded with spectators. The intersections were full of people so he couldn't turn down a cross street; and as if things weren't embarrassing enough, people along the curbs were laughing and cheering and applauding him, as if his disruption of the parade was part of the show, something planned and intended to add to the day's entertainment, instead of a terrible, terrible mistake, the result of his stupidity and clumsiness, another Gus bungle, he couldn't do anything right. He finally turned at Seventeenth Street and headed down the hill toward the river, the few people along the sidewalks and on their porches and front yards waving to him, children pumping their arms for him to blow the whistle. When he got to the steamworks, he thought he was safe, away from the public eye. He turned into the entrance, through the tunnel under the administrative offices, but news of his debacle had already reached the plant; the workmen who had prepared the machines for the parade all hooted and hollered as he pulled into the yard, clapping each other on the back and doubling over with laughter. When Gus came to a stop near the boiler shop, MacIninch the foreman came over, a wide grin under his ginger mustache.

"Aye, laddie. Well, you certainly did for yourself this time, didn't you, now?"

Gus stepped off the rear platform, pulled off the leather sleeves, threw them on the ground at his feet.

"Okay, Mac, have your day. I know I bollixed it up."

"Aye, you did that, sure enough. But don't fret, from what the lads tell me everyone upstreet got a big hoot out of it, you're the talk of the town."

Just what he didn't want to be, but there was no help for it at this point. He remembered he had promised to drive his grandmother home after the parade; he wondered if she could bear to be seen with him now. He went over and fired up his Lylemobile and headed out of the yard again, up the hill back to the scene of his fiasco. Traffic had resumed on Eighth Avenue but there was no one on the reviewing stand, his grandmother must have found another ride home. The sight of the statue in the park, still covered with a tarpaulin prior to her dedication, brought back his shame and guilt all over again, he had ruined the day for her. He would have done anything if he could to make it better, to relive the morning and his foolish choices, but all he could do now was add it to the ever-growing list of Gus' follies. And go on.

He remembered seeing Emma Edgeworth in the crowd before the parade turned up Tenth Street. On a whim, he drove up Fifteenth Street and headed back down Ninth Avenue to Eleventh Street, then turned up the hill and entered the alley, he wasn't going to hide the car this time. He parked in front of Emma Edgeworth's outbuildings, snuffed the engine, climbed out of the car, and went over to the backyard gate. And stopped. Bert Featherstone, in his shirtsleeves, was sitting astraddle the bench on one side of the wood picnic table in her backyard. As Gus watched, Emma came out of the kitchen door and down the back steps carrying a tray with sandwiches, a pie, and a pitcher of lemonade and glasses, unloading the tray on the table as Bert Featherstone rubbed her buttocks. Bert Featherstone said something and they laughed; then Emma happened to look up and saw Gus standing at the gate. She reached down and held Bert Featherstone's face with two hands and kissed him on the mouth, then sashayed back to the house. On the steps she paused and looked over her shoulder, giving Gus a little wave of her fingers, a gesture that Bert Featherstone thought was meant for him and waved to her in return. Emma laughed and went on into the house. Gus went back to his car, thinking, Well, it serves me right, what did I think was going to happen, what did I want to happen? Nothing that should. Good God, I'm a married man, like Father said, I love Lily, she'll come back from Kansas and everything will be all right, I've got to get hold of myself, I'm better than this, I have to be better than this. . . .

When he arrived at Sycamore House, he saw Dr. McArtle's Model T parked in front and guessed how his grandmother must have got home. He climbed out of the Lylemobile and walked over to the Model T, giving it the once-over. Could he really see his steam car in competition with this gas-fueled car? Probably not, he had to admit, they certainly could never match Ford's ability to turn out cars with his assembly line. But it's more than that, Gus thought. The Lylemobile is safer, better made, more economical to run, better and more responsible for the environment. Yet people have already made up their minds, they won't even look at the Lylemobile as an alternative, or if they do, see the value of the steam car, they choose the gas-fueled car anyway, who knows why? Wretched democracy in action: everything reduced to the lowest common denominator. How do you live with that, if you're trying to reach higher, do better, have ideas that don't fit the common mold? I guess it doesn't help if you're basically a bungler, there's nothing so simple that I can't complicate, nothing so straightforward that I can't put a kink in it. I've got a talent for it, that's probably what my father would say. But when does self-knowledge turn into self-pity?

He shook his head, this wasn't going to solve anything; he climbed the steps and entered the front door. And was greeted with his grandmother announcing, "Here he is now, the man of the hour!"

The little assemblage—his grandmother, Dr. McArtle, Perpetual, Margaret, with his mother listening from the living room—applauded and cheered and laughed, Dr. McArtle patted him on the shoulder.

"Grandmother, I'm so sorry—"

"Oh piffle, I won't hear of it. I wouldn't change what happened for anything. Oh, the looks of horror on the mayor and all those fancy-pants officials. And those decorations all needed to be re-placed anyway. Your father has been too cheap to buy the city new ones, now he'll have to. Isn't that right, Malcolm?"

Malcolm had emerged from his study at the front of the house, but he seemed dazed, uncomprehending. He held his hands in front of him as if he carried some small dead bundle.

"Malcolm, are you all right?" Dr. McArtle said, going over to him. "What's wrong?"

"The phone," Malcolm said, not focusing on anything, as if trying to see something in the distance. "That was a steamship company. In New York. There was a mine in the harbor . . . the ship John Lincoln was on. . . ."

"What happened?"

"They said he was standing up on the railing, waving at some-thing," Malcolm said. "The ship's okay they said. . . ."

"Malcolm," Libby said.

"He fell overboard," Malcolm said, looking at them all for the first time. "With the explosion. John Lincoln drowned. He's dead."

There was a scream from the top of the stairs. Mary Lydia was standing braced against the newel-post, the skirt of her blood-soaked nightdress hiked up to her waist, holding with one hand something bloody and slimy and awful spilling out of her from between her legs, screaming again, "John Lincoln! John Lincoln!"

Gus was the first one to react. He ran up the steps two at a time, reaching Mary Lydia as she started to collapse, gathering her up and lifting her in his arms, carrying her back down the corridor to her room. Dr. McArtle was close behind him and helped Malcolm get Mary Lydia onto the bed. Then McArtle took charge, calling downstairs, "Somebody get my case from my car.

And I need warm water and towels, lots of towels, hurry!"

Missy was on her way up the steps. "Perpetual, get the doctor's case. And you, Margaret—" But Margaret was already headed toward the kitchen.

Things were swirling around Gus. The moment of clarity he experienced when he knew he had to reach Mary Lydia before she fell was gone, now everything was a blur. Dr. McArtle was bracing pillows under Mary Lydia's legs and trying to reassure her, while Missy was on the other side of the bed helping to get her daughter arranged among the tangle of sheets. Then Perpetual was there with the doctor's case and McArtle was sterilizing instruments with alcohol, tending to the discharge and water and blood oozing out on the bed as Mary Lydia cried hysterically, screamed in pain and fear, still calling for her brother. Gus came to himself with Perpetual's hand on his arm.

"You should leave. If we need you we'll call. She's got the doctor and her mother."

"Yes, certainly," Gus muttered, aware now that he shouldn't be there, embarrassed that he still was. He backed out of the room as Margaret came laboring up the stairs and down the hall carrying a large bowl of water and a stack of towels. Gus, still dazed, Mary Lydia's screams in his ears, wobbled down the hall, physically shaken, braced on the banister, stopping at the top of the stairs. There was a stain on the floor where his half-sister had stood, blood and viscous liquid. At the foot of the stairs, his father was still standing where he was before Mary Lydia screamed, as if rooted to the spot. For a long moment father and son stared at each other, one at the top of the stairs, one at the bottom, as if separated by miles. Until Malcolm turned away.

26

I lay in bed with them sitting on either side of me, Perpetual on one side, Missy on the other, listening to them talk. Missy—I wanted to think of her as Mother, but couldn't, she never acted as a mother to us when we were growing up, and none of us children ever called her that; if anyone was called Mother in the household it was my father's mother, Libby; my mother was always called Missy. They must have thought I couldn't hear them, so I kept my eyes closed, peeking at them occasionally through half-open lids, wondering what they would say. Missy was there earlier and must have just come back into the room, maybe that's what woke me. I expected Perpetual to be there—she was always there, she who did all the mothering to John Lincoln and me growing up—but I was surprised that my mother would care.

"She's still asleep?" Missy said.

"She stirred a little while ago, but she's still out. Poor dear."

"She's had a hard time. Dr. McArtle said that what he gave her would keep her under for several hours. Rest is the most important thing for her now."

"You changed your clothes," Perpetual said. Missy was wearing a street dress, serviceable lace-up brown shoes. Practical, everyday clothes.

"Yes. I want to be ready if the doctor decides to move her to the hospital when he gets back." Missy was quiet for a moment. "Besides, I think it's time I put away the nightclothes, don't you? Except for nights."

"That probably be true. Perpetual thinks they served your purpose."

"I'm not so sure. Malcolm never seemed to notice."

"Maybe he noticed and decided if that was what you were going to do, if that's what you needed to do, he wasn't going to try to stop his wife. Maybe it be an act of love."

"Or maybe it was not caring enough to care."

"That be the prickly part of love, isn't it? Separating what's there from what you think be there. Maybe that's the prickly part of living."

Their voices were soothing, they were speaking softly so as not to wake me, but they were actually putting me back to sleep, I felt myself drifting off, so many memories coming back, those times so real again. We were eight or so, and your favorite song was "A Bird in a Gilded Cage," you'd play it over and over on our new phonograph machine. You were so serious about it that I couldn't help myself, I'd sing along, "I'm only a gild in a birded cage, a beautiful sight to see . . ." and you'd get so upset, your face would turn red and you'd yell at me, "No, Lybia, it's 'I'm only a bird in a gilded cage. . . .'" And I'd sing it my way all over again, and you'd get angrier and angrier, I thought it was so funny, the look on your face, I thought you thought it was funny too, that it was a game we were playing. Then one day I sang, "I'm only a gild in a birded cage—" and you hit me, slapped me across the face, it really hurt, but you just looked at me, as if you were both surprised and amazed at what you had done, as if you just discovered something. I started to cry and you didn't know what to do, you looked around afraid somebody was going to come to see what was wrong, then to make me quiet you kissed me full on the lips, like we'd seen in pictures, you kissed me and held your mouth on mine for a long time before you broke away and I'll never forget the look on your face then, the expression as if you'd just got away with something, took something from me, then you went away. . . .

"Did she say anything while I was gone?" Missy said.

"She said John Lincoln's name again a few times in her sleep," Perpetual said. "She must have been dreaming."

They were silent for several moments. "Well, it stands to reason, doesn't it? That she would call for him now."

Perpetual only sat there looking at the diminutive woman.

"After all," Missy went on, "she was always closest to John Lincoln. They were inseparable growing up. Like one half of the other. So, it makes sense that she would call for him now, when she was having the pain and the miscarriage and all."

All Perpetual said was, "Mmmm."

"What? You don't think that's why she's calling for him now? What other explanation is there?"

"It may be what you say. It may be also she be learning that with this baby she lost more than her baby."

Then I could hear them talking but I couldn't understand what they were saying, I was drifting again, their voices far away. I remembered there was a dance at the little amusement park at the end of the trolley line beyond Orchard Hill, you and I rode the trolley together that day, it was while we were still in high school, I think it must have been Founder's Day. I was wearing a new white dress, with a high bodice and lace around the shoulders like a cape and a long skirt, I felt very adult, and was so proud to be with you, you had on new clothes too, a checked sport coat and a shirt with a high stiff collar, you looked so dapper, I thought we were a beautiful couple, I told myself someday I'll have a beau and this is the way we'll look, people will see us together and they'll think we're special. But when as we got to the park you left me on my own, you went off to talk to some other girls and I didn't know what to do with myself, I thought people were looking at me and saying, What's wrong with her, why doesn't anyone want to be with her, I felt something was wrong with me. But Billie Gibson came along and he sat with me for a while, he waited for me while I rode the carousel and then we sat on the edge of the dance pavilion and listened to the music. I didn't really like Billie Gibson all that much, he lived in the one of the shacks at the foot of the hill and didn't have very nice clothes or anything, him and the other boys who lived there used to beat up John Lincoln all the time, but he was always okay to me and that day he was nice to keep me company so I didn't feel so bad. Then you came over with a pretty girl you said was visiting from Youngstown, Janet something, and you said to her, after you introduced me as your twin sister, "See? What did I tell you? I'm the pretty one," and Janet Something laughed with you as the two of you walked away. I was crushed that you'd say such a thing about me and I started to cry but Billie Gibson tried to comfort me, he gave me his handkerchief and then he got up and went after you and when I realized why I hurried after him. I caught up to you on the other side of the pavilion and Billie Gibson was saying something to you and you said something back and then Billie Gibson pushed you on the shoulder and you stumbled backward and started to cry and I told Billie Gibson to leave you alone and he looked at me and said, "You shouldn't care what this sissy says about you, he's a nobody," and I said, "No, he isn't, he's my brother," and Billie Gibson looked at me and then at you and at me again and shook his head and headed back to the dance pavilion and I thought you'd be with me after all, that we'd be together like we were supposed to be, but Janet Something and her friends were headed toward the carousel and you hurried after them. . . .

I heard my mother say, "Do you think we should step outside?"

"No, I don't think so. She'll have to hear anything we say sometime or other."

Just the way Perpetual said it, I knew she knew I was listening, at least some of the time.

"The only other reason I can think of that she'd be calling for John Lincoln is she heard what Malcolm said about the phone call from New York." When Perpetual didn't say anything, Missy went on. "She knows John Lincoln is dead, doesn't she?"

"Perpetual's not sure how much she heard. I think so but. . . ."

"My poor beautiful baby boy," Missy said. And for once she sounded as if she meant it.

"John Lincoln be the saddest of Perpetual's little ones. He was his father's heir without a father to tell him how. He was his family's hope for the future without a family around him to help him know what he was supposed to be. When he was a little boy he would sometimes come and wrap his arms around Perpetual's legs and bury his face in Perpetual's skirt, I think he just wanted to get away from the world for a while, and he knew Perpetual would let him hide there. John Lincoln be the love of Mary Lydia's life, truth be known. But Mary Lydia be the love of John Lincoln's life too, it's just he never let himself realize it. But I don't thing John Lincoln knew how he felt about anything."

"It's true, he didn't have a proper father. He didn't have a proper mother either." Missy fell silent again.

"Do we know about the arrangements for the body?" Perpetual said.

"Gus said he would go to New York and bring John Lincoln home."

"That sounds like Gus. He be the one always ready to help the other person. But he be never able to help himself."

How well Perpetual knew us children. How well Perpetual still knows me. The love of her life, she said. Well, how else could it be? The person she always depended on to help her. Foolish foolish heart. Deadly dangerous deluded children. We were upstairs in the attic and you told me there was a cuckoo's nest under the eaves of the roof and you said the cuckoo was the most beautiful bird in the world and I wanted to see it too, and you said you'd help me and you opened the small round window at the peak of the gable and told me I'd have to lean out and I did, I leaned as far as I could and you said, "Can you see it?" and I said I couldn't and you said I'd have to lean farther and I did but I still couldn't see the cuckoo so you told me I'd have to squeeze out the window with my leg over the edge and I did so, I was sitting on the sill and I looked down and the front yard seemed to be swirling around in a circle and I felt dizzy but you said, "Go on, Lybia, lean out farther, I've got hold of your other leg," and I leaned even farther, as far as I could go, and then you weren't holding me anymore, I felt you let go and I started to fall and reached back and grabbed the edge of the window and screamed and Gus was just coming home and he looked up and saw me, "Hang on, Mary Lydia, hang on, I'm coming!" and he ran into the house and I could hear him coming, running up the steps and calling to me to hang on and then he was in the attic, I heard him push you out of the way as he hurried over to the window and I felt his strong grasp of my leg and he was talking to me all calm and reassuring, telling me not to be afraid, that he was there, and I wasn't afraid then and he helped me climb back in the window and you just stood there across the room watching, you didn't help me at all and you didn't say anything, you just stood there with a kind of little grin on your face and then Gus exploded, screaming at you, "What the hell were you trying to do? Were you trying to kill her? What's wrong with you?" but you still didn't say anything, you just shrugged and then you went away, back down the attic steps, and yes, I know now that was it, you actually were trying to kill me, not because you hated me or anything or even that you wanted me dead but because you were just curious to see what would happen. I was never another person to you, I was just another half of you that you thought you could do anything you wanted to for your experiments, your amusements, your little setups just to see what would happen if. I thought I loved you but I didn't, not really, we were just halves of another person, a person known as the Twins, I thought I needed you to complete me, but I know now I didn't and I don't, you were just the only love I had known but now I know better, when you left me you left me to find I can be a whole person on my own without you, in fact I'm better off without you. I never thought I'd say this in a hundred years but I'm glad you're gone. Because now I'm me.

In the bed I opened my eyes.

"Oh look," Missy exclaimed. "She's back with us."

Perpetual got up, leaned over me, looked into my eyes. "No, this girl never been here before," she said, tucking the covers in around my shoulders, then kissed me on the forehead.

27

She was standing outside, at the railing of the balcony, looking at the night, the occasional fireworks reaching up into the night sky from the town below in the valley, when she heard the knock on her bedroom door. She decided it had to be Malcolm: Perpetual would have walked right in, and everyone else in the household knew better than to disturb Libby at this hour—unless it was an emergency, and there better not be an emergency associated with such a timid knock. No, it had to be Malcolm. Regardless, she stayed where she was, enjoying the night air, but wasn't surprised when she heard him come through the French doors behind her—his boot heel clacked on the threshold; Lift your feet, my son—and he joined her at the railing, standing beside her though not too close, looking out at the night as if he had been there the whole time.

"What did young Dr. McArtle have to say? I saw him leave a while ago," she said after several minutes, nodding toward the driveway below. She liked adding the "young"; it put him in his place, as well as differentiated him from the Dr. McArtle, his father, who she knew oh so many years before.

"He decided not to move Mary Lydia to the hospital. He's afraid it would do more damage, jostling her about, than if she just stays put."

"That sounds wise."

"He's sending over a nurse in the morning, and he'll be here himself after his rounds."

"He seems like he knows what he's doing. His father was a good doctor, despite his other, shall we say, shortcomings."

"I think I remember his father."

"I've wondered how much of those times you remember."

"Enough," Malcolm said.

Libby wondered how much was enough. She pictured a little boy standing in a dark upstairs hallway, looking through a half-opened door at the good doctor standing over his mother lying in bed half out of her mind on laudanum; she had no idea if he had any memories of Captain Walker and the other Rebels, even though Judson gave him a ride on his horse one evening, Malcolm never mentioned them after they were gone, after his father was injured blowing up the bridge and destroying the war engines. "Let's say young Dr. McArtle's father did what he could, with the information he had at the time."

"Things have a way of moving forward, don't they? Medicine no exception."

"It's called progress, so they tell me," she said, looking over at him for the first time, then back at the night. "Whether it's always for the best is debatable. Is Perpetual with Mary Lydia?"

"She was. But she went back to her room, after Missy said she'd stay with Mary Lydia."

"Missy?"

Malcolm shrugged. "I was surprised too. But Missy said she wanted to. Plans to stay with her in the room all night. She put two chairs together and is camping out."

"What do you suppose that's about?"

"I don't know. She also changed into regular clothes. Perpetual says Missy told her she was through with the frilly peignoirs."

"Did you talk to her?"

"Missy? No, but I'm going to. I want to. I think it's time we did."

"Past time," Libby said. Thinking of the final conversation she had with Colin, after he moved down to his office at the steamworks. After all the years she had been unkind to him with her relationship to Eugene McArtle, a relationship that meant nothing to her except as a way to get the drugs she craved; after the episode with Captain Walker, Judson, after she lost her heart to the dashing cavalry officer, just as Colin supposed she would. Why didn't you care when it still could have meant something? he said. I just want to be alone now, I just want to devote the rest of my life to my work, I don't have much time left. . . . Almost as an afterthought, she said to her son, "Better now than never."

Above the squares of lights of the town, above the glow of the furnaces from the mill along the river, against the black of a night sky, first a red starburst appeared, then a white one, their fragments raining down. In the distance came the faint whistle of the rockets. Malcolm was quiet for several moments, thinking about something.

"I guess this ends the question of who the baby's father is."

"Thank heaven," Libby said.

"It doesn't make much sense chasing after the baby's father when there is no baby."

"And good riddance. Nothing good was going to come from such an inquiry."

"We couldn't get hold of that Greek fellow anyway. Or Turk, whatever he was. The fellow who was in the photograph with her on that outing last spring. It sounds like he's not coming back to the college with the war and all at home. Gus thought he seemed the most likely candidate."

"Sending poor Gus on such a mission. It's a wonder he didn't tell you he wouldn't do it. I wouldn't have blamed him if he did. Gus always did get the short end of the stick around here."

"You're right—"

"I know I'm right," the old woman said.

"That's why I had a talk with him this evening."

"With Gus? I hope he's not still beating himself up about the parade."

"He is, of course. You know Gus. He'll never forgive himself. But that's not what I wanted to talk to him about." Malcolm thought for a moment, looking out into the night. "The steamworks was offered a commission to build a tank, an armored vehicle, like the ones the French have developed to fight the Germans. And I have to say the offer is very tempting—it would certainly assure the future of the company. But I told Gus I want him to pursue his development of the Lylemobile instead. I know that's what he wants. It will be his company soon enough, it should be the company he wants it to be."

"Are you sure he can handle it?"

"No, quite frankly, I'm not. And I'm not sure that the Lylemobile has a chance of success. But I'll never tell Gus that." Malcolm looked at his mother. "I know what it's like to have a father who doesn't have faith in you."

Libby started to respond, then kept quiet; there was obviously something else Malcolm wanted to say, was struggling to find the words. In the darkness, without being aware he was doing it, he rubbed at the scars on his hands.

"The night Lydia burned in the trench—"

"Malcolm, you don't have to—"

"Yes, Mother. I do have to."

Libby lowered her head and waited for him to go on; there was so much they hadn't said to each other over the years, she owed it to him to listen to what he had to say now.

"When Lydia tripped on the plank and fell into the trench and the lantern broke and splattered her with kerosene, I looked up at the house and saw Father standing in his study window watching us, watching what was happening. And I froze, the idea that he was standing there watching me, watching to see what I would do, I panicked, I couldn't think straight. I just knew he was thinking that I wasn't doing it right, that I wasn't doing what I should be doing. That I wasn't doing it the way he would do it. It was like I was blind, I grabbed the first barrel I could lay my hands on, if you had asked me I would have sworn it was salt from the groceries delivered that day but it wasn't, it wasn't. It was flour and it just made everything worse. The woman I loved, I would have done anything to save her. I tried to do everything I could to save her, I beat at the flames, I tried to scrape the flour off her but it only made it worse, I just kept spreading the flames around. I'm not making an excuse, nothing could ever excuse what I did. But I'm sure the fact that Father was standing there watching me, and knowing how Father felt about me, that I could never do anything right, had a bearing on how I acted that night. It's what I've devoted my life to, to overcome that feeling or maybe go on despite it."

"It wasn't that your father didn't have faith in you. The truth was he didn't have faith in anyone but himself. He thought it was up to him to do everything, that if he didn't do it, if he didn't control it, he couldn't trust it. It wasn't directed at you, it was directed at himself."

"It's a moot point. It felt as if it was directed at me."

"And he knew that and he wished more than anything he

could have changed it. But that would mean changing himself, and he was unable to do that. He trusted you enough to give you control of the company at the end though, didn't he?"

"Yes. . . ."

"And he was so proud of you, the things you were doing with the company, taking his ideas and getting them to market, making Keystone into an international company. I know this for a fact because he told me."

"I'm glad to know that. But I don't want Gus to have to guess at whether or not he has my support. I've already sent word to the government delegation that Keystone Steam Works won't be pursuing the development of their project. And I told Gus he should move forward with the Lylemobile starting immediately."

"I would think that would please him very much."

"I thought so too, but I'm not so sure."

"How so?"

"He got this strange expression on his face. Like he couldn't believe it was happening—no, it was more like he wasn't sure he wanted it to happen. I probably misread it completely."

No, my son, you probably didn't. Poor Gus. His father just handed him the keys to the kingdom, but no one ever showed him which key unlocked which door.

"It wasn't at all the celebratory moment I expected it to be," Malcolm went on.

"But at least I know I didn't fail him like I failed John Lincoln."

Libby looked at the figure of her son in the darkness. "How did you fail John Lincoln?"

"If I had paid more attention to the boy, he wouldn't have been so locked into his affection for his sister. And he wouldn't have been so devastated and disappointed in her when she got pregnant. I'm sure that's what's drove him away. With the results. . . ."

Libby thought, I'm not so sure there was any help for John Lincoln regardless. He was always too sensitive, but there was something else. Something darker. . . .

When his mother didn't say anything, Malcolm went on. "For that matter, I should have paid more attention to Mary Lydia too, I should have been more of a father. It would have helped her when the temptation of that Turk or Greek or whoever he was came along. But I have the chance now to try to make it up to Mary Lydia in the future, she'll need her family in the days to come. And I've set Gus up for the future as well. I can rest assured that my children know that they have a father."

Libby looked into the valley and the darkness and the scatters of light, thinking, Malcolm blames his father for not having faith in him, for not preparing him for the business of the world, and now he's done the same to his own son. Malcolm was lucky, he was able to overcome the difficulties and his own shortcomings by simple bullheadedness. But Gus doesn't have that. Gus is too nice a person. A quality that Malcolm was never encumbered with. I'm afraid Gus' good fortune from his father will eventually destroy him. As for Mary Lydia, I hope she can get away from this house, from this family. A family can be support and refuge for some who need it, but for others it can destroy them, it would seem sometimes for its own satisfaction, a sacrifice of one to maintain the others, and the others gladly witness and encourage the mental burning at the stake, the bloodletting in effect, in order to keep the family intact. She needs to get away, have a life of her own away from here, I wish I could tell her but now's not the time for that, there is no time for that now. For that matter it's a good thing Malcolm will never see what would have become of his sainted John Lincoln if he had lived. The boy wasn't encumbered with niceness, and being a son of privilege would have only taken him so far. He would have dallied around and wasted his life, and taken anyone close to him down with him—Oh Colin, what did we wrought with our half love?

In the darkness, the town below in the valley seemed to be disintegrating into smoke, the fireworks diminished to only an isolated flash, a few sputtering firecrackers, with the orange glow of the mill along the river. Instead, on the dark lawn, she became aware of the fireflies lifting from the dew-soaked grass like miniature skyrockets, tracing through the black bushes at the edge of the lawn. After several moments of silence, Malcolm sighed.

"Well, I guess I should be heading to bed. It's been quite a day. Good night, Mother."

As he turned to go, Libby said, "Malcolm."

Her son stopped by the French doors and looked at her. With the lights from the bedroom behind him, he appeared as a faceless silhouette, he could have been anyone. Then she shook her head.

"No, it's nothing. Go on to bed."

28

After waiting a while longer to make sure A. Crow wasn't coming back, the animals wended their way back through the dark wood toward home. Fox was the first to leave them, nose sniffing the air, tail like a plume, obviously happy to be on the hunt again.

"I think she said something about being cooped up," Turtle said.

"No," Rabbit said regretfully, "she was talking about a chicken coop."

"Oh dear," Turtle said. "Well, I guess you can say she's being true to who she is."

"Good for her. Bad for the chickens," Rabbit said, looking over her shoulder.

"Maybe that's what's called the cost of living," Turtle said.

When they got to the pond, Turtle said good-bye to the others and settled back in her place among the rocks along the shoreline. Taking A. Crow's words to heart, she decided as long as she always carried her home with her, she should make it as comfortable as possible— maybe get a new carpet inside her shell, some pictures for the walls. As for Rabbit, she said her good-byes as well when they arrived back at the spot where they first met her.

"Thanks for letting me come with you," she said, working her whiskers. "But now, as A. Crow would say, I've got to run." And with that she bounded off through the brush, practicing her jukes and feints at every imagined threat.

Which left Mole Rat and Hedgehog—Mole Rat holding carefully to Hedgehog's arm—walking alone on the path as the late afternoon sunlight filtered down through the particolored autumn leaves. When they got back to where Mole Rat first bumped into Hedgehog, she said, "Well, here we are, back at the beginning. Though in this case it seems to be an ending too."

"I was thinking," Hedgehog said, "that maybe it doesn't have to be an ending. I really enjoyed myself today. I didn't find the answer I was looking for, in fact I didn't find any answer at all. But I learned that if I let them, somebody else can help me hear what's going on. You helped me learn that. And though that isn't as close as a hug or something, that's a kind of closeness all of its own."

"And I was thinking that being with you was nice

for me because I didn't have to worry about bumping into things or falling down. You brought a kind of light into my life."

There was a log beside the path and Hedgehog guided Mole Rat over to it and the two little animals sat down, Mole Rat sitting close enough that Hedgehog's spines tickled her arm. As the day drew to a close, the birds all singing their evening songs, the autumn leaves overhead glowing in the half-light, Mole Rat and Hedgehog discussed all the things they might do the following day, the travels they might go on, the places they'd like to visit. Together. Closer than family. Friends.

. . . and as the evening grows darker the town continues its slow descent into smoke as thick as fog, the smoke of the fireworks with the smell of gunpowder lingering through the quiet streets, the smoke of the mill along the river carrying the smells of coke and coal, sulfur and ash and oil, drifting over the small frame houses, haloing the streetlights, ringing the headlights of the cars making their way to the change of shifts, the smells of the mill always present in the town along with the sounds, the ringing of steel on steel, the rumble of heavy machinery, the scream of whistles and sirens, but smoke this heavy in the town a peculiarity, the result of an approaching weather system that keeps the smoke from rising above the level of the valley's hills, pushing the smoke back down over the town, an indication that it will rain maybe later tonight, maybe early tomorrow, but soon, a harbinger of a change in the weather that everyone in town recognizes intuitively, the smoke as much a part of the town as the hills and the trees and the flow of the river . . . as in the new city park a sculptor named Ennio Scarpaletta pulls the tarpaulin from his statue to see his creation one last time before leaving town in the

morning, the figure on horseback towering over him in the smoke and the darkness like an avenging angel, the copper surface catching the dull reflections of the nearby streetlights, and thinks, So much for you, my friend, the lady has created a monument to a dream . . . as in her house on steep Fifth Street near the old lock on the river, Marie Pinnella sits at her kitchen table hoping her husband, Nali, comes home from the Panthers Club soon before he drinks away all the money he made the last few days working extra hours at the Keystone Steam Works, hoping against hope to have some extra for the savings she's been putting away for her fondest wish, a matching set of kitchen chairs . . . in his office on the first floor of his house on upper Seventh Avenue, Dr. James McArtle sits at his desk replenishing the vials of chemicals in his doctor's bag, the same valise of chemicals his father carried with him on his rounds, and thinks back to earlier today driving Libby Lyle around town when she put her hand on his knee, a eighty-nine-year-old woman and he almost drove them up a telephone pole, thinking, My poor father, he never had a chance . . . in his bedroom in Sycamore House, Malcolm Lyle dreams he is standing on a reviewing stand as a parade goes by in his honor of everyone who was ever affected in a good way by one of his decisions, even if they weren't, there's Gus and John Lincoln and Mary Lydia, there's Missy and Margaret and Perpetual pointing a finger at him, there's a young Turkish boy or maybe Greek and the two government reps and all the employees of the Keystone Steam Works, a dream that fills him with warmth and satisfaction though he knows someone is missing . . . while down the hall in Mary Lydia's bedroom, his wife, Missy, sits stretched out on the two chairs she's pulled together, a makeshift bed from which she plans to keep watch on her daughter, Mary Lydia, through the night, aware it's too late now to be a mother to John Lincoln, and almost too late to be a wife to Malcolm, but is determined

now to be a mother to Mary Lydia, finds herself singing a lullaby
as much to comfort herself as her child,

> *Bye-lo-bye,*
> *Bye-lo-bye,*
> *Bye-lo-baby, bye*

. . . as across the room Mary Lydia is asleep dreaming that she
and John Lincoln are riding in Professor D'Angelus' Balloon
Ascension, the two of them alone in the basket rising above the
town and the river and the hills, all the world, all their troubles,
far below them in the sunlight and the warm breeze and the blue
blue sky, John Lincoln standing behind her holding her, saying
into her hair, "Don't be afraid, Lybia," but that's the point, she
isn't afraid, and she knows she never will be again and that she
doesn't need John Lincoln to tell her . . . as in the darkness on
the hillside above the town, Margaret Moon walks through the
woods carrying a basket with the dinner she prepared for the Lyles
today but no one got around to eating after word of John
Lincoln's death and then Mary Lydia's aborted birth, when a
ghost child comes toward her through the trees, but she knows it's
only her ten-year-old granddaughter come to walk her grandma
home to Black Town, and thinks, The good Lord took both my
twin white babies today, it's just that the one is only finding it
out now . . . as in the stable behind Sycamore House Margaret's
husband, William, wakes as the horse he shares the stall with stirs
restlessly, listens to make sure nothing is prowling about, and tells
the horse, one of two matched grays left to the household, to go
back to sleep, his voluntary watch to keep his beloved horses safe
as long as possible from the march of progress, such as Mr. Gus'
Lylemobile lurking in the next stall . . . in the farmhouse that
serves as her father's manse outside of Wichita, Kansas, Lily

Richard Snodgrass

Lyle sits at the dining room table after dinner with her father and mother and little Mal, the nightly ritual of listening to her father read the psalms as they dodge the dozens of june bugs and moths and beetles and horseflies that circle the overhead light, thinking, All things considered, maybe my place is back in Furnass after all . . . as in his wing of Sycamore House, Gus Lyle sits in his living room holding a photograph of his wife, Lily, and their son Mal, thinking, All things considered, maybe it's best for everyone if she stays in Kansas now that she's there, with work on the Lylemobile going forward, he's going to be tied up at the plant more than ever, if she comes back he'd only disappoint her more, and he can't stand the thought of disappointing anyone anymore . . . on the Capital Limited heading back to Washington, D.C., two representatives of the United States government sit facing each other, Charles Adams finally breaking the silence as he says to Julian Taylor, "Well, with all the regulations he's going to face with his little steam car, Malcolm Lyle is going to regret ever turning us down, regret it very much" . . . in the living room of her tidy brick home a block from the campus of Covenant College, Elizabeth Quigley takes off her reading glasses and puts down her copy of Somerset Maugham's Of Human Bondage *and thinks about the visit she had yesterday from Gus Lyle inquiring about his sister, thinks she was probably too hard on him, that he was only doing his father's bidding as usual, poor hapless Gus, and regardless what she thinks of the Lyles, the college doesn't want to offend Malcolm Lyle, there is still money to be had there . . . in a poor district of Constantinople a young Greek man named Dimitris Papalas hides with his family along with other families in the basement of their makeshift Covenantor Church, listening for the sound of Turkish soldiers come to arrest them, thinks of the Scottish Covenantors in the Killing Time of the seventeenth century hiding in the moors from the soldiers of the king, and thinks back to his recent time in America, the picturesque college on the hill and a picnic on the hillside across the river where the only danger was getting grass stains on his pants and the girl he knew there, what was her name? . . . in her bedroom Emma Edgeworth abruptly gets out of bed, pulls her nightgown back down over her body, and says to Bert Featherstone, "Okay, that's it, get out of my house!" and Bert Featherstone looks at her and says, "What did I do?" and Emma Edgeworth repeats, "Out of my house before I call the police!" and as she watches Bert Featherstone reluctantly get up and put on his clothes she thinks, Oh Gus, if you had let me, I could have turned all those whimpers into growls . . . and on Emma Edgeworth's front stoop Bert Featherstone finishes tucking in his shirt and pulling his braces up over his shoulders, dancing on one foot and then the other as he ties his shoelaces, and thinks, Women, bloody women, you tell me, mate! as he heads off through the dark smoky streets back to his room above the Triangle Tavern in the Lower End . . . while in another saloon in town, the Iron Hearth, close to the mills along the river, Hugh MacIninch sits on his own but can't help overhearing a group of men farther down the bar having a good laugh as they recount the tale of Gus Lyle in a Keystone Well-Driller taking out the electrical and telephone wires along with the Fourth of July decorations on Eighth Avenue, and thinks, Och, 'tis sad but true, the lad's head is full of wee beasties, and they're all deid . . . as in one of the shack-like houses in a hollow at the base of the valley's hills, a young mill worker a few years out of high school named Billie Gibson steps out onto his family's porch, lights a cigarette, and looks up the dark hillside at the lights of the Lyle house through the trees, the windows haloed with the smoke drifting up from the town, and thinks that he's been looking at these lights glowing above him his entire life, imagines as he often does that somewhere in one of those lighted rooms*

Mary Lydia is sitting at a table or in a chair reading a book or is getting ready for bed, and realizes all over again that there will always be things in this world that are not meant for him, that there will always be pleasures and people that are beyond him, and that no matter how hard he tries he can never change it, and thinks, as he has many times before, Fuck you all . . .

. . . and in her room in the Lyle house, Perpetual puts the cap back on the fountain pen she took from Malcolm's office and makes a mental note that she should return it now that she's finished with her story, there's no more use for it now, gathers the pages she's been working on for the past few days and rolls them into a scroll, ties a ribbon around them, and leaves it on the blotter of her writing desk as she gets up and listens for a moment for movement in the room next door, hears Libby rocking slowly back and forth in her chair and smiles to herself, knowing from what they talked about earlier that it is time, that Libby is preparing herself as she waits for Perpetual to come to her, but not quite yet; Perpetual leaves her room and makes her way down the hall alongside the banister of the stairwell, goes to the door of Mary Lydia's room and carefully opens it, looks in at the young woman lying in her bed resting easily with the medicine Dr. McArtle gave her earlier, her mother, Missy, sitting beside the bed in two chairs pulled together, an afghan over her legs, who gives a little wave to Perpetual to let her know that everything is all right, that she'll be keeping watch through the night, and Perpetual closes the door again and continues on down the hallway to the landing at the head of the stairs and around the newel-post to the closed door of Malcolm's and Missy's bedroom but doesn't linger, pauses only long enough to hear Malcolm breathing heavily in his sleep and is satisfied, returns to the landing and starts down the stairway, the soft melodic Tunk! *of the aged wood under her footfalls marking her progress, down the stairs into the*

darkness of the first floor, only a few lights left burning here after Margaret closed up the kitchen for the night, Perpetual gliding in her out-of-fashion floor-length dress, a muted multicolored specter among the shadows, making her normal late-night rounds to ensure all is well in the house, her house to her mind, past the kitchen, listens down the hallway to determine if there is any movement in Gus' wing of the house but doesn't hear anything, considers for a moment going down the hall to look in the living room or even upstairs in the bedroom to see if Gus is there and okay, she's concerned for him after the events of the day, the fiasco of the parade and then Mary Lydia's miscarriage, but decides it is not her place and might upset him more, all things considered, he's liable to take such concern as a lack of faith, Gus being Gus, decides that she should leave him alone even though she senses that he needs her now, needs somebody, needs his wife and child to be home if anyone were to ask her, though of course no one does, it being her house perhaps, at least to her mind, but not her family; and having completed her rounds, she returns to the front hallway where she smells wood burning as she does each evening, the downstairs filling up with smoke and the glow of flames as she continues past the foot of the stairs and on to the room at the front of the house known as the study, the room that was originally the den and refuge of Colin Lyle and is now the same for his son, Malcolm, and will someday be the same for his son Gus, stands at the doorway to the room full of flames and smoke swirling around the figure of the man sitting in one of the tall wing-back leather chairs holding the scale model of a Lylemobile on his lap, the man and the model and the room and everything in it engulfed in flames the same as they are each evening as she closes down the house, Perpetual aware that there is nothing she can do to prevent or extinguish the fire decades before it will happen, turns away from the burning room and sees at the end of the dark hall as she does each evening a woman standing in a column of light, or rather is a column of light, a figure of luminous fibers, egg-shaped, woman-shaped, the woman standing there looking at Perpetual as if to ask her something, but Perpetual says to her as she does each evening, You go on now, Mrs. Lydia, you go to your rest, there's nothing you can do for these folks now, Perpetual she be here to help, and the woman of luminous fibers nods and turns and begins to dim, fading into the farther reaches of the house, and Perpetual looks around once more to make sure all is well, though she knows unlike every other evening that nothing from this night forward will ever be the same in Sycamore House, the Lyle House, climbs back up the stairs to the second floor and returns briefly to her room, takes from the windowsill the glass of dark viscous liquid she prepared earlier this evening, takes it to her secretary desk and picks up the scroll of her story and then opens the connecting door to Libby's room and goes in, smiles to the elderly woman sitting in her rocking chair who is waiting for her, waiting. . . .

29

"Did you walk the house?"

"I did, Mawm," Perpetual said, putting the glass and scroll on the stand beside Libby's chair.

"And how is the house this evening?" Libby said. She looked at the items Perpetual placed on the stand, then rocked back and forth a couple of times, as if in recognition.

"The house be fine, Mawm. As fine as the house can be."

"That's good. That's as it should be." She watched as Perpetual went to the French doors, looking out at the balcony and the night, then came back to her.

"I heard Mr. Malcolm talking to you outside. Did you tell him?"

"No, no," Libby said, looking at her hands, rubbing at her age spots. "He would never understand. No, that is all just between you and me."

"I'm sure he be worried about Mary Lydia."

"Oh, Malcolm. Poor man. He's still fussing about who the baby's father might have been. He says he isn't concerned, but then he brings it up again. He won't let it go that it was the Turkish or Greek boy Gus unearthed from Gus' talk at the college. I swear if Malcolm thought he could find the boy, he'd send Gus over on a steamer to ask him about it in person."

Libby paused, thinking of something. "Tonight I had the opportunity to tell him that I loved him. I thought he needed to hear that after all that's gone on, I wanted to tell him. And I found I just couldn't say it. The words just wouldn't come, I don't know why. Something in my nature."

"It be a scary thing to say to another person, Mawm. Everything changes then."

The two women looked at each other for a moment, before Perpetual picked up the previous thread of the conversation. "I think Mr. Malcolm be so concerned about the baby's father because he wants to make sure it wasn't John Lincoln."

"I know. I wondered the same. Afraid of that too. Particularly when John Lincoln ran off the way he did when he learned Mary Lydia was pregnant. And then when she kept calling his name when she lost the baby—"

"Perpetual knows he wasn't the father, Mawm. I know as sure as if Mary Lydia told me herself. I looked in her eyes and saw that John Lincoln was to her all in the past, he be present with her no more. When she call his name, it be a lament for all things lost in this world, all lost loves, all things that are different now."

"If you say so, then I know it's so," Libby said, leaning back again in the chair. "It's been a long day. But it's almost over now."

"*C'est mauvais* about the statue."

"As I told Malcolm, it's just as well I didn't go through with the dedication. I owe Gus that. I might not have been able to hold off telling those silly townspeople that they were honoring a group of Morgan's Raiders. Everyone seems to forget that those Union soldiers when they came to town were actually Confederate spies dressed in Yankee uniforms. They stole those uniforms on their way here."

"Our little joke, Mawm."

"I wonder if anyone will ever climb up there and see the CSA on Judson's belt buckle. Well, no matter. We know it's there."

"A fitting tribute to a man who was important to you," Perpetual said, going over to turn down the bed, then caught herself.

"You forgot what you were doing," Libby said, a tired smile on her face.

"Yes, Mawm." Perpetual came back to her, standing in front of the rocker. "And you could still change your mind."

"And have you lord it over me for the rest of my days, propping me up in bed when the time comes and wiping the drool off my face? Not on your life."

"I would, Mawm. You know Perpetual would."

"Yes, I know you would. But I care too much for you as a friend to put you through that. And I care too much for myself to put myself through it. To what purpose? Just to last a little longer? No, thank you. I've accomplished everything I set out to do these last days. It's unfortunate that it will come so close to John Lincoln's funeral, but it can't be helped. And it's probably best to get these unpleasant things out of the way all at one time, so the family can get on with the business of living." She rocked a couple of times back and forth, then nodded to the stand beside her chair. "And is that my drink?"

"It is, Mawm. It won't taste very good, Perpetual is afraid.

But it will cause you no pain. You'll just go to sleep."

"Right now, that sounds very welcome indeed. And no one will ever know."

"I'll take the glass as soon as you're through. And that be that."

"And that be that." Libby looked at Perpetual for a long moment. Then nodded, smiled, took the glass, and drank the contents, giving her head a little shake when she was through. "Brr. No, that isn't what I'd call delicious. Here, let me have a little whiskey chaser."

Perpetual poured her two fingers of rye in her usual glass and Libby drank it down, giving a satisfied "Ah-h-h-h-h" when she was finished. "Oh, I did love the taste of rye," she said, handing the tumbler back to Perpetual. Perpetual put it back on the stand, took the other glass and tucked it away inside the folds of her dress.

"So now," Libby said. "Pull that chair around and read me the story you wrote for me. I want to hear the sound of your voice as I drift away. What kind of story is it?"

Perpetual pulled up the straight chair and got herself settled, taking off the ribbon from the scroll of pages. "It be a story about some little animals who discover that what they're looking for is what they're looking with."

"It all sounds very human."

"Do tell," Perpetual said, her wrist crooked against her hip.

She and Libby exchanged looks, Libby with the slightest smile of understanding on her lips. She wanted to say more but she was getting drowsy, her eyes becoming little more than slits. But she leaned forward and took Perpetual's hand, the two women holding on to each other for a long moment. Then Libby settled back again, rested her head against the back of the rocker and closed her eyes. "Please read to me, Perpetual. I'm ready."

Perpetual felt the slightest makings of a tear. Oh no you don't, child. Don't you start that nonsense with me, not in your lifetime. Mrs. Libby, she be rising in glory this day, rising in glory. The woman cleared her throat, took a deep breath, and read from the sheaf of pages:

> *"Ow!" said Mole Rat. "You spiked me!"*
>
> *"Ow, yourself!" said Hedgehog. "You're the one who bumped into me!"*
>
> *Hedgehog ran her paws down the length of her snout as if to make sure it was still in place. The small animal had stopped on the path to admire the view of orange and yellow leaves as the trees changed in autumn. . . .*

ACKNOWLEDGMENTS

There are four people—friends, actually; dream catchers—without whom I could never have brought these books to publication:

Kim Francis
Bob Gelston
Dave Meek
Jack Ritchie

I also thank Eileen Chetti for struggling through my quirks of style and punctuation. For converting all the Books of Furnass to eBook formats, I thank Umesh of Vsprout (umesh@vsprout.in) who works such technical wizardry from half a world away. Doug Circle of Zerkel Creative has been invaluable for his work in publicizing the Books of Furnass in support of Kim Francis of Magpie Communications, LLC. Our splendid award-winning website at RichardSnodgrass.com was designed and maintained by Chris Nesci and Crew at My Blue Robot Creative Agency. I particularly thank Jack Ritchie who took on the task of designing the covers so I wouldn't, in his words, embarrass myself, and who has long served as a sounding board, bullshit detector, and all-round good friend. And then, of course, there's my wife Marty. . . .

⟨❦⟩

Richard Snodgrass lives in Pittsburgh, PA with his wife Marty and two indomitable female tuxedo cats, raised from feral kittens, named Frankie and Becca.

⟨❦⟩

To read more about the Books of Furnass series, the town of Furnass and its history, and special features for *All That Will Remain*, go to www.RichardSnodgrass.com.

11283310R00159